I0584378

Published February 2023
Published by Indies United Publishing House, LLC

Cover art by Leslie A. Piggott and Lisa Orban

ISBN: 978-1-64456-571-1 (paperback)
ISBN: 978-1-64456-573-5 (ePub)
ISBN: 978-1-64456-572-8 (Mobi)

Library of Congress Control Number: 2022949219

INDIES UNITED PUBLISHING HOUSE, LLC
P.O. BOX 3071
QUINCY, IL 62305-3071

www.indiesunited.net

ii

FORSAKEN TALENTS

The Cari Turnlyle Series: Book 2

by Leslie A. Piggott

INDIES UNITED PUBLISHING HOUSE, LLC

Dedication

To my own grandmas: Margaret and Treva. Thank you for cheering me on, for reading my books, and for always loving me. I will hold you both in my heart forever. Rest in peace.

Table of Contents

Chapter 1

J ade got into her car, a 2025 BMW convertible. Her dad had given it to her as an early birthday gift. She knew he was secretly hoping the luxurious gift would make her feel guilty about not going to college yet. *FAT CHANCE, DADDO!* She laughed.

She put the car into gear and backed out of her spot. It was a gorgeous summer day, so she hit the button to put the top down. She rubbed her lower jaw on the side where the hygienist had replaced the sealants on her molars. They hadn't done anything invasive, but her jaw was feeling a little bit tight. She shrugged it off. She'd probably been clenching it at night.

Jade looked at her watch. She was supposed to meet her boyfriend, Harold, for a picnic lunch soon. *Had the hygienist said anything about waiting to eat?* She couldn't remember. Her arm spasmed a bit as she put on her blinker to signal she was turning onto the highway. *I'm falling apart over here*! She laughed to herself. Harold lived out in the boonies on his grandparents' land. He'd taken over their farm after getting his degree in Agricultural Management a year ago.

Even though the wind tangled her hair in a million places, she loved driving out to the farm with the top down. It felt like she was flying. She was about to start singing along with the XM radio when a call cut in on the Bluetooth. When she tried to move her thumb to hit the answer button, she couldn't do it. *What the hell? Can I really not move my thumb?* She couldn't move either hand or her arms. She started to panic. Harold was calling her, but she couldn't answer. The big curve right before the turnoff for his farm was coming up and she couldn't slow down for it, let alone turn the steering wheel. She'd put the cruise control on and now she couldn't turn it off! *Help me!* She cried in her head.

Tears streaming down her face, she watched as cars passed her from the other direction, but she had no way to get their attention. Somehow, she was paralyzed! The turn loomed just ahead and she tried to scream as she saw an 18-wheeler coming around the bend. She was going to end up right in its path! She willed her body to respond, to move, to do anything! She wished she could close her eyes before it happened, but they were frozen open along with the rest of her body. All she could do was cry.

Chapter 2

Cari Turnlyle bent down to grab the edge of her yoga mat. She had joined a new power flow class as a way to get some cardio in when it was too cold to run outside last winter. She had loved the class so much she joined the studio and came for a class three or four times a week.

"Where was Jade today?" the instructor, Julia, asked her.

Cari winced when she heard the name. "I guess you didn't hear—"

"Hear what?" Julia asked, alarmed.

"Jade was driving out to her boyfriend's farm yesterday and was in an accident." Cari tried to keep her eyes from filling with tears.

"What?! Not in that sweet, new car of hers?"

Cari grimaced, her green eyes bright. "I'm afraid so; it was pretty bad."

"What do you mean? She's not..." Julia trailed off.

"I don't know what happened. She was hit by an 18-wheeler on the big curve north of town. She's...she's gone."

"No! How is that possible?"

"I don't know. I literally just saw her *here* yesterday. She was telling me all about some trip she was planning with her cousin. Going backpacking in Europe this fall or something like that."

"I know she was young, but she's driven that road dozens of times. How could she miss the curve?"

"I don't know, Julia. I was shocked when I heard it too. I'll let you know if I hear anything else. See you tomorrow."

Cari tightened the strap around her yoga mat and slung it over her shoulder. She didn't want to talk about Jade anymore. She hadn't known the young woman all that well. In fact, she only saw her at the yoga studio, but they were both regulars. She knew Jade was from a well-to-do family in the area and had taken a gap year after graduating from high school. The one year had turned into two, and she still had not applied to attend a school, much to her father's dismay. He had big plans for her to join his business; she had been an exemplary high school student. She was enjoying traveling the world and seeing things most people only dream of visiting. Her policy was that she should do it while she could, which was on her daddy's dollar. Jade knew he'd never tell her no.

The information about the wreck had come in over the police scanner at the newspaper office. Cari was a journalist at the *Brenington Beagle*. Earlier this year, she'd been promoted from sportswriter to one of the lead journalists for the paper after she uncovered a scheme in the athletic department at the local university. Her editor had been impressed with her dedication and bumped her up the ladder. Unfortunately, it meant sharing space on the front page with Lionel Cardian, the long-time lead reporter for the newspaper. He was arrogant and rude. Cari tried to steer clear of him whenever possible.

Jade's wreck had been classified as an accidental death by the responding officers. Cari was relieved that Cardian hadn't been in the office when the report came in; their editor, Mr. Ollaman, had asked Cari to write up a quick summary for the morning paper. She knew that if Cardian had gotten the assignment, he would have been unforgiving to the young driver. She sighed and tucked a rogue curl behind her ear. She needed to grab a shower and get to her office.

* * * * *

Detective Genevieve Viacorte tugged her wavy, dark hair into a messy bun at the nape of her neck. She really needed to make an appointment to get her hair trimmed; it was longer than it had ever been and hard to care for. As she fastened the elastic around it, she stared again at the blinking light on her desk phone. She knew who left the message without listening to it and was hesitant to hear the recording.

Her partner, Alex Runimoss—Roo-Nee-Mohs, as he always corrected everyone—had called on her way in that morning to say that a Mr. Frederick Kastener wanted to meet with them. His daughter, Jade, had been in an automobile accident around noon the day before. The county sheriff's office and the ME had both ruled the death to be just that: an accident. Kastener wouldn't accept that. He was certain that something besides a lapse in judgment had resulted in her death. Genevieve sighed and started to press the button. *Coffee first*, she thought and started to walk away from her desk.

"Hey, hey! Where are you going? You *literally* just got here." Alex chided her.

She lifted her empty mug in response. "I need some caffeine before I can handle Kastener. You read the sheriff's report. He is angry and wants answers. I don't have any of those."

"And you'll get some from the coffee?" Alex smirked, his dark eyes sparkling with humor.

"Ha ha, funny guy. No, but at least I won't get a headache." She went to the breakroom and grabbed the handle of the carafe, cringing a bit as she smelled the bitterness of its contents. They really needed to have a continuing ed course on how to brew a good pot of coffee. She poured some into her mug and squeezed in a tablespoon of honey from the little plastic bear on the counter. *Better than nothing,* she thought and walked back to her desk.

"Okay, before I hit play on this message, what did he say in the one he left for you?"

"Exactly what you would expect. He demanded a more thorough investigation, and threatened to call the mayor and the chief of police."

"Does he know the chief?"

"I'm guessing that he makes it his business to know everyone. I've lived here over fifteen years, Gen. The Kasteners have been here forever. They probably own close to half the town. Our lieutenant also sent us an email about Kastener, so obviously he either already contacted the chief or he knows our lieutenant. We're supposed to give it our full attention. Luckily, we don't have any *real* cases right now to shove onto the back burner." He rolled his eyes.

"Great. Well, it's now or never, I guess." She pressed the blinking light and had the message play on the phone's speaker.

"Detective Viacortez," he began, mispronouncing her name. "This is Mr. Frederick Kastener. I left a message for your partner as well; he can fill you in on the details. I will be at the station at nine a.m. sharp to meet with the two of you regarding my daughter's case." The recording clicked, indicating that he'd ended his message. Genevieve pressed the delete button and looked at her watch.

"Well, it's 8:35 right now, so I guess that leaves us twenty-five minutes to discuss how we're going to handle this."

"I vote that you do most of the talking. You're calmer than me."

"Oh, no you don't! One hundred percent this guy wants to talk to another dude. He is not going to take me seriously. He has *old school* written all over him."

Alex rolled his eyes and raked his fingers through his shortly cropped, dark hair. "He is going to hate both of us regardless of who speaks."

"Yep. We can't bring his daughter back and we can't hold anyone responsible for what happened."

"Let's read the accident report again. Maybe there's something in it that will convince him."

Genevieve shrugged and turned on her computer. She doubted

there was anything that could change this grieving father's mind."

* * * * *

Cari quickened her pace when she heard her desk phone ringing. She didn't want to miss a call with a potential story. She slung her messenger bag into her chair and grabbed the phone receiver at the same time.

"Brenington Beagle. This is Cari Turnlyle. With whom do I have the pleasure of speaking?"

A gravelly voice responded. "This is Mr. Frederick Kastener, father of Jade Kastener. I read your brief article in this morning's paper about her death where you called it an *accident*. Young lady, this was no accident!"

"Sir?" Cari asked, surprised at his tone.

"I spoke to the truck driver. Did *you* speak to the truck driver before you put out that drivel you call writing?"

Cari's eyes stung as she listened to the man's words. *Drivel*?

"Sir, I, uh, I'm very sorry for your loss. Mr. Kastener, sir, I knew Jade. We took the same morning yoga class."

"Then you know that she was a very responsible young lady who took very good care of herself."

"Yes," Cari said, drawing the word out a bit as she tried to gain purchase in what Mr. Kastener was trying to say. "She struck me as someone who was very punctual and organized."

"I know people think she was probably texting and driving or some such nonsense that young people are always blamed for when there's a car wreck, but my daughter DID NOT DO THAT!"

"Of course, sir. What was it exactly that the truck driver said to you that has you so upset?"

"He said that the young woman, my Jade, looked like she was crying when he saw her face. Crying. Now, if he could see that she was crying, then that means she wasn't distracted while she was driving. It couldn't have been an accident!" He growled.

Cari stifled a gasp as much as she could. *Why would Jade have been crying?* "That's very interesting, sir. I will do my best to track down the driver and see if he remembers anything else from the, uh, collision." She stopped herself before using the word accident.

"And then you will write a better article about how my Jade was MURDERED."

"Mur—? I will definitely keep you updated on my research, Mr. Kastener. Thank you." The dial tone rang in her ear as she realized he had ended the call before she responded to his declaration. *Murdered?* Cari wondered if Mr. Kastener realized that the trucker's words made the accident seem more like suicide than murder. Still, Jade had seemed like she was always on top of the world, carefree and happy. *Why would she drive in front of a truck?*

She sat down at her desk and logged into her computer. She needed to get her hands on the accident report. It would be a public record, but that would require a call, or more likely, a trip over to city hall. If she wanted to talk to the trucker today, she had to get his name today. She smiled and fished her cell phone out of her purse.

"Hey, Cari—what do you need this time?"

"I probably deserve that, Bob, but still, ouch!" She pouted. Bob was a friend of hers from college. He worked in the crime scene unit at the medical examiner's office.

"I couldn't resist, but I'm also not wrong, am I?"

"No. Sometimes, you're too smart for your own good, Bob Hursley. I'm calling because I just got off the phone with an angry father. He claims his daughter's death was not an accident as I reported in the newspaper. Any chance I could get a copy of the accident report? Please?"

"You must mean Jade Kastener's father, Frederick. I heard he was trying to meet with some officers or maybe even detectives too. I can't blame him; losing your only child must be horrific. You know you can get that report through city hall, Cari."

8

"I *know*, Bob, but then I have to wait over a day to actually get it. If I get it from you, I can get it now."

"I really can't send you a whole report; you know that."

"I know. I'm going to request my own copy from city hall after we hang up, but first, can you at least tell me the truck driver's name? I want to interview him and make sure that we've got this story right."

"That I can do." He clicked through some things with his computer mouse. "The man's name is Dave Minim. It says he's local, so you should be able to find him in the white pages."

"Thanks, Bob! You're the best!"

She ended the call and grabbed the receiver for her desk phone while using her free hand to look up the number for city hall. The system took her through several automated steps before she finally got a real person on the line.

"Hi, there. This is Cari Turnlyle calling from the Brenington Beagle. I would like to request a copy of the accident report from yesterday out on route 27. I believe it happened around noon."

"I know the one. Each public record report is free to the public, but we charge a quarter a page to print it for you. It's fourteen pages. How would you like to pay?" The operator responded.

"Is there any chance that I can get a digital copy emailed to me?" She asked sweetly.

"I'm afraid not, Miss. We aren't that high tech over here yet. You'll have to come pick it up or pay extra for us to mail it to you."

"When can I come get it?"

"Probably first thing tomorrow."

"Let me give you my *Visa* number."

She finished her request for the report and hung up the phone. *Someone needed to help city hall into the twenty-first century already!* Cari typed 'Dave Minim' into the database the Beagle subscribed to for all its reporters. She added Brenington, New York as his place of residence. Luckily, Minim wasn't a common name, and Bob was correct in saying he was local. She found his address and phone number and jotted both down in her notebook. Then, she punched the numbers into her desk phone and listened for it to ring. *Please answer!*

"Hello?" A nasally, nerve-grating voice answered.

"Mr. Minim?" She asked cautiously. She wasn't sure if a man or a woman had answered.

"Speaking. Who is this?"

"Hi, Mr. Minim. This is Cari Turnlyle with the Brenington Beagle. I was hoping I could chat with you a moment about the accident yesterday."

"You better not try and pin that girl's death on me. I told all those officers: she drove in front of my rig, not the other way around." He barked at her.

"Oh, of course not, Mr. Minim. I spoke with the young woman's father. He mentioned a conversation that the two of you had yesterday. Could you tell me about that?"

"That old man will scare the tar out of asphalt, I tell you what. He is *mean!*"

"Yes. Mr. Minim?"

"Right. Like I said, grumpy old cuss. He got to the crash site real quick before my wife could get over and bring me home. My rig had to be towed on account of her vehicle slamming into the front of it. Anyway, he was real mad, as you would expect, being her father and all. The police tried to keep him away from me, but I said it was alright. He could come on over and talk.

"He was real red in the face, you know? And real sad too. I could see it in his eyes. That's when I remembered. The girl driving the little car, I mean, uh, the young lady driving the car…she was crying."

"You could see her face?"

"Plain as day, my dear. She had the top down on her car and her eyes were as big as saucers. Big ole tears running down her face. I tugged on my horn and tried to get her to get back over. There's not a big shoulder on that part of the road. I couldn't miss her. It was terrible."

"I'm so sorry, Mr. Minim. That had to be a very hard thing to experience. Are you injured from the collision?"

"Nope. That big truck kept me safe. Is there anything else you need from me?"

"No, sir. I appreciate your time. Thank you." She replaced the receiver back into its cradle.

* * * * *

"Mr. Kastener is here. Dana is escorting him over to us." Genevieve said to Alex after hanging up her desk phone.

Alex took a deep breath. Genevieve knew he was trying to remind himself to be patient. His patience frequently grew short with people who were overly critical of his work, and he really didn't like people with money throwing their weight around.

"Grieving parents are some of the hardest people to talk to. Sometimes, an accident is just an accident whether they want to believe it or not." He sighed and looked towards the doorway. Their office administrative assistant walked a tall man with dark, close-cut hair down the hallway towards them.

"Thank you, Dana," Genevieve said to the middle-aged woman. Dana had been handling the front desk for as long as everyone could remember. She looked like a friendly grandma, but she was tough. Almost no one got past that desk without Dana's say-so.

"Mr. Kastener? I'm Detective Genevieve Viacorte. This is my partner, Detective Alex Runimoss. Why don't you have a seat? Can we get you anything? Soda? Water?"

"I'm just fine, thank you. Where are you in the investigation?" He asked as he sat down.

Genevieve was just rolling her chair up to her desk when he asked his question. She struggled to keep from leaning back in response to it, not wanting to offend him with her body language.

She glanced over at Alex, who was also looking at her.

"Ahem." She cleared her throat. "We were just reading through the, uh, report regarding the collision yesterday. It sounds like you arrived at the scene fairly quickly, sir. Could you talk to us about that?"

He narrowed his eyes at her. "It's quite simple. When I purchased Jade's car, I included the option to receive notifications if the vehicle is in a collision of any kind."

Alex raised his eyebrows. "I didn't realize the technology existed for that. Miss Kastener—"

"JADE. Her name is Jade." Kastener interrupted.

"Right, my apologies, sir. Did Jade have a history of traffic incidents?"

"No! She was a great driver. Very responsible. I wouldn't have bought her such a nice car if I thought she was going to wreck it. She's an only child and I lost my wife a few years ago when Jade was only 16. She was all I had left. I just wanted to know that she was safe."

"I understand, sir. I'm very sorry for your loss. So, there's an app or something that sends you a text or notification of some sort if the vehicle is in a collision and tells you the location too?"

"That's correct."

"Mr. Kastener, does it give you any other information about the collision?"

"What do you mean?"

"For example, does it tell you the speed the vehicle was traveling or the direction or anything like that in the moments before the collision?" Genevieve asked him.

He tilted his head as he thought about her question. "I didn't look through the entire report. I'm not sure what was included. I know that is probably surprising to you, considering that I'm demanding that you investigate her death. I just hadn't thought about what else might be in it. I can send it to you if you think it will help."

"My email address is on my card, sir. If you could forward the report to me, we'll check it out and see if there's anything helpful in it." Genevieve said as she slid one of her cards across her desk.

"In your voicemail, you mentioned speaking with the truck driver at the scene yesterday. What did Mr. Minim have to say?"

"Didn't they put it in the report?!" Kastener's face flushed with anger.

"I'm sorry, sir. They listed his name as the other driver, but—"

"Such incompetence!" Kastener shouted.

"Please, sir, we can't help if you won't talk to us," Genevieve said calmly, noticing Alex's jaw clenching.

"I'm sorry. My apologies. I know this isn't your fault." He took a deep breath. "Mr. Minim said that he saw Jade had tears on her face as her car sped towards him."

"He could see that?" Alex asked.

"That's what he said."

"That *is* interesting. We will give Mr. Minim a call and see if he can remember anything else."

"That's it? You're just going to talk to the trucker?" Kastener asked incredulously.

"With all due respect, sir, we will review the evidence and see if anything points to foul play, but at this time—" Alex started.

"At this time, as my partner was saying, we can't really tell you any more than that. We promise to update you as we learn more." Genevieve cut in over Alex. "Can you give us a list of her close friends or her typical weekly schedule?"

Kastener looked from Alex to Genevieve and back again, wondering what was being left unsaid. Genevieve hoped he wouldn't get upset with her interruption.

"Yes, I brought a list of contacts with me. I don't really know her schedule. She was always going some place and then coming back later."

"The list will be a big help. We'll start on it after we speak with

Mr. Minim."

"Okay. I will leave you to it. I want regular updates. Every morning."

"Mr. Kastener, we might not have something new every day, but I promise we *will* keep you in the loop," Genevieve explained before Alex possibly erupted.

Kastener opened his mouth then seemed to decide against speaking. He stared stonily into Genevieve's eyes as though challenging her somehow. She held his gaze and after a few seconds, he looked away.

"I understand. I dropped off her phone with the woman at the desk on my way in. If I don't hear from you soon, I'll be back here asking why." He got up from his seat, turned and walked out of the office.

Genevieve looked at Alex. "Well, that could have gone worse."

"It could have gone better. Why did you cut me off?"

"He was not going to listen to you say that his daughter might have committed suicide, Alex!"

"I wasn't going to say that exactly."

"Oh? What were you going to say?"

"I was going to say that evidence of her crying could be indicative of something other than murder."

"And how do you think he would respond to that?"

"Okay, fine."

"Should we give Minim a call? Or talk to the ME? They could definitely find evidence of tears on her skin."

"I'm fairly certain that her father is going to request an autopsy if he hasn't already. Let's start with the ME. Then maybe we can talk with Minim and see if he has anything to add."

Chapter 3

Cari brought her left hand up to the locket around her neck and ran it along the thin, gold chain. The locket was a gift from her grandmother; it held a photo from her childhood of the two of them in a field of sunflowers. She tapped her desk with the eraser end of her pencil. *Why had Jade been crying?*

She didn't know a lot about the Kastener family, so she decided to read up on them a little before plunging into Jade's *accident*. Luckily, the Brenington Beagle had several articles in its Health and Leisure section that talked about the family. She selected a few from various decades to read through.

Frederick Kastener was the son of Clarence and Sylvia Kastener. His grandfather, Sigmond, had married Harriet Winter, sole heir to the textile factory, Henri & Co. The textile factory had been the first to market a new-to-the-era fabric: denim. Henri was short for Henrietta, who was Harriet's grandmother. Her father was credited with the creation of denim when trying to make a different fabric called serge. When the family migrated to the Americas from France, they brought the material with them. What started as a mistake grew to become a very successful business passed down to the oldest son or daughter from generation to generation.

Cari skimmed through the rest of the articles and took a few notes. She wondered if her editor knew Mr. Kastener well. He seemed to be well-connected and someone who made it his business to know influential people in the community. She picked up her desk phone.

"Hi, Mr. Ollaman. Yes, it's Cari. Say, you wouldn't happen to know Mr. Frederick Kastener, would you?"

"Kastener? Yes, and I know he spoke with you earlier this morning. I sent him your way after he called to complain about the article you wrote."

Cari could hear a note of disdain in his voice. "Yes, sir. He did call and talk to me. I was just reading about their family, but wondered if you knew any more about them than the articles in our archives?"

"More about them in what way?"

"Well, sir, I knew Jade from a yoga class we both take in the mornings, but I only met her a few months ago. She seemed like a happy young woman. Would you agree?"

Ollaman coughed. Cari wondered if he was trying to keep from laughing. "Yes, I would agree. She was Kastener's little princess from day one. Ever since his wife died—"

"Oh no! I'm sorry for interrupting. I hadn't realized that his wife—please, continue."

"His wife was in a hit and run accident a few years ago. They never figured out who did it. She was up in the city. We all thought it would have been captured on a traffic cam or someone's cell phone, but unfortunately, they couldn't find anything. It was very tragic. Jade was still in high school then."

"How awful! And now his daughter too. The poor man."

"There is nothing *poor* about that man, but I know what you mean. Jade was his world. He doted on her quite a bit: the new car, limitless credit card charges, you name it, she had it."

"She mentioned once that she was taking what she called an extended gap year after high school. Do you think she intended to go to college?"

"I do. Jade was incredibly intelligent. I'd have to look it up, but she might have been valedictorian. Everyone expected her to get her business degree and take over for Kastener in under a decade, but she wanted to travel. He can't tell her no, so travel she has."

"How interesting. I think I remember her mentioning having a boyfriend. Do you happen to know who that was? Maybe he might know why she was upset yesterday."

Sensing Ollaman's confusion, Cari clarified. "Mr. Kastener told me that the truck driver observed Jade crying when her car was coming at his truck. I spoke with him and he confirmed the story. I have never seen Jade upset, so I'm not sure what would trigger that. Maybe the boyfriend has an idea."

"That's a good idea. I think it was the Sheely boy. What's his name?" Ollaman clapped his hands. "Harold! Harold Sheely. He manages his grandparents' farm out north. That's probably where Jade was headed yesterday when she, uh…" He trailed off.

"I will look him up. Thank you, sir!" She hung up the phone and turned back to her computer.

The database was still open from when she looked up Mr. Minim's information. She typed Harold Sheely into the name field and left Brenington for the city. Not surprisingly, there was only one Harold Sheely in all of Brenington. It listed both his home address and his cell number. Cari picked up the receiver again and punched in his number. After four rings, a voicemail recording picked up.

"This is Harold with Sheely Farms. Please leave your name, number, and a brief message after the beep."

"Hi Mr. Sheely. This is Cari Turnlyle with the Brenington Beagle. Please give me a call when you get this." She hesitated, then left her number, still debating whether she should mention Jade by name. The extended pause led the voicemail to believe she had finished, and it beeped in her ear. *Guess that settles it.*

* * * * *

The helper carefully washed their hands, then dried them on the terrycloth towel next to the sink. The incident with the girl yesterday had been mostly successful. Reading about it in the newspaper today, it seemed that everyone believed her death to be an accident. Reaching up, they pinched the bridge of their nose to try to relieve a headache. While they had successfully punished the girl, they had unintentionally put another soul at risk. Thankfully, that person was not hurt, but it had left the helper in a quandary. As penance for the mistake, they had undergone a twenty-four hour fast from food, water, and vitamin supplements. As expected, this resulted in a terrible headache. The helper would have to do better next time.

* * * * *

The medical examiner's office was in the basement of the police station. Genevieve usually tried to avoid it if at all possible. It wasn't just the smell of death and chemicals, or the cold temperatures, or the lack of windows; it was all of it. The place was always so dreary, but, unfortunately, when your chosen profession was detective, you went there often.

She looked over at Alex. He was wiping a little Vaseline right along the edge of his nostrils. It was his trick to avoid the smell getting stuck in his nose.

"Again with the Vaseline?" She asked him as they walked down the stairs together.

"Hey, if it works, it works."

"It's so greasy, though. The rest of the day, my face feels like I was ravenously eating tacos from Larry's, except I haven't had a taco, Alex. I just have a greasy face."

"You want to get tacos after this?"

"Are you crazy, man?" She couldn't believe he could consider eating anything after being in the morgue. Gross.

"I'll take that as a no. Want some?" He offered her a little packet of Vaseline.

"Ugh. Fine. Sure. It's better than that funky smell." She took it from him and squeezed a little out onto her index finger to rub under her nose.

Alex knocked lightly on the door, then after pausing a moment, opened it up. A blast of cold air hit Genevieve in the face. She stepped under Alex's arm and entered the room. Alex was six foot six, standing barefoot while Genevieve barely reached five foot two. The medical examiner was looking at something with his microscope. He turned around to greet them. His curly salt and pepper hair was in quite a state, as though he had pulled his mask on and off repeatedly throughout the day. Genevieve supposed it was possible that he just never combed it in the first place.

"Detectives. Come on in. I was just looking at something I found on our victim's cheek."

They stepped over to his desk to look at the screen, amplifying the image under the microscope. Genevieve could recognize skin cells after seeing them on the same screen several times over the last few years, but wasn't sure what else he was trying to show them.

"Hi Dr. Green. Sorry to be obtuse, but what are you looking at exactly?"

"I'll have to run a test to confirm it, but I think there was some DMSO on her cheek."

"In English, please?" Alex asked.

Dr. Green chuckled. "Certainly. DMSO is dimethyl sulfoxide. It has a myriad of uses, one being that it makes a good solvent to deliver other medications through the skin. It also has some analgesic properties."

"Why would it be on her cheek? Does that make you reconsider declaring the death to be accidental?"

"Not necessarily. The father of our victim wants a full autopsy, so I'm running a tox screen to see if there was anything in her system that shouldn't have been there. I might get those results before the end of the day, but it could be tomorrow. It could just be that she had a toothache or a sore jaw and rubbed some on there to relieve the pain."

"Did you find any evidence that she was crying?" Genevieve asked.

Dr. Green spun his chair away from the desk and got up. "I did. If you look right here along the side of her face, you can see the salt residue from her tears. I already tested the residue to make sure."

Genevieve looked at the young woman's face. She could easily see the line of crystals left behind along the side of her nose and both sides of her face running down towards her ears. It definitely made her death more suspicious.

"Did you find anything else noteworthy?" She asked.

"No, that's all I have for you for now. I will keep you posted on the tox screen."

"Thanks, Dr. Green," Alex said.

He flicked his head towards the door, indicating he was ready to go. Genevieve pushed on the crossbar to open the door and get back into the more temperate air.

"What do you make of the DMSO?" She asked Alex.

"It's interesting, right? We need to find out what she was doing before she got in her car to drive."

"Who would know her schedule? Do you think they got anything off of her phone?

"We could ask next door since we're already down here."

They walked across the hall and knocked on the door to the department's CSU office. It was technically an extension of the ME's office. The person nearest the door looked up and waved them in. Three women and two men sat at individual desks with computers. Only two of them looked up when Genevieve and Alex walked in.

"What can we help you two with this morning?" A young man in a button-up shirt and khakis asked.

"Hi, Bob. We were wondering who got the victim's cell phone from the collision yesterday?" Genevieve asked.

"That would be me." The wiry man next to Bob spoke up. He wore jeans with loafers and a green polo shirt. "What do you need to know?"

"Thanks, Chris. The ME found some sort of ointment on her cheek near her jawline. We were hoping to get a look at her schedule and see if we could figure out why it was there."

Chris had a cell phone connected to his computer's hard drive via a USB cord. He clicked around on the computer screen with his mouse until he found a folder labeled 'Calendar'.

"Let's see what we have in here. I had just started accessing her phone when you walked in. Her father brought it in this morning along with the cord. He didn't know the passcode, but we were able to bypass it." He opened the calendar.

The young woman's calendar was fairly empty. The entire month of August only had three appointments on it: one with the dentist, one with her father for lunch, and one with someone named Olivia.

"It looks like she went to the dentist yesterday morning. Do you think her father knows who her dentist was? Or is there a contact number with the calendar appointment?" Alex asked.

Chris clicked on the appointment, but it only made the details they could already see bigger. There was no phone number listed.

Alex groaned. "That means we have to call that guy back."

"Can we help you with anything else?"

"Why don't you give us a printout of all of her calls and texts for the last week, as well as a list of her contacts?" Genevieve asked.

"Could I send them digitally? We have access to her phone records."

"Perfect. I'll let you know if I think of anything else. Thanks, Chris."

They nodded their goodbyes to the CSU group and exited the room.

Chapter 4

C ari opened a new document so she could organize her thoughts about Jade and Mr. Kastener's insistence that the collision was not an accident. She was making a list of the people she had spoken with as well as what information they offered when she sensed someone was watching her. She minimized the window and looked over her shoulder.

"Can I help you with something, Lionel?" She asked the portly man who was peering at her over the edge of her cubicle wall. Not surprisingly, his ill-fitting toupee was askew and just as obvious as always.

He looked over the rims of his reading glasses at her. "I was just on my way out of the office."

"And?" She asked with a frown.

"Thought I'd see what you were working on so furiously over here. I could hear your fingers slamming into the keys from across the room."

She resisted the urge to roll her eyes, knowing he couldn't hear that well at all. "I'm following up on the collision from yesterday."

He raised his eyebrows. "The girl who was texting and driving?"

"I'm not sure there is any evidence of that, Lionel. Where did you hear it?"

"Oh, come on. Everyone knows kids these days never take their eyes off their phones. It's obvious what happened."

"Well, thanks for clearing it up. I guess I don't need to make any more calls." She was about to add a dig about him covering the local apple-picking festival rather than *real* news, when her desk phone rang. "If you'll excuse me, Lionel."

Thankfully, the old goat walked away and out the office doors. She still didn't trust the sleazy old man after he stole some of her notes from her story earlier this year. Lionel had taken advantage of Cari's hasty exit from the office one day and helped himself to her files when she left her computer unlocked.

"Brenington Beagle, this is Cary Turnlyle. How can I help you today?" She said into the receiver.

"Ms. Turnlyle, this is Harold Sheely. I'm returning your call." The young man had a deep voice with a bit of an accent that she couldn't quite place.

"Mr. Sheely—"

"Please, call me Harold."

"Harold, I'm Cari. I called about your girlfriend, Jade. I'm very sorry for your loss. I just had a few questions, if you have a moment?"

He let out a breath before speaking. "Certainly, though I'm not sure how much help I can be."

"Jade's father is convinced that the collision yesterday was not an accident."

"I'm aware of his opinion."

"You don't share it?"

"Ms. Turnlyle, uh, Cari. Jade's father would never believe a negative thing about his princess. I'm not being condescending. Don't get me wrong, but Jade walked on water in her dad's eyes."

"I assume she was driving on that road yesterday because she was going to see you?"

"That's correct. We had planned to have a picnic out at the farm."

"What time were you planning to meet?"

"She was hoping to get out here by noon, but she had a dentist appointment in the morning and wasn't sure how long it would take."

"Do you know what the appointment was for? Just a cleaning

or..." She trailed off.

"Hmmm...I think she mentioned something about sealants."

"Okay. Do you know who her dentist was?"

"I think everyone in her family sees Dr. Santer. That's who we both always saw growing up. I don't know why she'd switch."

"Harold, was Jade, um, was Jade happy?" Cari stuttered through the question.

"Happy? What? Why wouldn't she have been happy?"

"It's just that, well, the driver of the other vehicle says that he could see her face before her car, well, before the collision. He says that she was crying."

"Crying?! I don't think I've ever seen Jade cry unless we were watching one of those sad ads about the animals without homes. Jade was the definition of happy. How could she not be happy? She had everything she wanted and no responsibilities at all."

"What do you mean?"

"Her dad paid all her bills, bought her that fancy new car, didn't make her work or go to college...should I go on?"

"I had that impression of her too—that she was happy, but I didn't know her well. Did you resent her carefree life?"

"Wait. How do you know Jade?"

"We were in the same morning yoga class. She was always smiling and friendly."

Cari heard him sigh again.

"You asked if I resented Jade. Of course not. I *loved* Jade. I wanted to marry her. Her dad refused to give his blessing until she went to college, though. He was worried that if I married her first, she would never buckle down and get her degree."

"What was her hesitation regarding college?"

"Honestly, I wouldn't call it hesitation as much as I'd call it being spoiled. I know that sounds harsh, but it's the truth. Kastener never made Jade do anything. Sure, he set some boundaries, but he would never withhold anything from her. He wanted her to take over his company one day, you know?"

"I was reading about his company and had assumed as much."

"He wasn't going to sign it over to her without a degree. Don't get me wrong, Jade was no dummy. She was brilliant—the top of her graduating class. But she lived such a pampered life that she had no desire to step out of it and be more independent."

"I guess I can understand that."

"This other driver, the trucker, is he reliable? Are the authorities certain that he's being honest?"

"I didn't visit the scene of the accident, Harold, but I did speak with Mr. Minim—the other driver." She explained. "He sounded genuine to me. I don't think he's lying about what happened."

"She just drove in front of his rig? But why? And why was she crying?"

'I guess you can see why her dad is convinced it wasn't an accident."

"But if she was crying, does that mean she intentionally drove in front of him?"

"I don't know, Harold. I would like to believe that she wouldn't do that."

"I KNOW she wouldn't!" He shouted. Cari heard him draw a sharp breath. "I'm sorry. I just. I can't believe I'll never see her again. I can't believe she's really gone."

"It's okay. I understand."

"I need to go, unless you have other questions for me?"

"No, that's all I have right now."

"Can you keep me in the loop? I mean, if you figure out that this wasn't just a case of careless driving on Jade's part, will you let me know?"

"I will call you myself. Thanks, Harold." She hung up the receiver as she ran her locket along its chain.

* * * * *

"Let's call Kastener and see if he knows who her dentist was.

25

He might even know why she had an appointment." Alex suggested.

"When you say *let's* call Kastener, do you mean *you're* going to call him, or…?" Genevieve asked with a smirk on her face as she picked up the receiver for her desk phone.

"Hello, Mr. Kastener. It's Detective Viacorte. Yes. I—Yes. We have been going through Jade's movements for the last few days. We checked her calendar and were wondering if you know who her dentist was? She had an appointment yesterday morning."

"Dr. Santer, her office is over on Main. She took over her father's business when he retired last year. Do you need the phone number?"

"No, sir. Thank you. We'll be in touch." She hung up before he could grill her for more information.

"She went to Dr. Santer. Are you familiar with the office?"

"They don't take our insurance, but I've heard of them. Let me look up the phone number." He punched a few keys on his keyboard with his left hand while pulling the telephone receiver with his right.

Genevieve cocked her head at him. "How do you still not know how to type properly?"

"Shut it," he said as he keyed in the phone number. "Hi, yes, this is Detective Alex Runimoss with the Brenington Police Department. I'm calling in regard to one of your patients. Jade Kastener. I can hold." He put the receiver on his shoulder to cover the microphone. "Think they're gonna give us a hard time about HIPAA or whatever?"

"Tell them she is no longer living."

He rolled his eyes and put the phone back up to his ear. "Not my first rodeo. Still on hold. I'm going to put it on speaker." He hit a few buttons on the keypad and replaced the receiver into the cradle. Elevator music filled the office. Genevieve shrugged and looked at her notes.

"Where did Kastener leave that list of her friends we could talk to? I suppose we could check her phone records for frequent calls—" She stopped when she heard a click on the phone call.

"This is Dr. Santer. How can I help you?" Alex grabbed the receiver and put it back to his ear.

"Hi, Dr. Santer. This is Detective Alex Runimoss with Brenington PD. I wanted to ask you about a patient: Jade Kastener."

"Unfortunately, Detective, we can't tell you if Ms. Kastener was a patient here or not. The federal law mandates—"

"You do understand that Ms. Kastener was killed in a collision yesterday around noon, right? She's no longer living?"

"Be that as it may, we would need—"

"Excuse me, ma'am, but I don't need to know her health history. I just need to know if she made it to her appointment yesterday."

"We're going to need a warrant or permission from her next of kin to release that information."

"So, she was a patient of yours?"

"Detective—"

"Fine. We'll talk to her dad and be in touch." He hung up the receiver. "No luck, though I think it's safe to say that she was a patient there. We already knew that, I guess. But this was interesting."

"What?"

"Someone was talking in the background; it sounded like the receptionist who originally answered the call. She said something about getting two calls about Jade in the last hour. Who else would be calling?"

Genevieve frowned. "My money is on Cari."

"Cari? You mean the reporter chick?"

Genevieve's frown deepened.

"Sorry, the female newspaper woman?"

"The one and the same. I'll send her a text and see what she knows."

Genevieve took her cell phone out of her pocket and scrolled through her contacts until she got to Cari's number.

Cari, what is your interest in Jade Kastener's wreck?

Why? You investigating? Want to compare notes?

I would consider it. Tonight, 9:30, O'Zook's?

It's a date!

"Sounds like it was Cari. I'm going to catch up with her tonight."

"I bet Kastener is barking at her too."

"You're probably right. He's probably working every angle that he can. I get the impression that she was more than just his princess. She was his world."

"Agreed. At some point, he's going to have to accept that she isn't coming back, regardless of what caused her death."

Genevieve nodded. "And that might be the tallest hurdle of all."

* * * * *

Cari put her phone away, wondering what tipped Genevieve off to her involvement in Jade's accident. She cringed when the word *accident* crossed her mind. If she was going to get anywhere on this story, she was going to have to stop thinking about it like an accident and more like a wrongful death.

She went back to her document of notes. The truck driver, Mr. Minim seemed genuine and honest in his retelling of the collision. She couldn't think of any sort of motive that would have led him to smash into Jade's car. It only slowed down his day. The next person on her list was Jade's father, Frederick. She dismissed him immediately. The man was earnestly pursuing every possible path toward justice for his daughter. It seemed unlikely that he would have also been the one to cause her harm.

Harold Sheely followed Frederick on the list. Cari didn't think she could fully eliminate the young man yet. While she didn't see a clear reason why he would have Jade killed, she also didn't know enough about him to say that he wouldn't have done it. She tapped her pencil on her desk and thought about the dentist. The office was unwilling to concede that Jade was a patient of theirs because of HIPAA. Cari hoped that informing them about the fatal collision would have changed their minds, but they wouldn't budge. That was the only stop besides the yoga studio she could find on Jade's schedule for that morning.

Of course, all of this brainstorming could be a complete waste of time because it was all just an accident anyway! Something was tickling the back of her mind. She hadn't known Jade very long, but she had always seemed so happy at the yoga classes. People hide their feelings well, and maybe Jade was secretly depressed. Maybe that was why she was crying. *Did she purposefully drive in front of the truck?* Maybe something else had happened to upset her. Cari looked down at her hand and saw she was fiddling with her locket again. It was almost lunchtime; she decided it was time for a break and a phone call. She locked her computer and grabbed her purse, calling her grandmother as she walked towards the exit.

"Is that my Cari?" Her grandmother asked.

"Hi, Grandmother! How are you today?"

"Wonderful, my dear. Happy to hear your voice."

"I'm happy to hear yours too."

"What's on your mind, dear?"

Cari sighed. "Well, I wrote a short article yesterday about the young woman who died in the car crash…"

"I read it! Such a tragedy. She was very young, even younger than you! Do they know any more about what happened?"

"Not really. There is some speculation that she was crying right before the other vehicle struck her car, but everyone I've talked to says that she was a happy person. I *knew* her and I would also say that she was a happy person."

"Oh, you knew her too?"

"She went to the same morning yoga class as me. She was

29

easy-going, carefree, and happy. She would always breeze in and breeze out, like everything in life was roses."

"Who says that she was crying then?"

"The truck driver. Jade—the young woman—drove a convertible. She had the top down and he could see her face pretty well, I guess."

"You don't think she was suicidal then."

"I don't know what to think. She was *fine*, her normal, happy self when I saw her yesterday morning."

"What led you to look into this further? Your article called her death an accident."

"Her dad. He called and was very upset that her death was being referred to as accidental. He is certain that she was murdered."

Her grandmother gasped. "Murdered! By the truck driver?"

"No, I don't think he blames the truck driver, but he does not think this was an accidental death. He says that she was a very good and conscientious driver. He contacted the police department about it too. My friend Genevieve is putting in some extra time on it."

"Her father must have a lot of influence."

"He most certainly does." She explained what she had read about the family.

"Oh, yes. I recognize the name now. Well, if it wasn't an accident and you don't think she would hurt herself, then what happened?"

"That's the million-dollar question. I'm meeting with Genevieve tonight to compare notes, well, to hopefully compare notes."

"Hopefully?"

"Detectives aren't really supposed to share their information with the news media, Grandmother."

"But this is kind of an unusual case, so maybe she'll let you in?"

"That's what I'm hoping for. I just don't know what angle to look at, Grandmother. I think it will crush her father if we figure out that she took her own life."

"He is the one driving the extra investigation, though, right?"

"That's right."

"He probably knew her better than anyone else. No parent wants to outlive their child, nor do they want to believe their child would harm themselves. If he has been honest with you so far, then you have to seriously consider his perspective. Keep digging, girl. You'll figure it out!"

"Thanks, Grandmother. I hope you're right. I don't think he's going to let this go until he has the answer he's looking for."

"Go get some lunch. Food always helps me think."

"Okay, Grandmother. I love you."

"I love you more. Tell Bob that I said hi." She ended the call.

"Tell Bob—" She started to ask before she realized that her grandmother had already hung up. *We're just friends already!*

Cari tilted her head and almost laughed out loud. She did need to give Bob a call, but she was *not* going to tell him that her grandmother said hi. She pulled up his number.

"Cari, again! That's twice in one day." She heard his chair scrape along the floor as he pushed it back. "I'm going to head outside for a walk. I'll be back."

She listened as his steps echoed in the hallway outside of his office and in the stairwell up to the ground floor. Soon, she could hear the wind and knew he had made it outside.

"Okay, I found out from Jade's boyfriend that she went to the dentist yesterday morning. He told me that she sees Dr. Santer over on Main Street. The office wouldn't really tell me much because of HIPAA, but maybe she had a reaction to something from her appointment? The boyfriend said that she was getting a sealant replaced."

"Hmmm. Fixing a sealant is non-invasive; they wouldn't have even used lidocaine to numb the area, so I can't imagine that something from the dentist appointment..."

"What? I can *hear* you thinking, Bob."

"The ME discovered that she had some DMSO on the outside of her jaw. Maybe the hygienist used it on her."

"What is DMSO? Could that impair her driving abilities?"

"Oh no, nothing like that. It's fairly common; I think you can even order it online anymore. It has some analgesic, uh, pain reducing properties. Maybe she ground her teeth or clenched her jaw and they were trying to relieve some of that pain topically? It's hard to say, and we don't even know that it came from the dentist."

Cari heard her phone click, indicating that she had received a text message. "Okay, well, I think the DMSO is of interest. I'm going to look into it some more. Thanks, Bob!"

"You're welcome, Cari. Why are you so interested in this young woman's death anyway?"

"Two reasons, I guess. One, she was in my morning yoga class and two, her dad called my article about the, uh, wreck yesterday drivel. DRIVEL! I suppose I want to show him that I'm a good writer."

"I understand. You shouldn't let him get under your skin. You know you're a great writer, right?"

"Thanks, Bob. I gotta run. I'll be in touch."

"Don't I know it." He ended the call.

She looked at her text messages and reread Genevieve's texts. She detected a hint of annoyance in her friend's messages, but maybe Cari was just being self-conscious. She had every right to investigate Jade's death too.

* * * * *

Cari swung into the parking lot of O'Zook's and saw that Genevieve had already arrived, as usual. She knew her friend liked to get to the place early so she could get the back booth. Then, she could watch the door and whoever was coming or going. She was always on her detective game, even if she wasn't on the clock.

When she entered the restaurant, she immediately looked to the back right corner and made eye contact with her friend. Genevieve was dressed in her usual after-hours attire of a SUNY t-shirt and jeans. Cari wondered if Gen had anything besides SUNY shirts to wear. Her friend's dark hair was pulled back into a high ponytail and she could see the intrigue in her hazel eyes as she approached the table.

"Hey, Cari. How have you been? I ordered us some chips and queso. Margaritas too." Genevieve smiled.

"I'm doing pretty well. Switching from sports to general news has been an adjustment, but it's a welcome one." She responded as she slid into the booth.

"Congrats again on the promotion! You definitely worked hard for that."

"Thank you. So, Jade Kastener. I take it her dad is pushing for an official investigation on your side too?"

"Yeah. He scheduled a meeting with Alex and me this morning. I guess he told you that he doesn't think it was a traffic accident?"

"Actually, he called my writing 'drivel' and said I needed to do some real research before updating my story for the newspaper."

"He wants you to print a retraction?"

"He didn't go that far, but I think he was close. I understand. Jade was an only child. I guess his wife died unexpectedly as well."

Genevieve blinked, revealing to Cari that this wasn't news to her. "He mentioned that his wife had died a few years ago, but didn't elaborate."

"Yes, a few years ago. Kastener is familiar with my boss, as I'm sure he is with yours too. Anyway, I talked to him about some family background to get a better idea of the lay of the land. Ollaman told me about his wife's death. Hit and run."

"Oh, how terrible. I guess that must have happened right before

I started here."

Cari nodded. "They never figured out who did it. Now he has another tragedy piled on top of it. I can understand his need for answers, even if they aren't the ones he's looking for."

"So, you don't think there was foul play?"

Before Cari could answer, the waitress returned with their margaritas. She had her notepad out, ready to take their order. Genevieve raised her eyebrows at Cari.

"Let's see. I'm not terribly hungry, but how about a second appetizer, Gen?"

"Works for me. How about the crostini?"

"Perfect." They nodded at the waitress who took their menus and jotted the order down before walking away.

"Where were we? Foul play? I don't know what to think. I heard that the ME found some sort of ointment on her cheek." She watched Genevieve's eyes for a hint of recognition, but her friend had a good poker face this time.

"I guess since it isn't really an official investigation yet, it can't hurt to discuss details like that. Yes, it's something called DMSO. I haven't had a chance to read about it today. Do you know anything about how it's used?"

"I did read an article that said it could be used to deliver other drugs through the skin. It's a solvent or whatever."

"That's what the ME told us too. It can also be used for pain. We were hoping to find out from her dentist if she had something like TMJ or clenched her jaw a lot, but they wouldn't talk to us without permission from her father. He's hopefully taking care of that tomorrow for us. Alex called him this afternoon."

"What do you make of the dad?"

"He's pretty intense and *really* well-connected. Alex told me that he's in the 'old money' crowd of Brenington."

"I read that too. I feel like whatever answers I'm able to find for him are not going to make him feel any better."

"Agreed. It seems like he has somewhat of an unrealistic end goal, not closure, but that figuring out what happened can somehow change what actually happened." Genevieve sighed. "What is your next step?"

"Well, I spoke with her boyfriend earlier today. He had no idea why Jade would have been crying."

"We haven't made it through the list of friends Kastener passed along—"

"You got a contact list?!" Cari asked incredulously.

"We have her phone too; that's how we found out about the dentist. She wasn't a big fan of putting things in her calendar."

"Maybe she used a paper calendar? I know that seems archaic, but they do still exist. I didn't think to ask Kastener. Did she still live at home?"

"That's the impression I get; rent-free life and all that."

Cari nodded. "What about a purse? Maybe she had a little pocket calendar."

"Not a bad idea. I still can't believe she didn't use a digital calendar on her phone."

"It could be on a different app than the default calendar app. Maybe in her email app or something?"

"You're making me feel like a fool for not thinking of any of this already."

"I think we were all caught a little off guard with this. You asked about my next step. I think I want to talk to B--, a friend of mine about what could have been combined with the DMSO to incapacitate someone."

Genevieve tilted her head at Cari. "Your friend who?"

Cari smiled. "My friend who chooses to remain anonymous."

Chapter 5

*A*lex ran his fingers through his short, dark hair. "I hate this thing!" He flicked the computer screen.

"The computer?" Genevieve asked.

"No, well, yes! But this stupid app. It keeps logging me out."

"Sometimes when that happens, it's because someone or something else is logging in elsewhere."

"Like Kastener?"

"I kind of doubt it. He doesn't seem eager to impede our progress by sticking his nose into it every minute. Maybe the car is still connected?" She picked up her desk phone and dialed a number.

"Hey, Chris. It's Genevieve. Have you checked on the victim's car at all?"

"We were just getting started on it. Why?"

"Could you disable the Bluetooth or whatever communication system it uses to talk to the app that Mr. Kastener put on it?"

"Oh, sure! I didn't realize that you guys were trying to access that. Do you need any help?"

Genevieve looked over at Alex waving his middle finger at his computer screen. "Um, I think that we will be able to handle it once you guys disable the feature." She stifled a laugh.

"Consider it done."

"Thanks. I appreciate it." She hung up.

"Okay, log in again. It should stay active this time. CSU was going over the vehicle downstairs."

"Have you seen it? The car, I mean?"

"Only the accident, uh, photos from the scene. It looked pretty smashed."

"I can't believe it didn't catch on fire. It was *drilled* by that truck. I'm surprised they can even turn it on."

"They might just be hooking it up to a computer. It probably doesn't start anymore."

"Then what are we doing with this thing?" He gestured at the computer screen again.

"I'm not sure if they can pull the information on the app from the car or not, but cars have their own version of a black box nowadays just like planes."

"My car doesn't."

"You drive a ninety-nine Ford Escort." She rolled her eyes. "Does it even have Bluetooth?"

He rolled his eyes back at her. "It runs and no one knows where I'm driving it or when I'm driving it."

"Paranoid much?"

"Let's focus, shall we?"

"Lead on, captain."

"Okay, the collision occurred at 12:03 p.m. The activity log is…right here. Let's see. She was traveling at about 55 miles per hour. The cruise control was on."

"Click on the little map button. I think we can see her speed and other data in real time with her position on the road."

Alex clicked on the button and a cartoon vehicle appeared on a map. A text bubble above it stated its speed and direction of travel as well as the longitude and latitude. He clicked on the triangle-shaped button to make the car move forward.

"Pause it. Put it on half-speed."

Alex looked up at her. "Do you want to run the controls?"

"Move over." Genevieve clicked a few icons and changed the speed of the playback to fifty percent. Then she moved the vehicle back to just before the curve.

"She's still going 55 right before that curve. She's not slowing down at all. The brake is not engaged. The cruise is still on. She never braked, Gen. She didn't accelerate either. She didn't move at all."

"What does this mean?"

"I don't know, but it doesn't feel right. If she was suicidal, wouldn't she accelerate?"

"Where's her phone log? Maybe she was texting and not paying attention."

"It's minimized."

Genevieve moved the mouse to the bottom of the screen and found the document with the phone log. One page had a list of calls made on the morning of the collision. The other page had text messages.

"She wasn't texting, but a call came through at 12:02:38. It says she didn't answer it. Whose number is this? Spammer or someone she knew?"

Alex rifled through the papers on his desk until he found the list of contacts Kastener had given them.

"Who is Harold Sheely?"

"Where is he on the list?"

"He's first."

"Gotta be the boyfriend. Cari mentioned one last night."

"How'd she know about the boyfriend?"

"She didn't say. Let's call him. See if there was some reason he was calling her."

"Or if he knows why she wouldn't answer. She had Bluetooth and her phone was connected to it. It's obviously something she knew how to use."

"Let's give Mr. Sheely a ring. Maybe he can enlighten us." Genevieve said to Alex. "Are you dialing or am I?"

"I got this one," Alex said as he picked up his phone. He pushed a button to put it on speaker.

"This is Harold…hello?"

"Harold Sheely?" Alex asked.

"Yes, and this is?"

"This is Detective Runimoss with the Brenington PD. My partner, Detective Viacorte and I would like to speak with you. We can come to you or you can come to the station."

Genevieve raised her eyebrows at Alex in a questioning manner. She thought that they'd handle the interview over the phone.

"I guess this is about Jade." The young man responded, his voice a bit quieter. "I'm not getting a lot done today anyway. I can be at the station in fifteen minutes." The call ended.

"Why are you bringing him in for a face-to-face?" Genevieve asked.

"I think it's a little suspicious that he called her in the minute before she drove in front of that rig."

"It is a bit strange that he didn't tell anyone or come forward. Hey, do you think the phone call could have triggered something that gave him control of her car? Within that app? Maybe it can be controlled remotely."

"Don't look at me. You're the tech expert between the two of us."

"I'm going to go check in with Chris. Maybe he can tell us if something malfunctioned with the car or if the app can control the vehicle. Wait for me before you interview him."

* * * * *

Cari reviewed her notes from the day before. The dentist's office hadn't been particularly helpful when she called yesterday, but maybe if she asked general questions, they would answer those. She looked up the number and dialed it from her desk phone.

"Dr. Santer's office. This is Sonia. How may we help you?" A cheerful voice sounded in her ear.

"Hi Sonia. This is Cari Turnlyle. I have a question about anesthesia practices in your office. Do you use the product, uh, DMSO?" Cari asked as she double-checked her notes for the name.

"As a numbing agent…or?" Sonia sounded confused.

"Maybe? I have read that it's an analgesic. Is it used for pain in your office?"

"I'm not sure. Let me get you Dr. Santer."

Cari heard a click and realized she was on hold when the classical music started. After a few minutes, the line clicked again.

"This is Dr. Santer. You have a question about DMSO?"

"Yes. I was wondering if your office uses it as an analgesic or numbing agent?" She asked using Sonia's words.

"It's not our standard practice, no. I actually can't remember when we used it last. I'm not sure if we have any in the office right now at all. Occasionally, we'll have a patient who doesn't respond to lido or nox and we'll try that as a last resort. It's very rare."

Cari heard her ask someone, possibly Sonia, a question. She assumed she had covered the receiver with her hand to muffle it. The person responding to her had a raspy voice, making her wonder if it was really Sonia answering or someone else. She waited for the dentist to continue.

"Okay, it looks like we do have some. Of course, I can't tell you who we used it on."

"I understand. Would it be something that you applied or one of the hygienists?"

"One of our hygienists would do it."

"Okay, thank you, Dr. Santer. One last question. Would a hygienist always tell you if she or he administered DMSO?"

"It would be in the chart, but they also verbally update me before I see a patient."

"Thank you. I appreciate your candor."

"No problem." She ended the call.

Cari wasn't sure that this eliminated the dentist's office as the source of the DMSO. She wondered if she would have had more luck if she had gone in person to speak to the dentist or hygienists about using the ointment. It seemed like her questions had stimulated some sort of conversation. Obviously, Jade could have used it herself or she could have gone somewhere else where it was applied. She sensed this was an important piece of information. Bob said that DMSO was fairly common, but she had never heard of it, so how common could it be?

She wondered if Kastener would let her look through Jade's room and bathroom. Maybe Jade kept some at the house to use on occasion. She opened up her document that had her notes and musings on the story so far. Creating a new heading titled "Next Steps", she added calling Bob about the DMSO and Kastener about looking through Jade's belongings.

* * * * *

Genevieve hurried downstairs to Chris' desk within the CSU. While she was still a bit skeptical that the collision was anything but an unfortunate accident, she thought that someone having remote access to the victim's vehicle was a promising lead. Chris was seated at his desk and typing away at the computer.

"Hey, Chris," she started to say, but he jumped. "Sorry! I didn't mean to startle you or break your train of thought. I had a couple of questions about the car and the app that was associated with it."

"Shoot." He said, pushing his keyboard back under the desktop.

"Could someone have controlled the car remotely if they had access to the app?"

Chris tilted his head sideways at her. "Say more, I'm not sure I totally follow."

"Like, could they disengage the brakes or make the car accelerate or something like that?"

He shook his head. "No, the app didn't offer that type of control. Any approved users were only able to *see* where the car was or how fast it was going. They couldn't manipulate it or anything."

Genevieve frowned. "Rats. I was hoping we'd come up with a

reasonable lead here. Was there anything that malfunctioned with the car? The brakes, the steering…" she trailed off.

"No. The car's computer reports it was functioning properly in all capacities."

"Okay. Thanks for your help, Chris." She turned to leave the CSU when she stopped short. "What if she received an incoming phone call through the Bluetooth feature? Could that have jammed the car's computer or something and made it stop responding to the driver?"

"No, I have never heard of that happening. Regardless, we could still see if the driver hit the brake pedal even if the brakes did not engage. She didn't touch the brakes or the gas. She just kept driving…right in front of that semi."

Genevieve sighed again. "I guess it was a bit of a long shot. Thanks again."

* * * * *

"Chris said that the app is informative only. It can't regulate anything in the car. It can't start the vehicle or turn it off or anything else like that." Genevieve told Alex when she got back upstairs after what turned out to be a rather brief conversation.

"Okay, well, for what it's worth, that was a good idea. I guess that puts another point on the accidental death side."

"I didn't realize we were keeping score."

"You know what I mean." He shrugged. "What about the car itself? Was the app correct in saying that nothing was wrong?"

"Yeah, the car is fine; I mean, the car *was* fine before it met up with the 18-wheeler. Did we hear back from Green about the tox screen, yet?"

"Oh, yes. Got it right here." He shuffled the papers on his desk until finding the one he wanted. "Caffeine was the only *drug* in her system. He tested for a whole slew of things, but caffeine was the only positive result."

"So, she wasn't drugged. It's looking more and more like no one caused this intentionally, except for possibly the driver herself."

Alex nodded. "The boyfriend should be here any minute."

"I'm going to go wait for him by Dana's desk." She turned and walked toward the front desk.

Genevieve scanned the sidewalk and street outside the precinct, watching for the young man to arrive. She spotted him instantly. Harold Sheely was tall and broad-shouldered, with a rugged complexion most likely developed from working in the sun on the family farm. He had medium brown hair that looked like it might be curly if it was allowed to grow more than half an inch at any given time. As he drew closer, she could see that his eyes were a pale shade of blue that almost made them look grey. She signaled to him to follow her when he stepped inside.

"Mr. Sheely, I presume?"

He nodded. "Please, call me Harold. I take it you're Detective Viacorte. The person on the phone sounded much different."

Genevieve smiled. "That was my partner, Detective Runimoss. He's waiting for us right over here."

She led him into the detective bay and over to where Alex sat behind a desk. Alex stood up and they followed him down the hallway to the interrogation room. Genevieve sensed some tension in Harold when they bypassed the more casual setting of the desks. He stopped in the middle of the hallway.

"Wait a second. Is this like a formal interview, like an interrogation? Am I suspect?" His eyes looked panicked.

Genevieve placed her hand on his arm. "We wanted our conversation to be private. As of right now, Jade's wreck is classified as accidental. Is there something you know that would alter that classification?"

"No! I mean, uh, I don't know. Her dad doesn't think she would have an accident like that. He refuses to accept it."

"Mr. Sheely, why don't we sit down in one of these rooms

instead of having a frantic conversation in the hallway?" Alex asked him calmly.

Harold opened his mouth to speak again, then abruptly closed it. He nodded once at Alex and followed him into the first room. Genevieve gestured at the single chair on one side of the table.

Settling into her own chair, she laid a manila folder down and opened it. "Harold, as you know, we are investigating the collision at the request of Mr. Kastener. It has come to our attention that you called the victim right before she died. The phone records indicate that she did not answer the phone call, but let it ring to voice mail." She slid a sheet of paper with a highlighted section across the table to him.

"What?" Harold frowned, then picked up the paper and scanned it. "Oh, right. Yes, Jade was on the way to the farm. We were going to have a picnic together. I called to see if she was on her way. Usually, she calls to tell me she's coming, but I hadn't heard from her and wanted to check in."

Alex nodded. "Why wouldn't she answer your call? Had you been fighting?"

"Of course not! Jade isn't a fighter. Well, maybe with her dad about going to college, but she was the *easiest* person to be around. Happy, light-hearted. I have no idea why she didn't answer. Wait, do you think my call made her drive in front of that truck?"

Genevieve started to shake her head no, then stopped. "We can't really *know* anything, but it seems unlikely. The truck driver could see her face. She was looking straight forward."

"She was—what? She *chose* to do this?"

"Again, we don't know. That's what we're trying to figure out. You said that Jade was happy. Was anything bothering her or upsetting her?"

It looked like Harold was about to laugh when he cleared his throat. "Ahem, no. I don't know how else to say it. Life was good for Jade. She didn't worry about anything or want for anything."

"What else can you tell us about her? We're aware that she had a dentist appointment that morning. What was that for?"

"The reporter lady asked me about that too. I think it was for sealants."

Alex frowned. "What else did the *reporter lady* ask?"

"Uh, I think she might have asked if Jade ground her teeth at night or clenched her jaw."

"And?"

"And what?"

"Did she?"

"Um, I don't know, I guess. I don't think so. She didn't talk about jaw pain or anything."

Genevieve made a note and set her pen down. "Give us a run-down of a day in Jade's life. What time did she usually wake up, did she exercise, did she go out with friends?"

"Well, she still lived at home. I guess you knew that. She was taking a yoga class that she really liked. It was in the morning, um, maybe seven o'clock or so? I think she went to it Monday through Friday. She liked to go to the little shops downtown and browse or whatever. She might get lunch with a friend. I'm not sure what she did in the afternoons regularly. I always imagined her curled up in their big window seat reading a book, but I don't know that for a fact."

"Do you know the name of the yoga studio or instructor?"

"Hmmm, maybe Honest Practice or Always Practice? Something like that. I think the instructor was Julia something or other. She really liked her."

"We can look it up. Thanks. Is there anything else that she did regularly? Volunteering? Church?"

"No to church. She would occasionally join me and sit with my family, but it wasn't a regular thing for Jade. She has—um, *had* talked about volunteering at the soup kitchen. I can't remember the name of it. It opened a few years ago. Anyway, her dad really wanted her to do some charity work since she wasn't starting college yet, but she kept putting that off too."

45

"Is there anyone that didn't like Jade or anyone that seemed jealous of her?"

"I think the jealousy list is probably pretty long, but I can't think of anyone who was vindictive or angry about it. She was a really happy and friendly person. It kept people from hating her for her easy life."

Genevieve nodded and looked at Alex. One glance told her that he was out of questions too.

"Well, thank you for your openness, Harold. We appreciate you taking the time to speak with us. We'll let you know if we have any follow-up questions. Here is my card if you think of anything else. I'll walk you out." She stood up and opened the door for him.

Chapter 6

*T*he helper sat down to review the schedule for the week. Life had been less complicated when the primary role was taking care of the old man, but now life offered new opportunities to make the world better for everyone. Staring at the paper desk calendar, the helper entered a few items into their cell phone's iCalendar. The electronic calendar was essential to them. The helper had two part-time jobs with different weekly shifts.

The old man had suffered for close to a decade with debilitating multiple sclerosis. The helper was grateful that the family home had been bequeathed to them and not one of the younger siblings or left as something for the group of them to squabble over. During the seven years that the old man had been bedridden, the helper had amassed a significant collection of textbooks. They had been forced to withdraw from a prestigious university when the old man was no longer able to care for himself. The old man's wife had been gone long before that. She didn't approve of the old man's parenting demands and deserted the family when the helper was in grade school.

While caring for the patriarch, the helper had continued to study, hoping that one day a return to the university would be possible. The old man wanted all of his children to value education and gladly paid for the textbooks and online courses. The helper viewed it as a fair exchange: a nearly full-time caregiver position for continued educational funding. As the years wore on, the likelihood of the helper returning to school became smaller and smaller. The professors had been encouraging early on, but soon grew distant and stopped returning emails. Caring for the old man had drained much of the family's savings. The helper could no longer afford to go to the university. Glaring, the helper thought of a middle-aged man who had begun to coast through life, no longer making a living through hard work and dedication.

The middle-aged man, whom the helper knew to be about forty years old, had quit his job a few months ago. He had been a co-owner of a day-trading corporation, but had decided that he no longer wanted to work and sold his share to his partner of nearly twenty years.

Checking the clock on the microwave, the helper realized it was time to leave for their shift. It took a bit of time to set up the space before the business could open. Everything needed to be just right for their clientele. Luckily, the business was within walking distance from the home the helper had shared with the old man.

The helper gathered up their tools for work, including the small vial and syringe necessary to continue their mission. The middle-aged man would cross paths with the helper today. The helper would be ready to deliver the judgment required of all who neglected their calling in life.

Chapter 7

*P*eter Eskota pressed the button on the door of his Mercedes to lock it. He lived in a gated community, but you could never be too careful. He rotated his neck around as he walked up the steps to his brownstone. He had just enough time to grab a shower before his afternoon tee time with his golfing buddies. His shoe caught on the last step and he had to put a hand out to stop himself from falling. *The massage must have really relaxed me today!*

He entered the house and walked straight to the bar in his office to get a little snifter of brandy before showering. He knew he was running short on time, so rather than sip it as he usually would, he threw the whole glass back in one big swallow. The liquid burned as it went down and he felt the room spin a bit as the alcohol hit his system. He shook his head in an attempt to clear it, then set the glass down on the desk and walked towards the large staircase. His phone chirped with a new voicemail. He entered the passcode and hit play on the message.

"Mr. Eskota, this is Natalie Ellison with the Brenington MS Foundation. I'm calling to make sure you received our invitation for the fundraiser gala next month. We don't have a response from you as of yet and know how much you enjoyed the event last year. As a reminder, the seats are a thousand dollars each. Also, the luxury golf resort has donated another weekend getaway for four. I remember you won that in the live auction last year and wanted to be sure to let you know that it was on the docket again. I hope to hear from you soon. Thank you for your continued support of the MS Foundation."

He scoffed. "I no longer have a job, you fools! I can't afford fancy galas and fundraiser dinners. I need to save all my dollars for me, myself, and I."

He stomped up the stairs. The masseuse had been more chatty than usual today. The person always asked about how he was feeling, but today the masseuse had asked about his participation with the charity too. He almost chuckled out loud when he realized that two people had hounded him about his charitable giving within an hour. He would take it as a sign from God if he believed that God cared.

Peter peeled off his clothes and left them in a heap on the bathroom floor. He hit the button outside his multi-head shower system to fire it up. He had the system pre-programmed to 102°F when it was installed. Within moments, the light turned green, indicating that the water had reached the desired temperature. He reached out to grab the door handle and almost missed. *Maybe I should have skipped the booze today.* The steam was already building up inside the stall as he entered and turned to close the door behind him. *It's so thick, I can't see it. Did I forget to turn on the lights?* His mind seemed to slow down and it felt like his arm was moving in slow motion too. The room just kept getting darker and darker. He felt himself start to fall forward, but couldn't get his arms to lift to catch himself. They were too heavy.

Chapter 8

*G*enevieve looked around the brownstone and wondered how much it had cost just to decorate the space. Her own apartment seemed less than meager compared to the home of the late Peter Eskota. Alex seemed to be a little more on edge than usual.

"Who called this in?" She asked the officer standing near the front door.

He flipped through a small spiral notebook. "Mark Wickle. He said that Mr. Eskota missed their tee time this afternoon and wasn't answering his phone. They played without him, but Mr. Wickle was bothered that they hadn't heard from their friend all afternoon. He came by and let himself in with the garage code."

"Was the garage code common knowledge?" Genevieve asked.

"I think Mr. Wickle would bring in the mail and such if Eskota was out of town or whatever."

"Okay. Continue."

"Not much more to tell. He entered the home through the garage. Called out to his friend, but didn't get a response. He heard the shower running, so he went upstairs. Found him in the stall with the water running cold."

"Is he still here?"

"The friend or the body?"

"The friend."

"He's in the kitchen. He was pretty freaked out."

"Okay. Ask him not to leave. We'll talk to him after we look at the bathroom."

Genevieve looked over at Alex who was motioning towards

the stairs. She thanked the officer and quickly joined her partner.

"What's your take?" She asked him.

"Without seeing the body, I can't say for sure. I'm going to guess that he was probably a day drinker and he passed out in the shower. Hit his head. Something like that."

"He must have been a heavy day drinker if he passed out in the shower."

They followed the sounds of the voices to the bathroom. The mirror had streaks on it as though water droplets had run down its surface recently. The shower stall was bigger than the entire bathroom at Genevieve's apartment. There were nozzles in multiple places at multiple heights with one large shower head on the side wall.

"This must have cost a small fortune to install," Alex grumbled.

"I wouldn't know, but what I can tell you is that he expired around 12:30 p.m. It looks like he slipped and cracked his head open on this nozzle here." Dr. Green pointed to one of the nozzles on the third tier. Genevieve almost did a double-take when she saw Dr. Green. His hair was like a cloud of fuzz around his head.

Genevieve stepped closer to look at the indicated nozzle. It looked virtually identical to the other eight. She was about to take another step when a gloved hand touched her arm.

"Careful. I'm not sure how far the evidence sprayed without turning on the black light again." Dr. Green told her. "The nozzle doesn't look any different in the regular light, but when we looked at the whole room with the black light, you could see blood splatter emanating out from that nozzle. The contusion on his head is similar to the shape of the nozzle."

Genevieve nodded and took a step back. "Would you classify this as an accidental death or…?"

"Without running a tox screen, I can't say definitively. There isn't any sign of a struggle, but it's purely conjecture at this point. We'll get him down to the lab and keep you posted."

"Thanks, Green." Alex nodded and turned to exit the bathroom, then stopped near the sinks. Genevieve looked at him and nodded.

"We might as well see what's in the drawers and medicine cabinet. Maybe there's more than alcohol in his system."

They pulled up drawers and cabinets, finding typical items like a comb, toothbrush, toothpaste, and mouthwash. He had aftershave and a small first aid kit in the medicine cabinet as well as a small nondescript tube of something. Genevieve adjusted her gloves and picked up the tube carefully with just two fingers. The label read DMSO.

"DMSO. Interesting. This is the stuff that Kastener's daughter had on her jaw." Genevieve commented.

"CSU said it was common, right? It might not even take a prescription."

She shrugged and put it back in the cabinet. Next to the tube she noticed a carelessly folded piece of paper with colored graphics. She gently pulled it from the cabinet and opened it up.

"Alex, this is a little flier or something about how to use DMSO on your sore muscles. It has the name of a spa stamped on the bottom of it. Or maybe it's a massage parlor? Hard to say."

"Keep that in case we need to get in touch with them."

She pulled an evidence bag from her pocket and slid the paper inside. Then she snapped a quick photo of it before passing it over to the CSU team. The only other items in the cabinet were a bottle of ibuprofen and another one of Aleve. *Good to have options,* she thought.

Alex nodded. "Let's talk to his friends and see what they can tell us about his habits."

Genevieve nodded. "The officer by the front door said that Mr. Wickle is in the kitchen."

"That's the guy who called it in?"

"Yes, sir. He entered through the garage."

Alex strode across the entryway towards the rest of the house.

Genevieve had noticed an office behind the staircase when she had first entered the house. The kitchen and dining room must be further past the living room they were crossing now. She was taking three steps to every two of Alex's large strides just to keep up.

"Are we in a hurry?" She called out to him.

He slowed down and turned back to her. "Sorry, Shorty. I forget that you're only a half pint."

"Very funny." She saw a man in a royal blue polo shirt sitting on a kitchen stool in the adjacent room. He had thinning dark hair with a bit of grey at his temples. He seemed to be in a daze and hadn't noticed them approaching. Another officer was standing near the doorway.

Genevieve glanced at the dining room as they passed through it. The table was preset for two with elegant napkins, silver napkin rings, and layered ceramic plates. Two pieces of glassware were positioned with each place setting. She assumed one was probably for wine and the other for water.

"Think he was expecting someone for dinner or was this just a staged part of the house?" Alex asked her.

"Seems staged, but maybe his friends will know."

Alex cleared his throat to get the man's attention. His eyes popped open in alarm until he realized where he was.

"Sorry, I was just thinking…"

"We're very sorry for your loss, Mr. Wickle. We just have a few questions about Mr. Eskota. Thank you for waiting." Genevieve said to him.

"Sure, of course. Oh, and call me Mark. I'm not really formal." His brown eyes were rimmed red from crying.

"It seems like you and Mr. Eskota were close. Had you been friends long?"

"Since grade school. We always knew Peter would be a success. He had big dreams and goals. I never doubted that he'd reach them. I sure didn't expect him to get there by forty."

"What do you mean?"

"Well, Peter was a day trader. He and a couple of his college buddies started a company right out of school. I don't know if it was luck or skill, but they made it big pretty fast. He's always been a whiz with numbers and such, so he knew how much he would need to retire at any given age. He made it towards the end of the first quarter and set everything in motion. His partners bought him out and he retired at thirty-nine years old. Gotta be a record or something."

"And you and Mr. Eskota played golf regularly?"

"At the club, uh, the country club on the west side." He looked down at his feet. "My dad gets me a membership there for Christmas every year. I couldn't afford it on my own. Peter won some kind of luxury resort trip to this place out in Arizona last year and took us with him. I think that was when he got it in his head to retire into luxury sooner rather than later. I guess you never know with the stock market, right?"

Alex nodded. "Did Mr. Eskota have any enemies—?"

"Wait. You think he was *murdered*?"

"We don't know, Mr.—uh, Mark. We're just covering all the scenarios from the get go."

"Oh okay. Enemies? Um, well, no?"

"Is that a question?"

"Sorry. No. I can't think of any enemies."

"What about his business partners? Did they still get along?"

"They sure seemed to; we went golfing with them every Thursday."

Genevieve nodded. "Do you have their contact information? We'll want to talk to them too."

"Sure. I can write that down for you," he said as he got out his phone. "Their names are Billy, uh, Bill Richards and Jeff Astrada."

"Was Mr. Eskota seeing anyone? Any serious relationships?"

"Serious? Nah, he brought women home every now and then, but no one that he was dating or anything."

"You said that he won the golf weekend. Was that a raffle drawing or what?" Alex asked.

"Oh no. It was at a charity gala last year. They had a live auction. Peter went every year; he was one of their big donors."

"Charity for what?"

"Umm, let me think. Maybe it was for Parkinson's or Hodgkin's or one of those diseases? I can't remember. I'm sure it's in his records."

"We'll look it up." Genevieve looked at Alex.

"Was Mr. Eskota a big drinker?"

"I don't know if I'd say big. I mean, he could hold his own or whatever. He maybe drank a little more than the rest of us, but he rarely got drunk."

"Did Mr. Eskota ever golf with Frederick Kastener?" Genevieve asked, drawing a sideways glance from Alex.

"Who? The rich guy? No. We all knew of him, but we never met him."

"You're certain that they weren't even acquaintances?"

"I know it looks like Peter had a lot of money; obviously, he was doing well for himself." He waved an arm around, gesturing at the expensive home. "He wasn't even close to being in the same league as Kastener. He used to comment that one day he'd have as much money as that family, but that was the extent of their interactions."

"Was he jealous of Kastener?"

Wickle frowned. "Is there something going on with Kastener that is making you ask all these questions?"

A glare from Alex seemed to scare Wickle into answering the original question. "Sorry. Geez. No, Peter wasn't jealous. It was more like a little boy dreaming of being Steph Curry one day, you know? Look at his financials; you'll understand. He was successful as a day trader, but he didn't earn enough to have some sort of huge estate that would pass from generation to generation."

Genevieve nodded. "I understand, sir. Thank you for your

time. You've been really helpful."

"Yes, thank you again for your help. If you think of anything else, please give us a call." Alex handed him one of his cards as Genevieve picked up the piece of paper Mark had written the partners' names and phone numbers on.

They retraced their steps to the front door and walked back outside. It was almost seven o'clock, but the summer day was still warm. They had driven to the house separately since it was the end of the day when they had been called out.

"I think we should wait and see what the ME says. If he rules this is a homicide, then we can interview the other friends. Honestly, I think he just slipped and hit his head just right."

"Works for me. Did you go into his office? I noticed an empty glass near a bottle of brandy on the bar."

"Yeah, who knows how many of those he threw back before getting into the shower."

Genevieve shrugged. "Until tomorrow then."

* * * * *

Cari turned on the news while she ate her Chinese take-out. She had her laptop open on the coffee table and was mulling over calling Kastener after she finished eating. She mentally made a list of questions to ask him. The anchorman was giving the highlights in the background, but she wasn't paying much attention. She muted the TV so she could focus more on her potential phone call. She wanted to ask if Jade had jaw pain or if she was known for clenching her teeth. She also wanted to get his permission to look through Jade's things.

Cari set the carton of fried rice on the coffee table and picked up her cell phone. She found Kastener's number and hit send. He answered almost immediately.

"Ms. Turnlyle? Do you have an update?" He asked earnestly.

"Oh, um, not exactly, Mr. Kastener. I'm trying to figure out a few things about Jade. Do you have a moment?"

"Of course. What do you need to know?"

"Did Jade have a habit of clenching her jaw or grinding her teeth or anything like that?"

"She had to wear a guard of some sort in middle school, but I thought she had outgrown it. My wife usually dealt with the dentist. What's this about? The detectives were asking for access to her dental records too."

Cari sat up straight. *The DMSO!* "Well, it seems like maybe some kind of ointment or something was on her cheek or jawline and I thought it might mean something."

"Something like what? What does the ointment do? Why am I just now hearing about this?"

"It's got some kind of pain-relieving properties from what I understand. I thought maybe she used it whenever she was having pain possibly. If not, then maybe the dentist's office used it? That's probably what the detectives are looking into as well."

"I signed a release form for the detectives, so they should be able to look at her history at Dr. Santer's office now. Do I need to add you to the list?"

"That would be really great, Mr. Kastener. Would it be possible for me to look through some of Jade's things?"

"What would you be looking for exactly?"

"Well, this ointment for one. Other than that, I don't know what I expect to find." She glanced at the TV and saw a headline that read Local Multi-Millionaire Found Dead in Home. She stifled a gasp and returned her attention to Kastener.

"...time would you like to come?" He was asking.

"What time? Um, is Monday okay? Around ten?"

"I'll leave your name with the gate attendant."

"Thank you, Mr. Kastener." She responded as the call ended.

He's very abrupt. She grabbed the remote and unmuted the television.

"...Eskota had recently retired and apparently had plans to golf with some friends this afternoon at the country club. Unfortunately, he slipped and fell in his shower. The police have not yet determined if the death was accidental or a homicide."

Cari frowned. *How am I just now learning of this?* She checked her work email, but there were no messages from her boss or anyone else with the Beagle. She logged into their portal to check the virtual news board. *Unbelievable!* Lionel Cardian had taken the call regarding the suspicious death and marked it low priority. Cari only got notifications for certain types of calls, and low priority wasn't included.

Cari drummed her fingers on her leg and tried to gather her thoughts before calling Ollaman about the new mysterious death. She didn't want to sound hysterical or paranoid, but she thought Lionel was wrong to mark it low priority. Maybe she should call Bob first and see what he knows. She grimaced and decided talking to her boss first was the best move. The call rang and rang. She was about to just end it when he finally picked up.

"Mr. Ollaman! I'm glad I caught you. I was just watching the news..."

"And you think the death of that Eskota fella is more interesting than Cardian labeled it."

Cari bit her lip and waited to see if he would say more.

"Hello?" He barked into the phone.

"Oh, sorry, sir. I wasn't sure if you had more to say. Yes, I do think that Mr. Eskota's death is something we need to look at a little more carefully."

"I told Lionel to send it off to one of our junior copy editors, but I can get it pulled back. Do you think it's related to the Kastener girl's death?"

"I think it's something we should consider, yes." Cari heard a call coming through and looked quickly to see that it was Bob. She let it ring to voicemail rather than hang up on her boss.

"Why don't you see whose name is tagged on the virtual board? You're probably faster with the technology than me. The incident report should be accessible on there, right?"

"If Lionel logged it in, then it will be there."

"Okay, keep me posted." He ended the call.

She opened the portal again and clicked on the file icon to pull up the report. Nothing happened. It was greyed out, which meant that someone was accessing it or that it was never logged in the first place. *Was Lionel up to some sort of shady business again?* Her phone buzzed with a new voicemail. She selected the notification and put it on speaker.

"Hey, Cari. It's Bob. I'm sure you've already heard, but give me a call. I think there's something you might find interesting."

She pulled up his number and hit send. He answered almost immediately.

"Cari! I was just about to go back inside. Did you hear about the Eskota man?"

"I saw it on the news. Cardian took the call for the newsroom and logged it as low priority. I think he might be chasing it down without telling Ollaman though. He didn't log the incident report yet."

Bob didn't speak for a few seconds. Cari wondered if someone was nearby and he didn't want to be overheard. "That's interesting. I'm sure he has police sources too, but they might not get him too far. Everyone here is looking at it as an accident, but here's the thing: we bagged Eskota's clothing from the bathroom. His shirt had an oily stain on it, so I swabbed it. It's DMSO."

"Surely that caused a buzz with the detectives!"

"They found a tube of the stuff in his medicine cabinet, so they don't think it's strange. He was forty years old. I'm sure he had some aches and pains."

"Still. Two suspicious deaths in one week? And both victims used DMSO?"

"I thought so too. One of the things the detectives bagged was a flier for a local spa place. It tells you how to apply DMSO and also has their address on it."

"Do you think he applied it before he got in the shower? Wouldn't it just wash off?"

"I don't know, Cari. It would probably take a little soap and water to get it off. Anyway, I didn't think it was something to just forget about, so that's why I called you."

"Would you send me a photo of the flier, Bob? Maybe I can find out if Jade ever visited it too. Maybe our victims have a connection besides the DMSO."

She could almost hear Bob debating about whether or not he'd get in trouble for sharing the image with her.

"I'll send it to you in a bit. My break is almost over, so I've gotta run."

"Are you working the graveyard shift this week?"

"No, it's my turn to cover the weekend, so I'm here until seven-thirty. And again tomorrow and then the weekend days, but only eight hours each of those days."

"Do you at least get Monday off?"

"Yes, ma'am. Now I've really gotta go. Bye!" He ended the call.

She imagined him scurrying back inside, his loafers slapping the linoleum flooring. He always dressed in business casual: leather loafers, khaki pants, button-up shirt. On the weekends, he dressed down a bit by sometimes wearing a polo instead of his usual button-up shirt. She smiled. He was definitely a fan of his creature comforts.

Her phone buzzed with an incoming text. Bob had sent an image of the flier from Eskota's house. She enlarged it so that she could read the name of the spa: Relax and Relief Massage. Cari wasn't familiar with the business, so she typed the name into Google to see if they had a website. She was in luck. The website had an online scheduler that included a dropdown menu with the services they offered. Before selecting massage, she clicked over to the services page to see if they talked about DMSO at all. She found a small paragraph virtually the same as what was printed on the flier.

Maybe I'll book a massage for myself and see what I can find out about the place. She clicked back over to the online scheduler and picked massage as her desired service. They had several openings on Saturday. She picked the ten o'clock spot and entered her information. Maybe she would find something at Jade's on Monday that would help connect her with Eskota or the massage parlor. She didn't think Jade would have much in common with a retired day trader, but they were both people with money or from families with money. Was someone targeting the wealthy? And if so, why?

Chapter 9

*G*enevieve flipped through the ME's report. Dr. Green had declared the death to be accidental. The victim had alcohol in his system, which would have impaired his vision and coordination. The tox screen didn't reveal any other substances in his system, so he ruled out foul play.

"Looks like Mr. Eskota just took an unfortunate tumble in the shower." She told Alex.

"What was his blood-alcohol level?"

"Looks like point oh-four."

"That's all? Seems a little low to make you crack your head in the shower, but I'm not a doctor. What do I know?"

Genevieve raised her eyebrows. "Case closed, then?"

"Case never opened." He flipped the folder on his desk closed. "What about Kastener? Are we off the hook on that yet?"

"I haven't heard anything from the lieutenant as to whether we can officially declare her death an accident."

"We've talked to the boyfriend. We ran down her schedule for the day. The tox screen was clear. What else do we need to do?"

Genevieve heard her phone ping with an incoming text. She pulled out her phone and saw it was a message from Cari. She frowned and decided to open it later.

"Always with the texts." Alex sighed.

"How do you keep your friends and family from texting you during the day?"

"I told them that I have to pay per text."

"Stop it. You did not. Even your wife?"

He looked at her pointedly. "If you out me, I will give them your number for emergencies."

"You're serious? That's so, what—2004? Unlimited texting has been around literally for decades. No way they believe that."

Alex pulled out his phone and slid it open. "See this? I probably have to pay extra just to have this old model, but I don't get bothered by anyone that I don't want to hear from."

"Does that thing even have apps?"

"Who needs apps?"

Genevieve rolled her eyes. At least he wasn't razzing her about her own texts anymore. She wondered what Cari wanted.

"I think we should try calling some of her friends. Maybe they could tell us a little more about how she spent her time. Also, we need to talk to whomever Olivia is. She had an appointment with her this week."

"Do you really think the friends are going to know her any better than her long-term boyfriend? From the sound of it, he was ready to marry her."

"Sometimes women tell their girlfriends things that they don't tell their lovers."

"Kastener got us access to the dental records. I think we should go to talk to them first."

Genevieve thought about it. "Okay. Let's give them a call and tell them we're coming by. I'd like to speak with her hygienist and see if Jade had a history of jaw pain."

"I'm dialing them right now."

Genevieve waited while Alex put the phone on speaker so that she could hear too. The receptionist picked up on the third ring.

"Dr. Santer's office, can you hold?" The line clicked.

Alex glared at the phone. "She didn't even wait for me to answer."

"Excuse me?" The voice on the phone spoke. Alex turned red.

"My apologies, I thought you put me on hold. Yes, I can hold."

Genevieve tried to suppress a giggle and failed. "Smooth, Alex."

"Whatever."

They listened to the hold music for about four minutes. Alex was tapping his foot impatiently while they waited. Genevieve worried it would make him grumpier than usual. Finally, she came back on the line.

"Dr. Santer's office. This is Sonia. Thank you for holding. How may I help you?"

"Hello, Sonia. This is Detective Runimoss. My partner and I were hoping to speak with Dr. Santer and whoever worked on Ms. Kastener's teeth on Monday. We're planning to come by the office in just a few minutes, but wanted to make sure both people were there today."

"Both Dr. Santer and Isabelle are working today. Will you be here soon? Isabelle is about to finish with a patient. You could speak with her before she starts on the next one."

Genevieve was already on her feet. "We're leaving the station now and will be there in a few minutes."

"See you soon." The call ended.

* * * * *

Cari checked her watch and decided to send Bob a text. She figured he was already at work, but since it was most likely the start of his shift, she didn't want to interrupt a meeting with his boss.

Bob, I'm trying to figure out if there was some kind of drug that could have been in the DMSO, but wouldn't show up in a tox screen. Something that might break down quickly. Ideas?

Cari had Google open on her computer and was trying various search parameters. She didn't have a medical background at all and wondered if there was a poison or other drug that would paralyze someone. Would it have been a temporary paralysis? Permanent? Bob would know. She tapped her pencil on her desk, willing him to respond, but her phone remained silent. She wasn't sure what words would help her search for the drug, or if it even existed. She scribbled on her notepad, throwing around different possibilities. She jumped when her phone buzzed. *That's my Bob!*

Tell me more about what you're hypothesizing.

Cari sighed. She still didn't know how best to describe it.

I thought there might be a drug or poison that could be used in combo with the DMSO to paralyze Jade. Temporarily or worse.

Let me think. There are a few things that might break down fast enough, even after death that wouldn't be picked up on a tox screen.

Would they show up as something else?

The only thing on the tox screen was caffeine.

Can you give me the names of the drugs?

I'll get back to you. I gotta go.

Cari felt like she might be on to something. If Jade had been drugged, maybe she was unable to turn the wheel. Maybe that's what sent her in front of that truck and why she was crying. She made a note to ask Bob if there was a drug that could paralyze a person, but also still allow you to cry. He had told her the night before that Eskota visited a spa. She needed to find out from Kastener if Jade ever went to a spa. Maybe she had gone there on Monday too, and that was the connection!

* * * * *

Genevieve walked quickly to keep up with Alex's long strides. She sometimes felt a bit comical next to him, as though she was merely a child going to work with their father every day instead of their partner. He had already reached the door to the dentist's office and was holding it open for her.

"Thank you, sir."

Alex nodded and followed her inside the office. It was decorated with small ferns on pedestals in the corners of the waiting room. Genevieve had to restrain herself from touching them to see if they were real. Apparently, Alex did not have the same self-control. He was fingering one of the fronds already. She elbowed him and he dropped his hand. The walls had images of people with beautiful smiles: white teeth, all straight across. Near the receptionist's desk was a water cooler with little cups next to it.

Genevieve approached the desk. "Sonia? Detectives Viacorte and Runimoss. We're here to see Dr. Santer and Isabelle." She pulled out her badge for the young woman to see.

"Yes, of course. Please come around back." She motioned towards the double doors.

They entered the patient area and saw a woman with mousy brown hair and brown eyes standing next to the counter. Genevieve estimated that she was about five-foot-eight and in good shape.

"I'm Dr. Santer. How can I help you today?"

"Is Isabelle free too? We were hoping to speak with both of you."

"She should be finished any moment. Why don't you join me in my office?" She turned back to the receptionist. "Sonia, could you ask Isabelle to come by my office when she is finished with her patient?"

Sonia must have nodded in the affirmative because Dr. Santer turned and walked down the hallway. Genevieve and Alex followed behind her. She opened the first door on the left and stood back to let them enter ahead of her. Dr. Santer closed the office door behind her before sitting down at the desk.

"Thank you for taking time to meet with us, Dr. Santer. We will make this quick; we know you're busy too." Genevieve told her.

"No problem at all. I understand you have some questions regarding Ms. Kastener's appointment earlier this week?"

"Yes. Our medical examiner noticed an oily substance on Ms. Kastener's cheek and determined that it was DMSO. When we learned about its properties and that she had visited your office that morning, we thought it might have been applied here for a medical reason of some sort."

Dr. Santer jiggled the mouse on her desk to wake up her computer. After entering her login information, she alternated between typing and clicking before turning the screen their way. Jade's face stared back at them from the upper left corner. The screen showed a list of dates of appointments as well as an entry with a code and the brief text: sealant repair.

"Here is a summary of the treatments Ms. Kastener received here. One of the sealants on her upper left molar had cracked, so we removed it and replaced it. We don't charge for it if it cracks in less than eighteen months from when we apply it."

"Would someone use DMSO for something like this?"

"I have never seen it done and as you can see, there is no note of it being used in her file."

Genevieve glanced at the door, wondering if Isabelle would be joining them soon. "Has DMSO ever been used on Ms. Kastener?"

Dr. Santer turned the screen back around and repeated her series of clicks and typing. "It has not been recorded in her chart during her time as our patient. She has been a patient here since age two."

"Have you ever had a hygienist use something like DMSO and not record it in the chart?"

"Obviously, if it wasn't recorded, it would be hard for me to know about it unless I saw them do it and noted the absence in the chart. However, DMSO has a bit of a distinct smell, so I feel confident that I would have noticed it if it had been used without my knowledge. In the case of a sealant repair, I would not be called in to review the work. I did not observe Ms. Kastener on Monday. I actually didn't even see her here."

"Do you trust that Ms. Kastener's hygienist would have made note of using it if she had used it?"

"Isabelle is one of my best and most reliable employees. I have no complaints about her work. She is here on time for every shift and does a thorough job of cleaning our patients' teeth." Dr. Santer paused.

"Was there something else?" Alex asked.

"No, well, maybe. Isabelle is not the most outgoing hygienist you'll ever meet. It's not really a drawback because you can't really talk to someone when you're having your teeth cleaned, but she is a bit robotic about it."

"Not a people person, then?" Alex questioned.

"Exactly. She isn't unfriendly, but she doesn't really engage."

At that moment, a soft knock sounded at the office door.

"Come on in, Isabelle." Dr. Santer responded.

A tall woman with dirty blonde hair pulled back into a low ponytail entered the room. She had pale, grey eyes and even paler skin. She stared straight ahead without acknowledging Genevieve or Alex.

"You wanted to see me, Doctor?"

"Yes, Isabelle. Thank you for coming by. This is Detective Viacorte and Detective Runimoss. They are looking into the death of one of our patients: Ms. Jade Kastener. I believe you saw her on Monday."

"That's correct," she said simply.

Genevieve cleared her throat, hoping to draw the woman's attention, but failing. "Isabelle, how was Ms. Kastener on Monday? In good spirits?"

"She seemed fine. She was only here a few minutes."

"We were just reviewing her file. Did Ms. Kastener ever complain of jaw pain?"

"Not that I know of."

"What about grinding her teeth? Or clenching her jaw at night?"

This sent Dr. Santer into another flurry of clicks and taps on the keyboard. Genevieve noticed that Isabelle's eyes flicked to the screen briefly before resuming the blank stare.

"I'm not aware of any such issues."

Dr. Santer spoke up. "It looks like she used to wear a device to prevent her from grinding her teeth, but that was years ago. We don't have anything recent in her patient history about her complaining of jaw pain, nor have we observed overdeveloped masseters or temporalis musculature in her jaw. That would be indicative of clenching her jaw or grinding her teeth repeatedly."

Genevieve nodded. Alex stood up as Dr. Santer indicated to Isabelle that she could get back to work. The woman left the office and closed the door behind her. It seemed like they had reached another dead end, but then she remembered Eskota. His death had been ruled accidental, but if he had been a patient here, maybe there was a connection they should consider. "Dr. Santer, I'm not looking for medical history or anything private, but can you tell me if Peter Eskota was a patient of yours?"

"Eskota? I think I'd remember a name like that. Wait, is that the man who was found dead in his shower?"

Genevieve hesitated, which basically confirmed the dentist's question. She decided to count her losses. "I think that's about all we needed to talk about. Thank you again for taking time to meet with us. You have our contact information if you think of anything else."

Genevieve shook the dentist's hand before exiting her office. As usual, Alex was waiting by the door for her to go out first. She thanked the receptionist on her way by the desk, then pushed the door open and held it for him instead.

He glared at her as he exited the building. "You aren't funny."

"Just because you aren't laughing does *not* mean that I'm not funny." She grinned at him.

"Back to the station?" He asked as they got back into the car.

She nodded. "Yeah, let's try to call some of her friends and the person she was going to meet...I think her name was Olivia."

"Sounds right. What do you think the friends can tell us?"

"I don't know to be honest. What did you make of the hygienist we just met?"

"She was a little different, but that doesn't mean she wasn't

70

truthful."

"I didn't get the impression that she was lying, but something seemed a little off about her."

"Maybe she just doesn't have very strong social skills."

"Perhaps. It seems odd that she would have DMSO on her cheek or jaw or whatever if she didn't actually have a reason to put it there."

"She might have had a reason to put it there and just didn't share it with her dentist."

Genevieve shrugged. "I guess."

"Did you really think Eskota was going to have been a patient here too?"

"It was worth asking."

"Yeah, you never know."

* * * * *

Only 2 drugs fit the criteria that you're suggesting. One hasn't been on the market in years. The other is only available with a prescription and you have to get it from a compounding pharmacy.

Cari frowned when she got the text from Bob. He had sent her the names of the two drugs even though she could read between the lines and infer that he thought it was a long shot that Jade or Eskota had been drugged. Anerva and Divinagen. Anerva was the newer drug and Divinagen was the one that had been discontinued. She wondered why anyone would develop a drug that would cause paralysis. A quick Google search resulted in few hits with relevant information.

Divinagen had been developed in the sixties as a sedative of sorts to be used in psychiatric wards. Its primary use was in patients that were hard to manage with more common sedatives on the market. It allowed the person to stay alert where they could hear sounds, but not move in response to them.

Sounds a bit controlling, Cari thought.

71

Anerva was similar to its predecessor, but only resulted in paralysis if too much was administered. It was supposed to be a muscle relaxant that also *calmed* the central nervous system. *Whatever that means.* She decided that she needed to call Bob and get him to explain all of this a little bit better. Physiology was a mystery to her. Cari pulled out her phone and thumbed off a text to her friend.

Can we meet to talk about these? I'm utterly confused.

She put her phone back into her purse without waiting for him to respond. She wanted to call Harold and ask if he knew anything about the spa. She lifted the receiver from her desk phone to call the young man.

"Harold Sheely with Sheely Farms," he answered after two rings.

"Hi, Harold. It's Cari Turnlyle with the Beagle again. I had a quick question that I thought you might be able to answer."

"Sure, go ahead."

"Did Jade ever get a massage or go to a spa?"

"Oh yeah. She went all the time."

"Did she go to a particular place every time?"

"She liked to go to her cousin's place. Olivia is her name. She went every Friday, actually."

"What is the name of Olivia's business?"

"LIVing Well. She capitalizes the first three letters to highlight her name, if that makes sense."

"You said that Olivia was her cousin?"

"Yes, ma'am. First cousin on her mom's side."

"Is this the one she was planning the trip with too?"

He chuckled. "Oh no. The big trips were all with her cousin Mae on her dad's side. None of her mom's relatives could afford to travel like that, but Jade probably could have talked her dad into paying for Olivia. She and Jade were pretty good friends."

"I understand. That's all I needed to know. Thank you, Harold."

"I'm curious. Why are you asking about a spa or massages?"

"There was a possible connection to a massage place with the DMSO, but it sounds like it's a dead end."

"Connection in what way?"

"Please keep this to yourself, Harold. I don't want to get Mr. Kastener's hopes up for no reason."

"You have my word."

"Another person died recently who also had DMSO on their body when they were found. They had recently visited a massage parlor. I thought it might be related, but it's starting to sound like a simple coincidence."

"I understand. I won't mention it to Mr. Kastener. It's not like we talk anymore anyway." He ended the call.

Cari felt bad for the young man. She couldn't imagine losing the love of your life so young. She had never even been in love. As if on cue, her phone buzzed with an incoming text. She checked her Apple watch and saw that it was her mother.

Decided to come for a visit! We're driving up the coast. Be there in a few days.

How many is a few?! Cari rolled her eyes and ran her locket along its chain. Her parents could have the worst timing. Why couldn't they be normal and plan a visit instead of just showing up without warning? She looked at her watch and tried to remember how her apartment had looked when she left it that morning. Luckily, it was a single bedroom apartment, so her parents would not be staying with her. She still needed to make sure that the bathroom was clean...and the kitchen. She groaned. It was all a mess. She sent a text back to her mom.

Will you be staying up at Grandmother's?

Yes

I could try to come up on the weekend

We booked a hotel in Brenington for next weekend. We'll join you for church!

Cari felt like a child again. She went to church off and on, but it wasn't really something anyone would consider to be regular. Her mom was always razzing her about going. Now it seemed like she was coming to make sure that she went. She shook her head. She needed to focus on her investigation. She could figure out plans with her parents later.

* * * * *

Genevieve looked at the list of names that Kastener had given them. It was fairly short. She wondered how well the man knew his daughter.

"Do you want to split up the list or call them one by one together?" She asked Alex.

"None of these women are suspects. Let's come up with the questions we want to ask them and then split up the list."

Genevieve nodded. "We need to ask about her recent state of mind. Was she depressed? Was something bothering her?"

"Let's ask about her relationship with Harold. See if they really were as happy together as he claims."

"Do you still think he had something to do with her death?"

"Truthfully? No. I think she got distracted and wasn't able to correct her trajectory before it was too late."

"Are you prepared to share that with Kastener?"

"Oh, hell no."

"I guess we should add something about her driving habits."

"Good call. Anything else?"

Genevieve shook her head and then took a photo of the list with her cell phone. "Here, you can have the paper copy and I'll use this photo. It looks like he listed three friends, plus the cousin, Olivia."

"I'll take Teresa and Jill."

"Okay, I'll call Constance and also her cousin Olivia. I'm going to ask about the meeting that they had scheduled too."

Alex nodded as he picked up his phone. Genevieve pulled the receiver on her desk phone and punched in the number listed for

Olivia first. She thought Jade might have been close with her cousin if their meeting at least rated a spot in the calendar.

"If this is another telemarketer, I am going to lose my mind—"

"Um, excuse me?"

The voice on the line coughed and cleared their throat. "I'm sorry. I don't recognize the number, but this is my work line and—"

"Right. This is Detective Genevieve Viacorte with the Brenington Police Department. Is this Olivia Buchanan?"

"Police...? Oh, sorry. Yes. This is Olivia."

"Hi, Olivia. I have a few questions for you today regarding your cousin, Jade Kastener."

"Oh. Of course. What can I tell you?"

"Were you and Jade close?"

Genevieve thought the connection might have failed and was about to ask when the woman spoke up again. "You know, Jade probably thought of me as a sister. She's an only child. We're practically the same age, so we were frequently paired up as children at family gatherings."

"You are related through her mother, I take it?"

"That's correct. Our mothers were sisters."

"You are not an only child?"

"I'm not. I have both a brother and a sister. I'm the middle child."

"Are you familiar with her cousin Mae?"

"The international traveling cousin? Yes. They did all their trips together."

"She didn't like traveling alone?"

"Does anyone?"

Genevieve laughed. "Fair question. Jade had an appointment in her calendar with you this week. What was that for?"

It was Olivia's turn to laugh. "That was actually my doing. Jade never put anything in her calendar unless you made her. She said she could remember it and didn't need a digital reminder. She came for spa treatments pretty often. I can't believe she's really gone."

"I'm very sorry for your loss, Olivia. How would you describe Jade's behavior recently? Had anything changed?"

"Jade was always the same. She wanted to travel the world and see everything. Anything to not go to school and take over the business yet."

"Was she not ready to be independent or why was she avoiding that?"

"I think to Jade the family business wasn't going anywhere. She told me she knew she could make the business even more successful, but that there was always time to work later."

"I've heard that Jade was very smart."

"That's an understatement. She is, I mean, was the smartest person I know. I'm sure she would have aced college and doubled the Kastener business in no time. She was the president of our "Future Business Owners" association in high school. She actually got to give a speech once at a city council meeting about how Gen-Z was going to change the business world. She was trying to convince them to sponsor our club so we could go to Washington, D.C. for a conference over Christmas break that year. She put together this incredible talk, using her dad's business as an example. They were impressed. The council can't actually support something like that with taxpayer dollars of course. Jade knew that, but she also knew that all of the council members at the time were small business owners keen about supporting the community. She pulled it off. None of us had to pay a dime for that trip."

"And her plans for her father's business?"

"Who knows? Something for the future, I guess."

"What about Jade's relationship with Harold?"

"What about it? She loved Harold. Honestly, I think part of her just wanted Harold to marry her and support her. I know it sounds really 1950s, but that was Jade. It's not that she was manipulative or something. Yes, she had a lot to offer intellectually. She just didn't have a lot of motivation to do that yet. Maybe because her mother died so young? I'm not sure. She was happy with Harold, though. She truly loved him and wanted to be with him forever."

"Did you ever ride in the car with Jade?"

Another big pause. "Yes, why? I mean, you don't think she was a bad driver, do you? You don't think she drove in front of that truck on purpose, do you?"

"I'm really just trying to understand Jade better, Olivia."

"I'm sorry. I've just heard a ton of people saying that she was probably texting and driving, but Jade wouldn't do that. I mean, she would maybe check a text if she was at a red light or something, but she didn't text and drive. You know, your generation had the click-it-or ticket slogan?"

"Yes..." Genevieve said slowly.

"Well, ours has been bombarded about texting and driving since before we could read. Honestly, Jade was responsible as a driver."

"I understand. Thank you for answering my questions. If you think of anything else, you can reach me at this number or just call the station and they'll direct your call to me."

"Is her dad making you investigate?"

"Why do you ask?"

"I read in the paper that it had been declared an accident. They don't have detectives call potential witnesses or suspects if something is really just an accident."

Genevieve chose her words carefully, not wanting to incur any more of Kastener's wrath. "We're trying to be thorough."

"I hear you. Well, good luck. Jade was probably the happiest person I know. I really miss her."

"Again, I'm very sorry for your loss. I appreciate you taking the time to speak with me."

"If it gets us some answers, then ask any time." The line clicked dead.

Genevieve looked over at Alex who was still on the phone. She pulled up the list of numbers on her phone again and punched in the number for Constance. Kastener hadn't listed a last name for the young woman.

"This is Constance Pollifer with Golly Polly! Pirate parties with real parrots and parakeets. What day were you wanting to schedule a party?"

"Um, uh. Sorry. You said this was Constance?"

"Who is calling please?"

"This is Detective Genevieve Viacorte with the Brenington Police Department. I'm calling about your friend Jade Kastener."

"Oh! Oh. Not for a party. Sorry for the confusion."

Genevieve looked at their list of questions. "How would you describe Jade's mindset recently? Had anything changed?"

"Mindset? I mean, Jade was always happy. She had everything she wanted in life. Love, money, brains…" she trailed off.

"And this hadn't changed recently?"

"No. I just saw Jade last weekend. We went boating on the lake. She was planning another trip with Mae."

"Did you ever travel with Jade?"

"I went to D.C. with her in high school. That's how I came to own my own business."

"The pirate parties?"

"Yes, do you have kids?"

"No." She cleared her throat. "Did you ever ride in the car with Jade?"

"In high school some, but not much since. We live on the opposite sides of town, so it was never really convenient. She seemed like a good driver."

Genevieve could almost hear the young woman shrug in indifference to the question. "Did she ever talk to you about Harold?"

"Not really. I mean, we all knew that Jade loved Harold. They were made for each other. He adored her and she was ready to marry him as soon as he asked. Between you and me, I *heard* that he wasn't going to ask until Jade finished college. She hadn't even started college yet, so I guess that was a long way off."

"I see. Well, that's all I needed. Thank you for your time. If you think of anything else, I can be reached at this number."

"Do you have any nieces or nephews?"

Genevieve blinked, startled by the question. "I'm sorry?"

"Nieces or nephews. You said you don't have kids, but what about other kids in your family? Younger siblings perhaps?"

"I'm not really sure…"

"I get it. You're working and that's personal. Well, if you know anyone who wants a pirate party, send them over to Golly Polly! We have all your pirate party needs covered." The call ended.

Genevieve sighed. She tried to ignore Alex laughing at her from his desk.

"Did you call a pirate party line?"

"One of Jade's friends…never mind. I didn't really learn anything new. How about you?"

"Both Jill and Teresa thought that Jade couldn't be happier. She was a great driver. She loved Harold. Blah, blah, blah."

"Same. Guess we write it up and file it in the book for now."

"Just one dead end after another. It's looking more and more like an accident with every person we talk to."

Chapter 10

*T*he helper glared out the window. After initially declaring the Kastener girl's death to be accidental, it seemed like they were looking into it more thoroughly now. The news had indicated the police were investigating, but the general thought was that the man's death was an accident. *Good riddance, you greedy drunk!* A smug smile curved onto the helper's face at this thought for a brief moment but was quickly replaced by the usual frown. That newspaperman was also making a nuisance of himself. His nosiness might jeopardize the ultimate calling to rid the community of the lazy and uninspired. He hadn't seemed to connect the two people on his own, but he had shown up at one of the helper's jobs. A co-worker had texted to tell the helper someone had come in asking about the day trader. A large man from the newspaper had stopped by and asked if he could speak with whomever had worked with the dead man from the day before. He had left his card and asked that they pass along his message of wanting to meet. The man was not one of the wicked and lazy people that needed to be eliminated, but he could not be allowed to prevent the helper from continuing this work.

The helper lifted the padded envelope up to the light to see if any ointment had gotten on the outside of it. Sending a package of this sort elevated the risks of the mission. Wearing gloves had kept any fingerprints from transferring to the package, but it only took a small exposure to the medication for it to have an effect on someone. This was meant for the large newspaperman and no one else. Inside the padded envelope was a small card with a coupon for a free taco from the local taco truck, which just happened to be down the street from the newspaper's office building. The helper had gotten it in the mail when the old man died. He had loved those tacos and requested them almost daily, much to the helper's irritation. A simple sandwich from the house would have been much easier for everyone, but the old man was demanding.

The helper had coated the small card with the ointment and some liquid from a different vial. It should be stable for the duration of its time in the envelope before the man opened it. The helper would drop it in the mail receptacle once it was dark. Everything was under video surveillance anymore, but a hooded jacket and the cover of night should be sufficient to disguise their identity. Touching the card would cause the man to feel like he had taken too much of a laxative. It might not send him to the hospital, but it would definitely sideline him for a few days. He would more than likely blame it on food poisoning, possibly even on the food truck!

Chapter 11

Cari texted Bob after going for a run Saturday morning. Summer was winding down and the morning weather was perfect for a long run. It felt good to get in several miles and it gave her time to think about Jade's death and her parents' impending visit. She hadn't had any eureka moments about Jade, but she had devised a plan to make the family visit go more smoothly. She knew Bob had said he was working the weekend shift, but she had decided to go to the early church service on Sunday. That way, no one would make a comment the following week about having not seen her in a while. She rolled her eyes. All of this to avoid being honest with her own mother.

What time does your shift start tomorrow?
9
Join me for early church at 8?
Really?
I hate going alone.
I know. Meet you in the lot 5 minutes before.
Ok. Thanks!
Still going to the massage place?
Of course.
Be careful.
Always.

She knew he rolled his eyes when he saw that last text. She was usually so caught up in getting the story that she made risky, spontaneous decisions. She felt bad dragging Bob into her church escapade. Maybe he was planning on going anyway, but going alone was the worst. You had to sit by yourself and get pity looks from everyone who passed you. You didn't have anyone to talk to and you didn't really know anyone's name. She looked at her watch and realized she had better take a quick shower. She didn't want to make a bad first impression with the masseuse by being the smelly, sweaty woman!

She rinsed the sweat off quickly with a little soap and then toweled off. She grabbed a lightweight maxi-dress from her closet and threw it on while slipping into her flip-flops. Her hair was curly enough to look okay when it was wet, so she ran a pick through it and called it good. Luckily, the spa was only a few minutes from her apartment. She cringed as she looked around her unit on her way out the door. Her mother would be abhorred with the current state of affairs if she were to visit today. *After the massage, it's deep cleaning time!*

She used the maps app on her phone to find the spa and arrived with a few minutes to spare. The business was located downtown amongst several other shops that sold clothing, jewelry, or art. Cari realized that she had never been to any of the shops in the two years she had lived in Brenington except for the large bookstore down the street a block or two. The limestone exterior probably kept the row of buildings cooler during the summer months. She parked in the public lot across from the businesses. Traffic was light, so she hurried across the street and entered the spa. The interior was dimly lit with relaxing music playing quietly in the background. The receptionist looked up when Cari stepped inside.

"Welcome to Relax and Relief! Do you have an appointment with us today?"

"Thank you. I do have an appointment. Cari Turnlyle."

The woman typed on her keyboard and smiled. "Yes, here you are. You will be with Julie today. The locker rooms are just through the door to your right. Here is a key to a locker that you can use. The number matches the locker, of course. You can leave your belongings in the locker and then put on this robe. There are further directions on the other locker room door as to how you get to your massage room. Any questions?"

"No, thank you." She took the robe and the key from the woman and pushed the adjacent door open. It opened into a small alcove which had two more doors: MEN and WOMEN. Pushing through the women's side, she found rows of lockers and benches. She could hear water running and assumed there must be showers around the corner to the left. Her locker was number twenty-six and closest to the door on the opposite side of the room. She seemed to be the only person in that part of the room for now. She had always been a bit modest and didn't really want to change out in the open. She followed the sound of the water to the showers and was happy to see that there were some bathroom stalls as well. She slipped inside one and quickly changed into the provided robe. She had brought her small clutch and hoped she could easily bring it into the massage room. She wanted to record her time there with her digital recorder in case something was said that was relevant to her story.

Cari stowed her clothing and her cell phone in the provided locker and used the key to secure it. The key came with a spiral elastic band to slip onto your wrist. She opened her clutch and pulled out her recorder. She quickly flipped the device on and slid it back into the purse. The elastic band with her locker key slipped around it nicely.

The door next to her locker had a laminated page adhered to it telling clients to proceed directly into the hallway behind them. They would see the name of their masseuse on the door of the room they were to enter next. Cari stepped into the hallway and looked at the names on the doors. Alli, Delilah, Julie, Savannah, and something with an I or maybe an L. Cari couldn't quite see the name on the last door. Some of the doors were closed, but a few were open as though they were waiting for a client to enter. She walked past the first three doors to Julie's room. Just as she was stepping inside, she heard a vaguely familiar voice ask if anyone had an extra towelette she could use. Cari nearly collided with a woman who was shouting out, "I do" as she moved to exit her room.

"Oh! Sorry!" Cari exclaimed, stepping aside.

"Oh dear! That's my fault." The young woman said. "I'll just be a moment. You can lie face down on the table and pull the blanket up to your shoulders."

Cari wondered where she had heard the voice before, but couldn't place it. She shrugged. It could have been anywhere, even at a restaurant or coffee shop. She took off the robe and folded it. She slipped her clutch inside the sleeve on top so the microphone wasn't too muted. She had just pulled the blanket up when a slight knock sounded at the door.

"Ready," she called out.

"My name is Julie and I'll be your masseuse today. Are there any areas of concern that you would like me to focus on or treat more carefully?"

Cari had anticipated this question. "I always have quite a bit of tension in my shoulders, probably from talking on the phone with it cradled between my ear and my shoulder."

"Are you under a physician's care for this or is it just a discomfort?"

"Oh, just a discomfort. It's never been debilitating or anything."

"I understand. Anything else?"

"I have read a little bit about DMSO and wondered if it was something you would recommend."

"We *do* use DMSO at the spa, but we encourage our clients to give massage a chance first before turning to a medicated approach. Many times, regular massage over a period of weeks will relieve the pain more organically and you won't need something like DMSO. Are you ready to get started?"

"Yes, ma'am. Thank you."

Cari wondered how long Eskota had been coming to the spa if he was already at the point of using DMSO. She needed to get her hands on the report that Cardian seemed to have lost, so she could contact potential witnesses or friends. She made a mental note to look for the report again when she got home.

The remainder of the hour passed quickly and soon Cari was back in the locker room gathering her belongings. She had stopped her digital recorder once she was certain she was alone. Her trip to the spa wasn't a total bust; she had at least verified that they would use DMSO on a client if it was warranted. Rather than use the shower at the spa, Cari just put her clothes back on. She could take a real shower with all of her soaps and accouterments back home. She double checked that her keys were still in her clutch and put her phone back inside it too before exiting the locker room.

"How was everything?" The receptionist asked as Cari entered the front of the business.

"Lovely. It's always great to get a massage." She smiled.

"How did you hear about us? We like to thank a client any time they pass on a good word on our business."

"I ran across one of your fliers at work the other day and thought I'd check you out."

"Oh, where do you work?"

"At the Brenington Beagle. I'm a journalist there."

"What a fun job! Well, thank you again for choosing us. Would you like to book a follow-up appointment?"

"You know, I have family coming to town on an indefinite schedule. I don't want to have to cancel. I'll give you a call once life gets back to normal. Thank you!" She waved goodbye and walked outside. Her to-do list was growing. She needed to talk to Bob about Jade some more, as well as the pharmaceuticals he had mentioned. She wanted to get a copy of the contact list from Genevieve too. Kastener should have given her one too. She frowned, trying to remember what else she wanted to do. *Figure out how often Eskota visited the spa!* She started her car and felt like she was forgetting something else important. It wasn't until she unlocked her apartment door that she remembered her promise to deep clean. Her shoulders sagged. Maybe she should find a cleaning service.

Chapter 12

G enevieve tried to distract herself by working in the community garden on the roof of her apartment building. The management company had built several raised beds for its tenants a few years ago. Gardening was a stress reliever for her. Her mom had taught her how to grow plants from seeds. One year, they even successfully grew a hearty crop of tomatoes from the previous summer's tomato seeds! She smiled remembering how delicious the marinara sauce was that year.

The building's roof had enough space for eight beds that were each ten feet by ten feet. When Genevieve moved in, three of the plots were unclaimed. Each tenant was only supposed to get one row, but the landlord had allowed her to take over all three plots when she offered to share the vegetable harvest with him. She had planted flowers in the middle of the three beds: digitalis, chrysanthemums, and marigolds. She gently pulled a few weeds from around the digitalis. The flowers probably wouldn't bloom again this summer. She paused, suddenly remembering a case they had reviewed at the academy that involved digitalis or foxglove.

The man, Charles Cullen, was known for being possibly the most prolific serial killer in the United States. He was a nurse and had injected patients with unprescribed medications which led to their death, often within twenty-four hours of when he injected them. One of the medications was digoxin, which was derived from the digitalis plant. Genevieve couldn't remember all of the details of the case. Instead of finishing her work in the beds, she gathered up her tools. Maybe Cari was right to think the two victims' deaths were related and not accidental.

She put her tools away and got out her cell phone. She wondered if digoxin could be administered on the skin. She frowned, regretting again not taking a biology class in college. This wasn't the first time she felt ignorant about a case because of her limited knowledge of science. She opened a browser window and searched for digoxin on the skin. None of the links that came up looked helpful to her. She sighed. She couldn't call Alex and ask him; he had less biology knowledge than she did. She wanted to call one of the CSU people, but felt guilty doing it on the weekend.

Calling Cari felt like admitting she was wrong. Plus, Cari was no scientist either. Genevieve only knew about digoxin because of growing foxglove flowers with her mother as a child. She figured that was the only reason the facts of the Cullen case had stuck with her so well. That killer hadn't used digoxin every time he killed a patient, but that was the method Genevieve remembered most. She had read some crime novels where the author used it as a weapon for the "bad guy" too.

Maybe Alex would have an idea of who she could call. She punched in his number and waited.

"It's the weekend, G. What's up?"

"Sorry. I was just thinking about the Eskota case—"

"Not a case anymore, remember? Just an accident."

"Right, whatever. It's just, I was in the community garden earlier and…" She could feel Alex getting annoyed with her being too detailed. "Anyway, there's a plant called foxglove that you can derive a drug from—"

"Digoxin."

"What?"

"Everyone in law enforcement knows that one. That Cullen guy or whatever."

"I'm impressed. I actually learned about it from gardening before I studied the case at the academy and…sorry. That's not important. Do you think it could have been used to paralyze our victims?"

"Through the skin or whatever? I mean, I have no idea, G. That's way over my biology level."

"Who would know?"

"One of the CSU guys probably, but you're not supposed to be working right now. It's the weekend. We're off, remember? No over time."

"I know. I know. Ugh." She groaned.

"Save it for Monday."

"Okay. Thanks, Alex. See you then." She hung up.

Cari had another source within the department. Genevieve suspected it was Bob Hursley. The two had gone to the same university and started in Brenington around the same time. She didn't know Hursley very well. For whatever reason, Chris was usually the person working on her cases when she called CSU for help or information. She knew Cari protected her sources pretty tightly and didn't want to jeopardize anything for her. She started to set her phone down and just let the weekend be the weekend, but the digoxin theory kept nagging her. She gave in and sent Cari a text.

Are you still working on the DMSO angle?

She stared at the screen, but Cari didn't respond. She thought about calling, but then remembered that her friend had said something about getting a massage at the spa Eskota had been using. She wondered if Cari had learned anything new from that experience. She set her phone down on the coffee table and picked up the TV remote instead. Maybe she could find a movie to watch and forget about the "case". She mentally put the word in quotes.

* * * * *

Cari heard her phone buzz out in the living room. She set down the toilet brush cleaner and started to pull off one of her rubber gloves so she could see who it was. She had already scrubbed the shower and bathtub as well as the sink. The mirror was freshly Windexed, and the floor was mostly dry from being mopped. In hindsight, it probably would have been a better idea to mop last. Only the toilet remained. She picked the brush back up and decided to finish the job before allowing her phone to distract her further. She couldn't remember the last time she had cleaned her apartment this well. *Probably the last time my parents came.* She wasn't sure when they would stop by, but she did not want to be caught unprepared, or she would never hear the end of it. Her sister, Beatrice was a stay-at-home mom and somehow kept her home spotless. Cari's mom was always commenting about how nice Bea's house looked. If Bea could keep a house overrun by two children clean, surely Cari could keep a one-bedroom apartment at least in a livable state.

She stood up and assessed her work. No clothes on the floor, no toothpaste smears on the counter, and extra rolls of toilet paper in the little basket. Check, check, and check. The kitchen was another story. She peeled off the rubber gloves and stomped off to see what other tasks awaited her.

She grabbed a trash bag from under the sink and shoved all of the empty takeout containers into it. Fortunately, she had grabbed takeout more often than not recently, so only a few dirty dishes cluttered her sink. She quickly rinsed them off and put them in the dishwasher. She still needed to vacuum and wipe off the countertops, but maybe she should save those jobs until her parents were a bit closer. Her phone buzzed again. Glancing around, she decided it was time for a cleaning break. She grabbed her phone off of the coffee table and unlocked it. Two unread messages.

Are you still working the DMSO angle? (Genevieve)

We made it to North Carolina! Visiting Asheville for a day or two. Love you, Mom.

She drummed her fingers on her knee. Genevieve had seemed to blow off her idea of the DMSO being a connection between the victims. What had changed her mind? She responded to her mom first.

Sounds like fun. See you...Wednesday?

It was next to impossible to tie her parents to a schedule, but Cari always tried. Her sister lived just under an hour away from their parents and never seemed bothered by their random drop-ins. Cari always panicked that she was going to disappoint them. Her mother didn't respond, so Cari went back to Genevieve's text. She hit talk instead of responding.

"Cari! I wasn't expecting you to call." She heard background noise and wondered if Gen was watching TV.

"I figured it would be easier to talk than text. I am still looking into DMSO. Why do you ask?"

Genevieve sighed. "I was working out in the community garden earlier and remembered something about digitalis."

"Digital-what?" Cari asked confusedly.

"*Digitalis.* You know, foxglove. It's a flowering plant. Purple flowers?"

"I got nothing. Zero gardening skills."

"Oh. Okay. Well, digitalis is a purple flowering plant that also has some medicinal properties. You're not supposed to eat it and wildlife will avoid it because they somehow just know this."

"Interesting. What kind of properties?"

"A long time ago, like centuries ago, people figured out that they could use the plant to help with several different ailments, but that too much of it was toxic."

"Like poison?"

"I suppose so, yes. Anyway, this drug was developed called *digoxin* and this nurse a few decades ago actually killed some of his patients with it, amongst other things."

"A nurse? What?"

"It's a really crazy case. As I was saying, I started thinking about how it was easy for him to *hide* the fact he was overdosing these patients because it's not something that would show up in a typical autopsy back then."

"What about now?"

"I'm not sure. I think if a person showed signs of a heart attack when they have lived a relatively healthy life, the ME would probably test for it."

"So, it causes a heart attack? Did Jade have a heart attack?"

"Yes, no. Ugh. Digoxin can cause a heart attack if someone is given too much of it. No, Jade did not have a heart attack."

"Then why are we talking about this?"

"Because I thought maybe someone had used something less common and hard to detect along with the DMSO in both victims."

"Yes! I was thinking that too. I asked…a friend of mine," Cari stopped short of saying Bob's name again.

"Yes?" Genevieve encouraged her to continue.

"I asked this friend of mine who knows about medicine and science if there were any drugs that might act in this way. I have two names, but I haven't been able to find out much about either of them yet. One is virtually a dead end because it's no longer manufactured or distributed."

"And the other?"

"You have to get it from a compounding pharmacy. I'm planning on calling some in the area on Monday."

"That could be a good lead, actually. I'm impressed, Cari."

"They probably won't tell me who they sold it to because of HIPAA, but I should be able to find out if they have compounded any recently."

"You said you were going to visit the spa today. Have you been yet?"

"I went this morning. I'm not sure if I really gained anything from going, but the massage was nice."

"Did they use DMSO?"

"I asked about it and they said that they wouldn't start using it on a client until after they had tried a more organic approach."

"Organic? Like, just getting massages?"

"Yep. It was a nice place. The receptionist was friendly and so was the masseuse."

"Do you think the spa is a dead end?"

Cari paused. Something was bothering her about her time at the spa, but she couldn't put her finger on it. "I'm not sure...I mean, it seemed pretty normal, I guess."

"But...?"

"I don't know. I can't put my finger on it right now. I brought a digital recorder with me. I'm going to download the file and listen to it in a little bit. Maybe it will jog my memory."

Cari waited for Genevieve to respond. She was curious about her friend's about-face. Yesterday, she had seemed pretty convinced that Eskota's death was an accident and unrelated to Jade's crash.

"Okay, well, I guess that's it. Thanks for listening to my plant theory."

"Sure."

"Have a good weekend." She ended the call.

Cari stared at the phone screen in bewilderment. If the police thought Eskota's death was an accident, why was her friend still thinking about it so much? She wanted to call the compounding pharmacies and ask them about the two drugs, but knew they were closed for the weekend and it would just be a waste of time. She stood up to grab her laptop out of her bag, but stopped short when she saw the vacuum sitting next to her table. Her shoulders sagged as she remembered her promise to herself that she would get the apartment cleaned today before doing any more work. She looked from the vacuum to her messenger bag and back. *First vacuum, then one call to Bob about Jade and the drug names he gave me. Seems like a fair deal!* She loosened the power cord on her vacuum and got back to cleaning.

* * * * *

Bob answered her call on the second ring. She was

multitasking by wrapping the cord around the back of the vacuum with her right hand while holding her phone in her left hand. Thankfully, her apartment was relatively small, so there wasn't a lot of carpet to vacuum.

"Hey, Cari. I'm glad you called. I've been wondering how things went at the massage place."

"It was pretty non-eventful. I made a recording of my time there and plan to listen to it later, but I think it was mostly a dead end."

"Why mostly?"

"Something is nagging the back of my mind about it, but it's probably nothing."

"I see. What else have you been doing today?"

"Ugh. Cleaning."

"Are you feeling okay?"

"Not funny, Bob. I clean sometimes."

He didn't respond immediately and Cari felt her cheeks flush in embarrassment. Maybe she was a bit of a slob!

"Right, so who's coming to visit?"

She laughed. "Um, rude. Sometimes you just need to clean up your space, you know?"

"Of course. I'm betting it's your parents. It got too hot for them down south, so they're driving north to cool off."

"Fine. Yes, my parents are en route, but they aren't staying with me! They're staying at my grandmother's."

"And now I know why you asked about church for tomorrow."

Cari felt guilty. Was she really so transparent? And shallow? "I mean, yes, but I do want to try to go more often. I just don't really know anyone there and...this is not why I called!"

"Sorry." He chuckled, obviously amused that she was flustered. "What do you need today, Cari?"

"I wanted to talk about Jade and those two drugs you told me about. I found some compounding pharmacies in the area that might make the one that's still on the market, but didn't get a chance to call them yet. What else can you tell me about it?"

"I'm not a pharmacist, but I can tell you what I read yesterday. I don't have my notes with me and I'm off for the rest of the day, so I'm at home."

"Whatever you remember is great." She had her notebook out ready to take down anything he said.

"Anerva is stable at room temperature when it's still in the powder form. Once it's combined with the solvent—"

"Would that be DMSO?"

"No, you're right in thinking of DMSO as a solvent, but that's not how they usually compound drugs."

"Okay, sorry, go ahead."

"Once it's combined with the solvent, it has to be refrigerated. It sounds like they typically divide it out into small vials that are administered with a syringe."

"Directly into a patient's bloodstream? I thought this could be used topically."

"You interrupt a lot."

"I'm sorry. Please continue."

"I think it would typically be added to an IV with patients, but it can have an effect through the skin. This would be amplified if you used it in combination with an oily solvent, like DMSO that helps it go across the skin. That's about all I remember. I'm sure a pharmacy can tell you a little more."

"I'm hoping they'll tell me if they sold it to anyone recently."

"They can probably share that with you."

"Do you think they would tell me who they've sold it to?"

"Now that might be a different story. It depends on the place and how tightly they follow HIPAA policies. It sounds like you're really convinced that these deaths weren't accidental."

"I feel like Jade's dad deserves to know that someone at least tried to find him some answers. Also, the trucker said she was crying. Why would she be crying?"

Bob didn't respond right away, so Cari plowed ahead.

"Everyone I have talked to has said that she was the happiest person they knew. She was planning a trip to Europe for crying out loud!"

"I don't have a psychology degree, Cari. I have no way of knowing her mindset. I agree that not everything seems to add up nicely. It's good of you to keep looking into it."

"Thanks. Something else is going on here and eventually, I'm going to figure it out." Cari started to say goodbye when Bob spoke up again.

"You know who does have a bit of psychology background?"

"No—"

"Detective Viacorte took some psychology classes in college."

"Genevieve? I mean, she did?"

"Yeah, there's a rumor that she wants to be a profiler in the long run."

"Really? That's…good to know." Cari felt caught off guard by Bob's revelation. She should probably know these facts about her own friend!

"Well, I guess, unless you have more questions, I will, um, see you in the morning."

"Oh, yeah. Do you want a ride or, I suppose you have to go straight from there to work, so—"

"I do, so I'll just, uh, see you there."

"Okay, thanks again, Bob." She ended the call.

Cari wrote down Genevieve's name and the word psychology in her notebook. She circled the two words and underlined them as she thought about the ramifications of her friend's skills. Maybe Genevieve also saw that Jade did not fit the mindset of someone who is suicidal nor did the evidence indicate that she was a distracted driver. And *maybe* Genevieve knew what kind of person they were looking for that would kill two seemingly different people.

Chapter 13

C ari looked around her apartment and nodded. It finally looked mostly clean. Not spotless by any means, but it no longer looked like it might have been inhabited by squatters. She shoved the vacuum cleaner back into the coat closet and pushed the door closed before it tried to topple back out. She checked her watch as she sat down on the sofa. It was almost six o'clock. She looked at her cell phone and drummed her fingers on her knee. Maybe Genevieve would be free to chat about the investigation some more. Surely, she wasn't the only one without weekend plans.

Free for O'Zook's tonight?
Why not?
7 pm?
See you there.

O'Zook's was close to her apartment, so she hopped up off the sofa to take a shower and get ready for dinner. It was still fairly warm out, so she picked out a sun dress and some flip-flops to wear. Cari paused as she hooked the dress' hanger over the doorknob in her bathroom. Genevieve usually wore a SUNY shirt and jeans when they met up at O'Zook's. She rolled back and forth on her feet trying to decide if she was overthinking her outfit. *Just get in the shower already!* She yelled at herself.

After cleaning all day, it felt good to wash the residue of the chemicals off. She toweled off quickly and wrapped her hair into a messy bun, leaving a few tendrils around her face. She decided that Genevieve wouldn't care what she wore and slipped into her dress and sandals. She rarely wore makeup and didn't want to scrub it off later. She had already gotten in the shower three times today as it was. She grabbed her clutch and stuffed her phone and her wallet inside. *Where did I leave my keys?*

She looked on the kitchen table and the coffee table, but came up empty. She usually threw her keys on the table when she walked in the door. She was going to be late if she didn't find her keys soon. *This is why I shouldn't clean my apartment!* She stomped back into her bedroom and pulled her shorts out of the hamper. No keys. She looked around the room, trying to remember where she had stashed them while she was cleaning. *I went running, I went to the massage place, I came home...* Cari rolled her eyes and put her hand back inside the clutch. Her keys and the small digital recorder were still tucked inside. She grabbed the recorder and put it into the small drawer on the front of her coffee table.

She was only a few minutes late to O'Zook's. Genevieve was already there in the back booth, as usual. Genevieve was watching for her and waved as Cari stepped inside. She hurried over to the booth. Her friend slipped out of her seat and gave her a hug.

"I'm sorry I'm late. I couldn't find my keys." She grinned.

Genevieve smirked at her.

"Turns out they were already in my purse!" Cari shrugged.

"Ha ha! No worries. I ordered us some drinks. Should we get chips and guac or queso?"

"Feels like a queso night to me...hey! You're dressed up! You didn't already have plans that I interrupted, did you?"

"I decided that I didn't need to look like a college student every time we came here."

"Well, you look cute!"

Genevieve was wearing a bright turquoise sleeveless top with khaki capri pants and ballet flats. Her wavy dark brown hair was in a low ponytail off to one side. She smiled at Cari's compliment.

"Well, I didn't put on makeup, but I did put forth a little effort."

"Who needs makeup anyway?!" Cari agreed.

They looked up as the waitress started placing drinks on the table. Genevieve had ordered each of them water and a frozen margarita. The waitress stood next to the booth with her notepad and pen out.

"Ready to order? Appetizers? Burgers? What can I bring you?"

"We'll get some chips and queso to start, please. And I'll have your cheeseburger with ketchup and tomatoes."

"No lettuce or onion? Or pickles?"

"No, thank you."

"I'll get a double cheeseburger, all the way, please." Cari told her.

The waitress started to tuck her pen and notepad into her apron. "No fries?" Both women shook their heads no. "Okay. We'll get those right out. Thank you."

"I'm guessing you weren't just looking for a fun night out. You're itching to talk about something, so spill. What is it?"

Cari paused to gather her thoughts. "Well, I know you have a psychology degree—"

"I don't."

"Oh. Wait. I thought you took some psychology classes in college?"

"I did, but I have a criminology degree."

"Oh, okay. But still, you know a little basic psychology, right?" She continued when Genevieve nodded. "I am trying to understand Jade's mindset at the time of the collision. On the one hand, it seems like she didn't make any attempt to keep her vehicle from running in front of the truck. That makes me wonder if she did it intentionally."

"But she didn't accelerate. Don't you think someone would have accelerated if they wanted to get hit?"

"Yes! That's puzzling too. And the trucker said she was crying, which is not the type of person I knew from our yoga class."

"Everyone we've interviewed has described her as happy, easy going, etcetera."

"Right. So, why didn't she make that turn?"

"You think she was drugged. You think Eskota was drugged too."

Cari nodded and started to respond, but Genevieve flicked her eyes up and barely shook her head. The waitress was back with the chips and queso. As soon as she walked away, Cari spoke up again.

"I do. Jade wasn't suicidal. I don't know this Eskota guy, and I haven't been able to look at the case report yet. Cardian didn't file it correctly in the system. The ME said his death was an accident, though, right?" She grabbed a chip and filled it up with queso.

"That's the conclusion. He had some alcohol in his system, so they think he got disoriented and the blow to his head when he tripped was fatal."

"Has anyone tried to find any overlap between Jade and Eskota?"

"We asked his golfing friend if they ever played with Kastener or if Eskota ever worked with him. He said that they, of course, knew who he was, but they didn't ever interact with him. He felt like Kastener was still pretty far out of their league."

"I asked Jade's boyfriend if she ever visited the same spa as Eskota. He was under the impression that she always went to her cousin Olivia's business. I suppose someone could check her financial records." She raised her eyebrows.

"That spa wasn't on the list of contacts that Kastener provided. I asked the dentist if Eskota was a patient. She hadn't heard of him except for seeing his name in the news. So, we can cross the dentist's office off the list along with the spa."

"If we can't find a point of overlap, then what else do they have in common?"

"I've been trying to figure that out too. I mean, obviously, they were both very financially stable in their own ways, but other people have more money and have not been hurt or killed."

"What about their wealth would make them a target?"

"I'm not sure. My gut says that these aren't accidents, but

there's nothing overtly obvious that gives me any clue as to why either of these people would be targeted. When you only have two people to compare…"

"It's hard to find similarities, but we can't just wait for them to kill again!"

"I'm not suggesting that we quit investigating. I'm just saying that we don't have a lot to go off of right now." She scooped up some of the last of the queso with a chip.

Cari nodded. "The only things I can find that overlap between the two of them is that they both had a lot of money and the DMSO. Other than that, they are almost as different as two people could be."

The waitress set their burgers down and refilled their waters with a pitcher she had balanced on her tray. "Can I bring you some more chips? Another round of margaritas?"

"No, thank you," Genevieve said after glancing at Cari for confirmation. "I think we're all set for now."

The waitress tucked the tray under her arm and walked away. Genevieve and Cari both picked up their cheeseburgers and silently ate for a few minutes. Cari wondered if they were asking the wrong questions or looking for the wrong answers. She couldn't think of another angle to approach the circumstances. Genevieve finished off her burger and took a drink of water.

"Did you listen to your recording from the spa? Any hint as to what you heard that seemed off or whatever?"

"I haven't had a chance to yet. I had to clean my apartment. My parents are making a surprise trip up here, and, well, things were a little rough inside."

"They're staying with you?"

"No, with my grandmother. She lives about an hour from here."

Genevieve nodded. "Did you bring the recording?"

Cari shook her head. "No, I almost did by accident, but I left it at home. Do you want me to send it to you? See if you can recognize what I'm missing?"

"I can't imagine it would mean a lot to me since I wasn't there to see what was making the sounds you recorded, if that makes sense."

"Oh right. Yeah. I'll listen to it tonight and keep you posted." She paused, looking down at the tabletop. "Hey, check it out! They have a QR code that you can scan to pay now."

"I didn't think this place would ever be that up to date with technology, but what do you know?"

"Mind if I pay with my credit card and you Venmo me the difference? I got a new Marriott card and I earn points with purchases. Maybe one day, I could go on vacation."

"And leave work behind? I'll believe it when I see it."

Cari scanned the code and entered her payment information. "I rounded up to the nearest dollar when I added in the tip, so it's twenty-two dollars each."

Genevieve pulled out her phone and tapped the screen a few times. "Done."

"I'm not sure we're any closer to figuring this out."

Genevieve chewed on her lip. "I'm a little worried that my lieutenant is going to pull us off the investigation soon. The ME already declared Eskota's death an accident. Kastener's daughter can't be too far behind. I think it's really only because her father demanded we give it a second look that the file is still open."

"Did your lieutenant set a time limit on it?"

"I'd be surprised if he has us work it more than a week. I know Brenington isn't really crime-ridden, but we do have our fair share of robberies and such that have to be investigated."

"So, you'll just drop it?"

"Cari, if I think there's a reason to keep looking into it, I will give it as much attention as I can. Okay?"

"Thanks. Well, I'm pretty beat after cleaning all day. I don't know how people do this every week."

Genevieve stifled a laugh. "I think most people do a little

cleaning every week rather than a lot of cleaning…however often you clean."

"Fair enough. Thanks for meeting me. I'll be in touch."

"See you around, Cari."

They both slid out of the booth and walked outside to their cars. Cari drove a Toyota Camry and hadn't realized she had parked right next to Genevieve's Ford Expedition.

"You're still driving this?"

"What do you mean *still*?"

"Didn't you drive this in high school?"

"Oh! This is a newer model. I loved that old Expo though. I didn't give it up until I made detective here and only because it was constantly in need of repairs. My dad is pretty good with cars, you know, but even he was like, *Genevieve, it's time.*" She laughed.

"Too funny. Well, have a good weekend or what's left of it anyway."

She waved goodbye and got into her Camry. She wanted to get back home and listen to the recording before she went to bed. Maybe it would reveal the clue she needed to get this investigation moving forward again.

Chapter 14

Cari woke up to her phone buzzing on her nightstand. She rubbed her eyes with one hand while blindly feeling around for her phone with the other. She grabbed the phone and saw it was Bob calling. She fumbled with the screen, trying to answer the call.

"Hey, Bob. Please don't tell me I'm already late."

"Late? No, I just, uh, I thought you might want to get breakfast first? I didn't wake you up, did I?"

"Oh, no. I mean, yes, breakfast sounds good. What, what, uh, what time is it?" She tried to shake herself awake. *It must be five in the morning!*

"It's just after seven. I did wake you up."

"It's okay. I think my alarm was about to go off any second. What time should I meet you for breakfast? And where?"

"How about the coffee shop near your apartment?"

"Perfect. Give me twenty minutes and I'll see you there." She ended the call and threw her covers back sending something flying across the room in the process. Whatever it was, it could wait until later. She was going to have to focus to meet Bob on time. She flipped through the clothes in her closet before settling on a bright, yellow dress with cold-shoulder sleeves. She pulled on her strappy sandals, trying not to fall as she walked back to her bathroom to brush her teeth. Her hair was a little wild, so she wrapped it into a bun again and called it good enough. She hastily fastened her locket around her neck and took one last look at her appearance before rushing out the door.

Bob was just getting out of his car when Cari pulled up in front of the coffee shop. She congratulated herself on making it on time. He waited by the entrance as she got out of the car. He was wearing his standard khaki pants and a light blue button-up shirt.

"You clean up pretty well, sir." Cari smiled at him.

He tilted his head in confusion. "I wear this basically every day."

Laughing, she said, "Oh, I'm aware of your wardrobe, Bob."

"What's that supposed to mean?!"

"Nothing. You look good. Let's get some breakfast." She grabbed the door handle and pulled it open.

The coffee shop wasn't too busy yet. Cari figured it took a bit longer for the place to fill up on a Sunday morning. Most people were probably sleeping in or relaxing at home with their families. She ordered a piece of coffee cake and a large cappuccino. She started to pull her wallet out of her purse when Bob stopped her.

"These will be together," he said to the barista.

"You don't have to buy me breakfast, Bob," Cari said to him.

"I dragged you out of bed early. It's the least I can do."

She shrugged and waited for him to order. The barista rang up the total and he paid from his phone. Bob had picked out a yogurt parfait to go along with his drip coffee. He picked it up along with Cari's coffee cake and nodded toward a table to the left.

"Want to sit here? They'll call my name when they get the coffees ready."

Cari took a seat and hung her purse over the frame of her chair. Thankfully, they had provided a fork with the coffee cake, so she didn't have to worry about getting crumbs all over her dress. She smiled as she watched Bob try to juggle the items without spilling anything or dropping the fork.

"Do you want some water too?" Bob asked.

"Oh, sure! Thank you."

He filled two plastic cups with water from the water cooler and turned around to set them on their table just as they called out his name for the coffees. He grabbed both cups and handed Cari hers before sitting down.

"Thanks for breakfast, Bob! I think the church is about ten minutes from here, right? What time do we need to leave?"

He looked at his watch. "We should probably be on our way in about ten minutes. Kind of a fast breakfast. Sorry."

She smiled. "I talked to Genevieve last night. She wants to keep looking into possible connections between Jade and Eskota."

"She better find something soon. I heard at work yesterday that the higher ups are not wanting to keep putting hours into those cases, especially the Eskota case. His death was already declared accidental."

"Genevieve thought that might be happening soon. Hopefully, they'll hold off for a few more days. It hasn't even been a week yet!"

Bob nodded knowingly. "It will help that Kastener is so well-connected in this community, but even that will only go so far if no new evidence is found. And it would have to be evidence indicative of foul play." He paused. "You mentioned that your parents were coming for a visit. When do they arrive?"

"I'm not completely sure. You just never know with my parents. They are driving up the east coast right now. All I know for certain is that they will be in Brenington next weekend."

"Will your grandmother join them?"

"I wish! But, no. She doesn't usually come down and stay since she only lives an hour from here."

"I know you are close with her." He cleared his throat. "How is your coffee?"

"It's really good. How is yours?"

Bob smiled. "So much better than what I get at work."

Cari laughed and glanced at her watch. "I guess we should finish up and drive over to the church, huh? Thank you again for coffee. This was fun."

"You're welcome. See you at the church?"

"See you there."

Chapter 15

C ari pulled into the parking lot and easily found an open spot. Early church must not be the most popular service to attend. Bob was right behind her and pulled into the spot next to hers. She tried to calm her nerves. It had been a few weeks since she'd come to a worship service and she hated feeling like an outsider when she walked into the sanctuary. Bob locked his car and walked around to where she was waiting. They started walking towards the main entrance. Luckily, it was marked with a large sign that hung below the bell tower.

"Ready?"

"Thanks for joining me, Bob. How often do you usually come?"

"I make it over here more often than not, I guess."

"Oh really?"

"Yeah. Sometimes I'll skip when I have the, uh, weekend shift."

"Oh, so you weren't going to come today. I'm sorry!"

"No, don't feel bad. It's all good."

They entered the building and walked down the hallway to the sanctuary. Cari started to slide into one of the back pews, but Bob was walking confidently towards another row. She followed him down the center aisle and into a pew only six from the front.

"Hey, Bob. Good to see you!" An older man shook Bob's hand. Cari looked around and saw that several people were waving hello to him or nodding to him from across the large room.

"You're like a regular here, huh?"

He blushed. "Something like that."

They sat down and almost immediately the organist started playing. Cari looked through the bulletin she had been given to see what was planned for the service. She was happy to see that she recognized both of the hymns. The scripture listed was from Matthew 25:14-30 and the sermon was titled, "We're All Talented". Cari turned her head to the side, trying to remember what that Bible story might be about. She was about to grab a Bible out of the pew when the organ stopped and someone was speaking. She sat back in the pew and listened.

After singing a hymn and listening to some announcements, the man Cari remembered to be the pastor at the church walked up to the front. He had a sheet of paper in one hand and a handheld microphone in the other.

"Out of pure vanity, I'm reading our gospel passage today from a piece of paper rather than from my Bible. I can't see the words well enough and hold the microphone at the same time, so I'm compromising. Hear the words of Matthew…"

Cari listened as he read the passage and recognized it as the parable of the talents. Three people were each given talents or money in varying amounts. Two of them were able to double the money while the master was away, but one had buried the money in the ground out of fear or possibly laziness. The pastor explained the parable and how he interpreted it but said that there were many ways to understand the parables of Jesus. Cari had kind of zoned out for a moment but refocused when she heard him say something about volunteering your talents.

"…we all have gifts, or talents, if you will, that we can share with our communities. In fact, our congregation has been a dedicated supporter of the local soup kitchen and homeless shelter. We are currently in need of some more regular volunteers on Saturday mornings. If you can operate a soup ladle, you can serve this community." He smiled at the congregation.

I guess if you aren't a busy, working person, then you could volunteer like that. She flipped her bulletin over and looked at Bob who was scribbling something down on his bulletin. *Was he considering volunteering?!*

Soon, the service ended and Cari awkwardly followed Bob out of the sanctuary. It seemed like he knew most of the people there and said hello to many of them on his way out. When they reached the back of the sanctuary, he shook the pastor's hand and stopped to talk again. Cari tried to avoid eye contact and be inconspicuous.

"Great sermon, Sam! That's one of my favorite parables."

"Thank you, Bob. I wasn't expecting to see you this Sunday; I thought you said you had the weekend shift."

Cari cringed, knowing what was coming next. She glanced up at Bob, but he didn't look at her.

"Well, my shift doesn't start until nine, so I thought I'd squeeze in the early service before heading over to the lab. By the way, who can I contact about the soup kitchen volunteering? That sounds like a good opportunity for me."

"The information is all on the church website. That's probably the easiest way to get connected. Thank you, Bob!"

They shook hands again. Cari smiled at the pastor and followed Bob toward the exit. She was still pretty shocked that he wanted to work in a soup kitchen or at a homeless shelter.

"Bob, are you really going to volunteer at the shelter?"

"Why not? Want to go with me? It sounds like they could use the help."

"What about the weekends you work? Aren't you too busy to do this?"

"I'm sure they can accommodate any hours I'm able to offer."

"That's probably true."

"So, are you going to join me?"

"Let me think about it. I'll get back to you. Thanks for coming to church with me. I hope your shift is low-key."

"See you around, Cari."

She waved goodbye and got into her car. She was about to call her grandmother when her cell phone rang with an incoming call.

It was her mother. Cari realized she hadn't silenced her phone for the service and was relieved that it hadn't gone off and embarrassed her.

"Hi, Mom. How's North Carolina?"

"It's so beautiful, honey, have you ever visited? We went to Asheville and saw the Biltmore. Oh my goodness, the gardens there are amazing. You absolutely have to go some time."

"I'll put it on my list."

"We're back on the road today. Your dad made a reservation at a bed-n-breakfast in Washington, D.C. for tonight. I think we're going to tour some of the monuments and museums tomorrow. It's been ages since we've been there. Probably since your fourth-grade field trip!"

"That sounds fun. I'm glad you're getting to see a lot of things on your trip."

"We should be at your grandmother's house by Wednesday. We'll meet for dinner? Maybe halfway so that none of us have to drive too far in the dark?"

"I'll find a place that will work and text it to you. Safe travels, Mom."

"Thanks, dear. We love you." Her dad shouted the same from the driver's seat.

"Love you both, too." She ended the call and fingered her locket. Wednesday was going to get here fast. She wanted to call her grandmother and chat but knew that she would either be on her way out of her church service or on her way to brunch with her friends. She would have to catch up with her later.

As she started her car, she thought about the church service some more. Something about the parable was tickling the back of her mind. Talents. It was bothering her the same way her trip to the spa had. *Trip to the spa!* She had intended on listening to her digital recording last night but couldn't remember getting all the way through it. That must have been what she sent sailing across the room when she got out of bed. Cari buckled her seatbelt and pulled out of her spot. Now that she was clear-headed, she could listen to it again.

* * * * *

Genevieve had spent the morning in her garden again. She had hoped that peacefulness of the rooftop garden would help her sort through her thoughts and come up with a new lead. She knew the department was not going to let the investigation drag on much longer without any evidence. It had been ruled an accident already and no one liked to say they were wrong. The only thing she had achieved by gardening was a few blisters from pulling all the weeds. She wondered if Cari had listened to the recording from her spa trip and if it had refreshed her memory. She pulled out her phone and texted her friend.

Did you listen to your recording?

I think I fell asleep listening to it last night. Gonna try again today.

Keep me posted.

Will do.

Genevieve sighed and set her phone down. She hadn't been able to find a single similarity between Jade Kastener and Peter Eskota. It didn't seem like they had ever met, nor had their lives overlapped in any meaningful way. Regardless, her gut told her that their deaths were not accidental. There had to be a clue somewhere. They had something in common; she just needed to comb through the evidence again and find it.

* * * * *

When Cari got home from church, she immediately went to her room to look for her recorder. She should have downloaded the file before she just started playing it back, but she always saved that kind of thing for later. She was feeling around under the bed when she heard her phone buzz with a text. Of course, Genevieve was curious about the recording too.

Since she had her phone in her hand, she turned on its flashlight to see if she could locate the little recorder better. Several dust bunnies and cobwebs were lurking around deserted magazines and old yearbooks. She even found a couple of socks that had taken a wayward turn from the clothes hamper. Satisfied that it was not under the bed, she crawled across the floor to look under the dresser. It had its fair share of dirt and cobwebs too, but no recorder. She tried to remember if she had heard it hit the floor and grimaced knowing she hadn't even listened.

Ten minutes later, her bedroom in complete disarray, she discovered the recorder inside one of her shoes she had kicked off after cleaning yesterday. *Phew. That could have ended badly.* She grabbed the recorder and padded off to the kitchen where she had left her laptop the day before. First, she would download the file so that she wouldn't risk losing it again.

She plugged the USB end into her laptop and waited for the device to be recognized. When the folder popped up, she dragged the file to her desktop to save it. Then she double-clicked the little icon to make it play. The first few minutes were almost silent and must have been when she was first getting into the hallway. She thought about doubling the playback speed, but it distorted the sounds, so she left it alone. Soon she heard a muffled voice ask for something. Her arms tingled with goosebumps. That was it. That was the voice, but where had she heard it before?

She paused the recording and went back a few seconds to listen again. *I must have been really tired last night to have fallen asleep before I heard this part.* As she listened again, she was certain she had heard the voice before, but still couldn't remember where. She usually remembered names and faces well too, but no face emerged in her mind in association with the voice.

Cari pulled out her notebook and wrote herself a few notes. Familiar voice. Where? She tapped her pencil on the notebook trying to will her mind to make the connection, but nothing came of it.

She added a note about the parable of the talents from church. Maybe it would be enlightening to Genevieve.

It was almost noon, so she shut the laptop down and went into the kitchen. As usual, her fridge was pretty bare, but she found some peanut butter, honey, and sandwich bread in her pantry. She lightly toasted the bread, then spread on the condiments. Before putting the two pieces together, she grabbed her last banana and sliced part of it onto the honey. She knew most people found this type of sandwich to be a little odd, but it was her go to meal when she had neglected going to the grocery store. She tore out a blank page from her notebook and started a grocery list. The store would be terribly busy on a Sunday, but she didn't have time to put in a curbside order. She finished her list and her sandwich just as her cell phone rang.

"Grandmother! I was just thinking of calling you. How are you?"

"So good, my dear. So good. I guess you heard your parents are on their way up the coast?"

"Yes, I talked to my mom this morning."

"I just spoke with your dad. They had stopped somewhere for lunch on their way to D.C. He said that you were going to find a place for us to meet for dinner?"

"Yes!" Cari said a little too emphatically. "I have that on my list to get done," she said as she scribbled a note onto her grocery list.

"Let me know where you make the reservation and what time. You can *text* it to me."

Cari smiled. "I will do it."

"Have you solved your mystery yet?"

"No, I feel like I'm getting closer to really unraveling it, but I'm not there yet."

"That sounds promising. I do hope you are being careful. If you're right that someone is intentionally harming people, you don't want to get in their crosshairs."

"I'm being careful. I even went to church today!" She told her proudly.

"Oh, that's wonderful, sweet girl. What was the sermon about?"

"Uh, the parable of the talents. The pastor encouraged us to use our gifts in our community and so on…"

"You know, back in my day, some people used to think that parable was telling us not to squander our God-given talents. That you were sinning if you were too lazy or didn't work as hard as you could at something."

"Oh wow. That seems pretty harsh. Some people don't even know what they're talented at until they're like forty years old!"

"That's true, sweetheart. Did your pastor have a specific suggestion for how one could use their gifts in the community?"

"He seemed to be recruiting volunteers for a local shelter or food pantry."

"And? Are you going to volunteer? It sounds like a lovely ministry."

"Oh, Bob—I saw Bob at church too…" Cari stuttered. "Bob was going to get some more information on it."

"Oh! So, you're going to volunteer together? That's wonderful. It will be fun to do that with a…friend. Well, I know you're busy. I'll let you get back to your day."

"I love you, Grandmother."

"I love you more."

Cari ignored her grandmother's insinuation that Bob was something other than a friend. She felt guilty for implying that she had any intention of volunteering at a soup kitchen or some homeless shelter. She couldn't even keep her apartment clean; she definitely didn't have time to volunteer. She picked up her grocery list and tried not to look toward her bedroom. All of her hard work cleaning up her apartment had been dashed by her clumsiness with the recorder. She sighed. It would have to wait until later.

Chapter 16

Cari slung her yoga mat over her shoulder and walked quickly to the yoga studio's entrance. She was right on the edge of being late. Not technically late, but she still needed to take off her shoes and unroll her mat. She didn't want to disrupt the start of class. She slipped into the classroom and gently set her flip-flops to the side. The instructor, Julia, heard her mat hit the floor and immediately looked her way.

"Cari! I'm so glad to see you. Some of the others were talking earlier. They heard that Jade's death was an accident. Is that true? I thought you were looking into it?" Julia tried to speak quietly, but everyone's eyes were on Cari.

"Um, I am looking into it. I don't have any updates really at this point."

"So, it wasn't an accident?"

"Someone killed Jade?!"

"Do we need to implement a curfew?"

Everyone was speaking at once. Cari lifted her hands above her head to try to calm them down. Her attempt to not be disruptive had fallen distinctively flat.

"Please, I can't really answer any of your questions right now. I just don't know. I promise, if I learn of any reason for any of us to be concerned, I will let you know immediately."

Everyone nodded and went slowly back to their yoga mats. Cari sighed. She hated that people were scared, but she didn't know what to tell them. Julia returned to the front of the room and turned on the music. Cari tried to focus on the exercises and poses, but her mind was a blur of thoughts. So much for a centering practice. Rather than be bombarded with another round of questions, Cari skipped the final meditation portion. She rolled up her mat and silently exited the studio. She had already run four miles before the class and was ready for a shower before settling in at her office.

The newsroom was abuzz with activity when she arrived around 8:30. She glanced at Cardian's desk as she walked past and noticed a small manila envelope on it. She wondered who sent him packages like that at work. He had been behaving more abnormally than usual and Cari still didn't trust that he wasn't trying to dig into Eskota's death without telling anyone. He was a ruthless journalist, and while he had earned numerous accolades for his work, he had burned many bridges in the process. She inwardly shuddered as she reached her own space.

Her first item of business was calling the compounding pharmacies in the area. She felt certain that one of them had made Anerva in the past two weeks. She hoped they would also be willing to tell her who purchased it: a hospital or maybe a hospice center. If it was an individual, she knew it would be a long shot for them to give her a name.

She was just about to dial the first pharmacy's number when she heard an outburst across the newsroom. Cardian had arrived and was waving something in the air. It must be from his little package. She hesitated with the receiver and tried to hear what he was saying.

"...appreciates hard work. Free breakfast taco on the house!"

Cari shrugged and wondered which restaurant was trying to butter Cardian up with free food. She watched as he rubbed his fingers together and then wiped them on his pants. *Funny that they would send a greasy coupon as thanks!* She had been with the newspaper for over two years now and had never heard about someone getting a free food coupon in the mail. She absentmindedly shook her head and went back to dialing the phone number.

117

"Real-Extra Medicines, this is Shonda. How can I help you today?"

"Hi, Shonda, this is Cari Turnlyle with the Brenington Beagle. I'm doing some research on some medications that can only be acquired from compounding pharmacies. Does your pharmacy ever compound Anerva?"

"Anerva? Let me see, just one moment."

Cari could hear her typing on a keyboard. She crossed her fingers as she waited for the woman to respond.

"Well, I see it in the database, but I don't have any records of us ever making it for anyone."

"Oh, rats. Thank you for looking—"

"Were there any other medications that you were interested in?"

"No, just the one for today, thank you."

"Have a nice day."

Cari ran her finger down the list of pharmacies in the area. She grabbed a pen and crossed Real-Extra off her list. She had three more to try that she had found within a twenty-five-mile radius. She was working off the assumption that whoever was responsible for drugging Jade and Eskota hadn't traveled too far from home to get the drug. She picked up the receiver and was about to dial when Cardian returned to the newsroom.

"That taco truck makes THE BEST breakfast tacos. They gave me one for free." He licked his fingers. "Just goes to show what good journalism practice can get you: free food." He laughed and stomped off to his desk.

Cari tried not to roll her eyes as she reminded herself what she was doing before the taco announcement distracted her. If Cardian was back from getting his taco already, it must have come from the truck down the street. She tapped her pencil on her desk. The pharmacies! The next two on her list both made Anerva, but neither of them had distributed it to anyone in the last six months. Trying not to feel discouraged, she dialed the last number on the list.

"Brenington Compounding, this is Rick. How can I help you?"

"Hi, Rick. This is Cari Turnlyle with the Brenington Beagle. I'm looking into a medication called Anerva that is only available at compounding pharmacies. Has your pharmacy dispensed Anerva to anyone recently?"

"Let me see what I can find for you." The familiar noise of clacking keys sounded through the earpiece. "Looks like we've made it a few times in the last six weeks."

"Really?" She tried not to sound too hopeful. "Would it be possible for you to tell me who you sold it to?"

"Hmmm...we didn't dispense it to any individuals, so there shouldn't be an issue with me sharing that information. We have compounded it for Home Hospice twice and Mercy Hospital once. Do you need their phone numbers?"

"That would be fantastic, Rick. Thank you so much." She wrote the two names and waited for Rick to read off the numbers to her. They both had familiar area codes, so Cari knew they were local.

"Can I help you with anything else today?"

"I've done a little reading about Anerva. I understand that it's stable at room temperature as a powder, but needs to be refrigerated after it's compounded."

"That's correct."

"What is its, um, shelf-life?"

"We don't store it—"

"Of course, but how long can the hospice center, for example, use what you've compounded before it expires or loses its, um, effectiveness?"

"The potency and efficacy start to wane after about a month. You can give more to achieve the desired effect, but eventually, it breaks down completely."

"Could someone overdose on this?"

"Whoa, are you planning a hit, or what?" He laughed

nervously.

"Not at all; I'm looking into potential scenarios for a story I'm writing. Purely hypothetical." Cari lied.

"Oh, okay. Interesting. Overdose? I mean, yeah, you can overdose on something as simple as Tylenol."

"What would the symptoms of an overdose look like?"

"It would look a lot like paralysis. The person would still be aware of their surroundings, but they wouldn't be able to move or speak."

"Would they be able to cry?"

"Cry? What kind of story are you writing exactly? Sorry. Yeah, I think the tear ducts would still activate accurately."

"Thank you so much, Rick. You've been a big help. I really appreciate it."

"Any time. Are you going to quote me in your story or...?" He trailed off.

"Oh, uh, possibly. Is that okay?"

"Sure! My last name is Sawyer, like Tom."

"Got it. Thank you kindly, Mr. Sawyer."

"You're welcome. Happy to be of service."

Cari replaced the receiver and tapped her pencil on her notepad. Anerva sounded like it definitely fit the bill for what happened with Jade, if not also Eskota. She couldn't imagine a hospice nurse or any person in the medical field being responsible for these deaths. Both Jade and Eskota were perfectly healthy. No one had mentioned a trip to the hospital, nor could she come up with a scenario that would involve the hospice center. She was running through a list of possible scenarios when she heard someone groan. She stood up to look over the cubicle wall. Cardian was stumbling between the cubicles clutching his stomach.

"What did they put in that taco? My stomach—" He lumbered away towards the men's room.

Cari tried not to feel satisfaction at his misfortune. *Couldn't happen to a nicer guy.*

She grabbed her phone and thumbed off a text to Genevieve.

Interesting news on Anerva, the compounded medication. Can cause paralysis. Also, one of the local places sold some 3x in the last 6 wks.

While she waited for Genevieve to respond, she wrote the words Suspect Characteristics on a blank page of her notebook. Someone who would possibly have access to Anerva either worked at the hospice or the hospital, or they had a loved one who had been in need of the medication. She wondered how easy it would be for someone to get their hands on a medication like this if it was being administered to their dying parent or grandparent. It seemed like something that would need to be monitored closely and not left out for anyone to use. Maybe if someone had been a hospice patient for a while, a nurse would become more lax around loved ones and the medications. She hoped Genevieve would respond soon. She might have some good insights into a person's mindset if she knew how they were incapacitating their victims.

* * * * *

"Rumor has it that the ME is going to declare the Kastener woman's death an accident." Alex said to Genevieve as she returned with her second mug of coffee for the day.

She frowned. "Even with Kastener breathing down our necks, wanting updates?"

"It's been almost a week. We haven't found any indication of foul play."

"I know, but something really feels off about her death. I don't know if I can call it an accident in good conscience. Did you look into my digitalis idea at all?"

"I did, actually, even though it was the *weekend*. I couldn't find any place that said that digitalis would paralyze a person if applied topically."

"Topically is on the skin, right?"

"Yes. I looked that up too." He grinned.

121

"What if there were another drug?"

"What other drug? The ME tested for drugs. He did a *full* tox screen."

"What if there were another drug that wouldn't show up on a tox screen, and there was a killer using that one to off people?"

"You think we have some kind of genius, mastermind out here in Brenington with such a vast knowledge of medicine that he—*or she*—has found the perfect way to leave no trace of evidence? The perfect murder. Twice?"

"I mean, don't you think we should at least consider it?"

Before Alex could answer, they heard their lieutenant shout their names from inside his office. She looked at Alex and then over at their lieutenant's office door. She wondered why he was so agitated.

"After you, G." Alex motioned towards the door.

They pushed back their chairs and stood up. Alex knocked on the door and they waited for the lieutenant to wave them in, which he did as soon as he saw who was knocking. Alex held the door for Genevieve. She tried not to squint as she entered the office. The lieutenant's head was completely devoid of hair. He almost always had his window blinds open, which made the sunlight glare off of his scalp. She blinked as her eyes adjusted to the brightness.

"Always the gentleman, Runimoss," Lieutenant Grusky said.

Alex grinned and closed the door behind him.

"Have a seat. I just got off the phone with the ME. He wants to rule the Kastener woman's death an accident. Officially. Again. The chief feels like we need to be using our time and resources elsewhere. He gave me a little latitude to have you pursue it, but he is very conscientious of the community's tax dollars. I promised Frederick, uh, Mr. Kastener that we'd run down every lead and it sounds like you've done that. What is your take? Is it time to move on?"

"Sir, we've run down several avenues regarding the collision on Monday. The tox screen was negative, stomach was empty, the car wasn't tampered with. It looks like it was a case of distracted driving."

"You're certain? Nothing else can explain the circumstances?" He asked.

Genevieve glanced down before making eye contact again.

"Viacorte? You holding back?"

"No, sir. It's just, well. It could have been suicide. No one that we interviewed seems to think she was depressed, so that seems unlikely as well. All of her friends told us that she was happy and making plans for the future. Also, the car didn't accelerate into the collision either. It continued on a path as though the driver did not realize that the road curved. Still, the eyewitness swears she was crying, which makes me wonder. I know Kastener is convinced it wasn't an accident, but we don't really have evidence that would suggest he's right."

Lt. Grusky nodded. "I understand. I take it that you would like me to speak with Mr. Kastener about this rather than meet with him yourselves?"

Alex spoke up. "He was a little intense. I don't want to get on his bad side or put the department in his crosshairs."

"I will give him a call and deliver the news. Thank you for looking into it. I know this isn't how we typically do things." He cleared his throat. "And Green told you that Eskota's death was accidental as well?"

"Yes, sir. Diminished capacity due to alcohol consumption." Genevieve told him.

He nodded. "Okay, well, write up a summary and file it with the case."

Alex nodded and stood up to leave. "Thank you, sir."

He waited for Genevieve to exit first. She gave him the side eye as she stepped past him to walk back to their desks.

"What?" He asked once they were out of earshot of Grusky's office.

"Always with the 1950s gentlemen stuff."

He shrugged. "Some habits can't be broken. Are you sure you're okay with calling this investigation closed?"

Genevieve thought back to the text from Cari. That woman was relentless. "I'm sure. Mostly sure." She cringed.

"That doesn't sound very sure."

Genevieve's phone pinged again. Alex raised his eyebrows at her. "Sounds like someone wants to make plans with you."

She pulled out her phone and unlocked it to read the messages, both of which were from Cari. She seemed to have found a pretty good lead from the compounding pharmacies. Genevieve hesitated. She didn't want to get on the chief's bad side by working a case he wanted to call closed.

"Your face doesn't look too excited about whatever this other person has planned." Alex teased.

She sighed. "It's not plans. It's—"

"It's what?"

She knew that Alex didn't like that Genevieve had a friend in the news business. He didn't trust them at all after something that had happened before she came to Brenington and joined the department. Cari had helped them solve a case earlier this year, though, so maybe he tolerated her more than the others.

"It's Cari. She thinks these two deaths are related."

"What?! Slow news week or what is her deal?"

"I don't know. She thinks because of the DMSO—"

"He had that sh—, uh, stuff in his house! No one put it on him."

"We don't actually know that."

"Green said that it was an accident. It's an accident."

"You don't know Cari. She is like a pit bull. She won't let something go until she figures it out."

"What is there to figure out? Green says both were accidents, so they were accidents. No reason to keep stirring up trouble."

Genevieve nodded. "Right. It's not on our plate anymore, so we don't need to worry about it."

In the back of her mind, she wondered if the chief was being too quick to dismiss things. It would really make the department look bad if people continued to die and the police had done nothing to stop them. Maybe she could work the case on the side when she was off the clock. She pocketed her phone for now. She would send Cari a text after they wrote up their summaries.

* * * * *

Cari was finally able to pull up the Eskota report. Whatever Cardian had been up to, he had at least realized that it was suspicious to keep the report to himself. She clicked through the brief report and found the name Mark Wickle as the person who called the police about the death.

Cari wondered why Genevieve was ignoring her texts. She needed to leave for the Kastener house soon, but wanted to talk to her friend about the case first. Maybe they had found a new lead to track down or learned something new after looking into Eskota's death.

She looked at her notes. She still wondered if Cardian was trying to investigate things on the side without anyone else realizing it. She decided to look up Eskota's friend and typed his name into the database to see if his contact information was listed. He might be able to give her some more background on Mr. Eskota and his habits.

Mark Wickle was listed in the database. He was married to a Suzanne Wickle. It looked like they had moved to the area straight out of college. Mark worked at a local branch of Bank of America as a loan and mortgage officer. She decided to call him at the bank rather than get ignored by using his personal number. If he picked up now, she could talk to him on her way out to meet Kastener.

"Bank of America, mortgage and loan, this is Mark. What dreams can we make a reality today?"

Cari was relieved they were not on a video call as she was certain her face belied her true response to his question.

"Hi, Mr. Wickle, this is Cari Turnlyle with the Brenington Beagle. Do you have a moment?"

"Are you calling about Peter?"

"Yes, sir. I'm very sorry for your loss. I understand that you two were friends, golfing buddies, right?"

"Yes, ma'am. Every Thursday more or less, but we were friends before Mark started golfing regularly. I've known him for close to thirty years."

"I see. How did you meet?" Cari grabbed her purse and put her computer to sleep as she continued listening.

"Well, we knew each other in grade school. We kind of lost touch as we got older, then I ran into him at some sort of charity event a while ago."

"Was Peter philanthropic?"

"Yes, well, he used to be. He, uh, ran into some luck about a year or so ago and got his partners to buy him out. He retired a few months ago or thereabouts. Retired by forty! I couldn't believe it. Anyway, he said that he couldn't afford to donate to charities now that he didn't have a *real* job anymore."

"Oh, I see. What other hobbies or habits did he have?"

"Let me think. He said something about maybe starting a brandy collection. I didn't even know that was something people collected. I think he was still tossing that idea around. Two months ago, he started getting a weekly massage. Does that count as a hobby?"

"Sure, why not?" She laughed as she unlocked her car. "Mr. Wickle, this is kind of a weird question, but do you know which dentist's office Peter used?"

"Dentist? That *is* a weird question. Are you serious?"

"I am. I can't really explain why I'm asking." She cringed. She should have just asked if he knew where she could get a list of contacts for the man. Besides, Genevieve had already told her that Eskota wasn't a patient of Dr. Santer's.

"I really have no idea. It honestly never came up."

"That's okay. Do you know where I could get a list of contacts or his schedule from the last week or two?"

"This sounds like you're trying to track down someone that might have wanted to hurt Peter. I thought they said his death was an accident?"

Cari frowned. She didn't want to alarm someone unnecessarily. "Yes, Mr. Wickle, that's correct. I, uh, I wanted to include a little background about him in the article for the paper. I'm sure there will be an obituary, but I thought I'd try to learn a little more on my own first." She rolled her eyes. She had not prepared for this phone call well at all.

"Hmm, well, his parents are both gone and he was an only child. I'm not sure who is in charge of his estate. I didn't even know who to tell the detectives to call when they asked about next of kin."

"I understand. Thank you for your time, Mr. Wickle. I appreciate it."

Cari ended the call. She started to call Bob and then decided she had done enough multitasking already. She needed to focus on one thing at a time or risk muddling the whole investigation. She turned on her car and mentally reviewed everything she wanted to talk with Mr. Kastener about.

Chapter 17

While driving to Kastener's house, Cari really wanted to use the Bluetooth to call Genevieve and find out where the department stood on Jade's death, but she wasn't sure her friend would answer. *Worth a shot!*

"Hey, Cari. What can I help you with?"

"Genevieve! Thank you SO much for answering. I'm going over to Jade Kastener's house to see if she had any DMSO or a journal or anything that might shed some light on her mental state. Everyone keeps saying that she was happy-go-lucky and everything, and, I mean, honestly, that was my impression too, but—"

"Whoa, easy there. You're talking a mile a minute. What is your question?"

"Oh, sorry. I was speaking with Mark Wickle, the man who found Peter Eskota on Thursday, and—"

"I don't even want to know how you found that man's name."

"Good. He seemed to be a pretty good friend of Eskota's, but I think I kind of spooked him by asking him a lot of questions about his habits and where he'd been in the last few days.

Cari listened as Genevieve let out a long breath. "Wickle was pretty rattled when we spoke with him on Thursday, so that isn't surprising. Plus, I'm sure the department called to tell him that the death was ruled an accident; probing questions might make him wonder if that's really true. And, Cari, you might as well hear it now. We're closing Jade's file too. Accidental death."

"What?! Kastener is not going to like that. Or did you already tell him?"

"My lieutenant is taking care of that, thankfully. Not a conversation that I wanted to have."

"What about the DMSO?"

"What about it? The ME says it's commonly used. Nothing more to it. Her tox screen was clean. No drugs. Her car wasn't tampered with. She drove in front of the truck, either by accident or intentionally. I don't think Kastener is going to accept intentionally any better than accidentally, so we're just leaving it at that."

Cari sighed. "Well, thanks for the heads up. At least I can expect him to be grumpy today. We should talk about Anerva, but I don't have time to get into it right now. I'll try to touch base with you later." She ended the call as she approached the gate at the Kastener house. She hesitated before rolling her window down. She didn't want to look like a fool for chasing a story that didn't exist, but she was already here. She opened the window.

"Cari Turnlyle to see Mr. Kastener. He should be expecting me."

The gate attendant silently hit a button and the large, wrought iron gate swept open. She could see the house up on the hillside at the end of the circular drive. She had never ventured over to this part of Brenington and was astonished at the size of the home. It was virtually a small mansion.

The white-trimmed, red brick house had three stories and each of the rooms on the second floor appeared to have its own balconies. As the road curved toward the house, she glimpsed some sort of garden in the back. She wondered how many people it took to keep the house looking its best. She pulled her car in front of the house just as Kastener himself was coming out the front doors. She could see that he was already scowling.

"Hello, my dear. I hope you got in okay."

"Yes, thank you." She closed her door and locked the vehicle, then wondered if that was the wrong thing to do in front of a house with its own guarded gate.

"You wanted to see Jade's room, where she lived here?"

"Yes, sir. Thank you. I noticed that you have a garden behind the house. Did Jade spend much time out there?"

"In the garden?" His demeanor softened noticeably and he chuckled. "As a child, yes. She loved to make little, uh, flower crowns and twirl around in party dresses like she was a princess."

Cari smiled, imagining the scene. "What about as an adult? Did she still enjoy the garden?"

His smile faded. "I think it was a place that she enjoyed with her mother. After...ahem, well, she hasn't really been in the garden in a few years."

"I'm very sorry for your loss, Mr. Kastener. I can't imagine."

He motioned towards the steps. "Shall we?"

She nodded and followed him inside. As she expected, the floors were hardwood and decorated with expensive looking rugs. She almost felt like she had entered an art museum as large paintings adorned the walls. The curved stairway gave her a perfect view of the garden, where she saw a few sculptures as well. She wondered what sort of parties the Kasteners had hosted in the past. It was a lovely place.

"Jade's room is, uh, was in the back. It looks out over the garden. Her bathroom is connected to the room."

"Thank you," Cari murmured as she stepped into the space.

"I'm going to go back down to my study. If you need anything, there's an intercom system on the wall. It's self-explanatory." He turned to go back towards the stairs, then stopped. "I trust that you won't disturb the room? You will leave it mostly as it is?"

Cari nodded. "I will be very careful, sir. Thank you."

She looked around the room. There was a cedar chest at the foot of the bed. A delicate lamp sat atop a nightstand made of a reddish wood. Cari wasn't familiar with all the types of wood used in furniture and couldn't hazard a guess as to the correct one. The bedspread was a pale blue with sunflowers along the hem. A large desk that she suspected was hand-carved sat in the corner. She sat in the chair and looked at the neat space. Jade hadn't left anything out on the surface except for a black ball-point pen and a framed photo of her with Harold. Cari gently eased the drawers open to see if there was a diary or journal hidden away somewhere. The top right drawer had a spiral notebook. Cari pulled it out and set it on the desk. It felt weird to be looking through the young woman's belongings. The notebook was about an inch thick and the corners were a bit dog-eared. She turned to the first page and felt her pulse quicken as she saw the contents. It was a journal! She wondered if Kastener would let her keep it for a few days. She closed it for the time being and looked in the other drawers to see if there was anything else worth her time. She found a passport, some jewelry, and a few photos that Jade must have intended to hang or frame at some point.

The door to the adjoined bathroom was open, so Cari stepped inside and turned on the light. Just like her bedroom, the bathroom was tidy and uncluttered. An electric toothbrush sat in the corner near the sink. A white, claw-footed tub was to the left next to a more modern looking shower. Cari wondered if the shower had been installed at a later date, possibly after Jade had outgrown taking baths as a child. She opened the medicine cabinet but only found a bottle of ibuprofen and a tube of toothpaste.

The linen closet held an assortment of white, teal, and pink towels, all of which seemed to be brand new and softer than any Cari had felt before. She looked through the drawers around the sink but didn't find any DMSO. Jade didn't wear a lot of makeup, but the little that she did use was in the top drawer along with some makeup remover and cotton rounds.

Cari closed the drawer and turned in a circle to make sure there wasn't anything she was missing. At least she had found Jade's journal. Maybe it would have a link to Eskota or the massage parlor. She re-entered the bedroom and walked over to the intercom system. One of the buttons was marked STUDY and another read SIMMS. She wondered if Simms was the butler or housekeeper. Kastener hadn't mentioned paging the butler, so she pressed the STUDY button.

"Mr. Kastener?" She said towards the little box.

"I will be right up, dear," came the quick response.

She looked around the room and didn't see anything that she had left out of place. Soon, she could hear his footsteps in the hallway. She stepped out of the bedroom to greet him.

"Hi, Mr. Kastener. I found Jade's journal and was wondering if I might borrow it for a few days?"

He looked at the notebook in her hand. "Journal? I didn't even realize that she kept a journal. If you think it will help you figure this out, certainly. Keep it for as long as you need."

Cari could see the weariness in his eyes. "Thank you, sir. I promise to be very careful with it."

"You might as well know that the police have officially ruled her death an accident. I'm not sure if you will be able to dissuade them. I can't believe that Jade was careless behind the wheel. After we lost her mother…well, she was all I had. She didn't want to cause me more pain."

"I understand. I will do my best. If there is another answer out there, I will find it for you."

His eyes were shiny with tears when he spoke. "I will show you out. Normally, Simms is here to escort people through the house, but I gave him some time off. Neither one of us wanted to look at the other and realize that we were the only ones who would ever be in this big house again. He will be back next week."

"I saw his name on the intercom system. Has he been with you a long time?"

"He started here when I was fairly young. In some ways, we are like brothers. My father hired him away from the old meat market. His father was a butcher, but Simms never had the stomach for it. He's been here since he turned eighteen. I was only twelve at the time. We were never close in the way you might expect. He was terrified of being sent back home and I was a bit of a spoiled snob at that point. He has been a faithful employee over the years."

"He got along with Jade?"

"What? Oh, yes. He drove her places before she had her own license and participated in tea parties that she held in the garden. Jade adored Simms."

Cari wondered if Simms adored Jade or not but didn't want to upset Kastener anymore. She could look into Simms on her own later.

"Thank you again for allowing me to look through Jade's room. I will let you know if I find out anything new."

"You are most welcome. I apologize if I came off in a hostile manner on the phone a few days ago. I really appreciate your willingness to investigate her death."

They had reached the entrance to the house. Kastener pulled one of the large doors open for Cari. She thanked him and hurried down the steps to her car.

"The gate will just open when you get close to it. It opens out, so don't worry about it running into your vehicle."

She nodded and climbed into the driver's seat. She carefully laid the journal into the passenger seat and started the car. It was almost lunchtime. As she drove around the curved drive, she wondered if she could talk Bob into meeting her for lunch.

Chapter 18

*C*ari got to the deli early and brought the journal inside with her. Bob couldn't get away for lunch for another half an hour, so she ordered coffee while she waited for him to arrive. She had requested they put her coffee in a disposable cup with a lid as she didn't want to accidentally spill anything on Jade's journal.

She opened it to the first page. It was dated October 10, 2022. Cari thought this must have been Jade's senior year in high school. She started skimming through the entries.

...wish Harold could take me to Homecoming! No non-high school students, though. I already picked out a dress. Daddy thought it was a bit low cut and too short, but he's old and knows nothing about what's fashionable!

...wants me to take over the family business. What a snooze. I'm not even a real adult yet.

...talked Daddy into a gap year. Gonna be the longest YEAR of his life.

...VALEDICTORIAN! Maybe this will get Daddy off my back about college. I didn't even have to work hard to be the best in my class. I can't believe he thinks I want to run the company. I could probably make some improvements, but why? It is doing just fine and I have a lot of traveling to do first...

Cari was still reading when Bob sat down. He cleared his throat.

"Looks like a real page turner, Cari."

"Oh! Hi, Bob. I'm sorry. I got this from Jade's father. It's her journal. I was just reading some of the entries. She started writing in it as a senior in high school."

"Anything interesting?"

"Not really. It sounds like she was really intelligent. I already knew that her father wanted her to run the family business one day. She had no interest."

"What did she want to do?"

"Travel."

"I mean, for a career? You said she was intelligent. Surely, she had dreams or goals?"

The waitress walked up before she could answer. Cari ordered an egg salad sandwich on honey wheat with tomatoes and Bob got a Reuben with a water to drink.

"Reuben? Doesn't that have sauerkraut?"

"It's quite tasty."

"Sure it is. Where were we?"

"I asked if there were any entries in the journal about her goals in life."

"I haven't come across anything like that yet. She was really looking forward to traveling the world."

Bob nodded. "You said that you wanted to talk about Eskota. Did you find something that links him with Jade?"

"Well, the DMSO, of course, but nothing else. She went to a different spa, according to the boyfriend. Now that I know Anerva could be what was used to paralyze the two of them, I'm trying to find some overlap in their lives as well as figure out who would have had access to the drug."

"Did you ask her dad if they knew Eskota? Maybe he spoke at one of her business things when she was in high school or something."

"I didn't want to mention it to her dad, yet. I didn't want to get his hopes up. He is so certain this wasn't an accident. I still don't really have anything that supports that idea."

"What about the boyfriend?"

"I could probably ask him without it getting back to Kastener.

I'll give him a call later."

"What will you do if he can't link Eskota to Jade?"

"I'll just keep digging. I'm on to something with this Anerva, Bob. I just know it."

The waitress returned with their sandwiches and two waters. Cari slipped the journal into her bag to keep it safe.

"Thank you so much for bringing me a water too," Cari said to her.

"No problem. One check or two?"

Cari raised a finger. "I'll take it."

Bob grimaced. "You don't have to buy me a meal every time you have questions about an investigation, Cari."

"The Beagle is buying." She grinned at him.

He sighed.

"Okay, Eskota. Why did the ME rule his death to be an accident too?"

"Alcohol in the system. No signs of foul play. No defensive wounds. Nothing under his nails. He had a little extra alcohol and lost his footing."

"But the DMSO!"

"It is a fairly common thing. Cari. I agree, I thought they might dig into it a little more, but when it looks like an accident and smells like an accident..."

"The smell! I was reading that DMSO has a distinct smell. Could you smell it on his clothing? Is that why you tested his shirt?"

Bob turned his head and considered her question. "Come to think of it. It didn't really have the usual smell. I just saw the oily stain on the shirt and assumed it was something he'd rubbed onto his back or whatever."

"But why would he rub it on his back right before he got into the shower? And with his shirt still on? That doesn't make any sense."

"Maybe they used it at the spa. I don't know."

"That's why I want to find out how often he visited the spa. They said that they didn't use it until you'd tried a more organic approach first. I really thought it would be easier to find something that overlapped between the two of them." She folded up her sandwich wrapper and set it aside.

"Please be careful."

"Why do I need to be careful if everyone is just accidentally dying?" She asked him pointedly.

He frowned. "Cari. Please. You know what I mean. The department isn't always right. There could be more to this."

"See? You're coming around. I wish the department hadn't ruled the deaths to be accidental. It always comes down to the bottom line, I suppose."

"But Cari, please, if you're right and there is a connection, you could alert the person and endanger yourself."

"Okay, okay. I will be careful who I talk to and what I say."

* * * * *

When Cari got back to her office, she pulled up Mark Wickle's number again. She didn't want to bother him again, but she was curious about Eskota's DMSO usage. She punched in the number and waited for him to answer.

"Ms. Turnlyle? I recognized your number from before."

"Yes, Mr. Wickle. This is Cari. I thought of another question for you. The report we received about Mr. Eskota's death mentioned that he used DMSO. Were you aware of that?"

"Well, I, um, how is this helping you write an obituary? This really sounds like you're investigating a crime or something."

Cari frowned. She knew if she pushed too hard, he might call Genevieve or Detective Runimoss to complain. She tried a different tactic. "I'm sorry, Mr. Wickle. I *am* going to write an obituary, but there were a few things about his death that struck me as odd. I want to be thorough as an investigative journalist."

Leslie A. Piggott

"Okay. That seems...believable. When Peter retired, he started playing golf a lot. As with any activity, you can overwork a muscle group if you don't build up the muscle usage slowly. He was having some back pain, which is why he started going to that spa. I think if he'd just taken a little break from swinging the club, it would have gotten better. Peter was never patient, though. He always wanted the immediate fix. After a few massages, the pain persisted, so he talked them into using that ointment, DMSO you said?"

"Yes, sir."

"Honestly, I wouldn't be surprised if he had started using it on his own too. Is it not safe? Is that what made him disoriented?"

"Everything that I've read about DMSO says that it's safe to use." *Unless it's combined with a paralytic.*

"Oh okay. Well, that's about all I know as far as the back pain goes. Did you have any other questions?"

"Not right now, sir. I appreciate you speaking with me again."

"Do you really think someone hurt Peter?"

"I honestly don't know. That's what I'm trying to figure out."

"Okay. Well, good luck with it or whatever." The call ended.

Cari pursed her lips. Eskota's DMSO usage seemed to point towards accidental death, but it didn't eliminate someone at the massage parlor drugging him by using the Anerva with DMSO. On the other hand, Jade had never visited that spa. She turned to a new page in her notebook and made a list of all the scenarios that fit the evidence she had so far.

Accident
Poisoning by Anerva
More than one criminal at work
Jealous hospice/medical worker
Unknown person with unknown motive
Person with possible hospice connection
Spa worker with access to paralytic
MOTIVE??

138

She wrote the last one in all caps. She was struggling to find a common thread between Jade and Eskota. She felt certain if she could link them somehow, the rest of the story would become clear. She tapped her pencil on the page; there was something else that fit in the picture, but she couldn't put her finger on it. Maybe Bob could help her think through these options. She pulled out her phone and texted him.

Would a spa be able to use a drug like Anerva?

What? I don't think spas would have access to any prescription medications.

Okay. Don't people get botox at spas though?

I'm pretty sure that's done at a medical facility of some sort.

Okay, ty.

Cari felt like she had heard of spas using Botox. She didn't think Bob had ever looked into getting a Botox injection, so maybe he didn't really know where people could do that. Then again, neither had she, so maybe she was the one who was wrong. She decided to call Rick back and see if he could settle it once and for all. She picked up the desk phone and dialed the number again.

"Brenington Compounding, this is Rick. How can I help you?"

"Hi, Rick. It's Cari Turnlyle again. I have another question about Anerva and well, paralytics in general, if you have a minute."

"Okay, let's hear it."

"Would you ever dispense something like that to a spa?"

"Like a medical spa?"

"Um, no, just a regular spa. Are medical spas the only ones, um, licensed to dispense things like that? I mean, is Botox available anywhere or...?" She trailed off.

"Oh, I see where you're headed with this. No. Regular spas cannot dispense or administer any prescription medications, including but not limited to Botox. A physician has to prescribe the medication and it's almost always a physician that injects it too."

"Got it. Thanks so much for your help, Rick."

"Definitely. Feel free to call back any time." He hung up.

Cari smirked. She should have known better than to doubt Bob when it came to something medical or scientific. She felt like she was zeroing in on the type of person that could be responsible for the two deaths, but she was really no closer to figuring out who that person really was.

Chapter 19

*T*he helper stared at the TV screen blankly. The broadcaster had mentioned the death of the local man during the headlines, but they hadn't gotten to the story yet. They grabbed the remote to turn up the volume when the man's name flashed on the screen.

"...local man's death was ruled an accident today by the Brenington police..."

Smiling, the helper turned the TV off and sat motionless on the couch. The young woman's death had not been perfect, but the day trader's was without any flaws. The arrogant man would no longer be wasting space with his life. The helper had made it possible for someone else to succeed where he chose to stop trying. Laziness could not be tolerated.

The helper looked at the framed photograph on the wall. The old man surrounded by his family. He had taught them all how important it was to live up to your potential—to use your God-given gifts to their full extent. The helper's siblings had been allowed their own successes, but as the eldest, the helper had been expected to care for the ailing old man as he slowly languished. It was now their calling to rid the community of those who chose to not use their gifts.

To celebrate, the helper decided to splurge and buy Starbucks on their way to work one day this week. The barista at the location between home and work was always friendly. The helper did not like to use the drive thru and always went inside to buy coffee. It was important to interact with others.

Chapter 20

When Cari arrived at the newsroom on Tuesday, she saw a basket on the front desk. She stepped closer to read the attached sign. Get Well Fund for Lionel. She felt a little guilty for enjoying his misery the previous morning. She pulled out her phone to look for an email with more information.

"EMS event at the Newsroom on Monday" read the subject line. She opened the email and read on. Cardian had apparently gotten sicker and sicker as the day progressed. At some point, he had gone to the men's room but not returned. An intern discovered him mid-afternoon and called 911 when he didn't respond to his name. He received fluids and was kept overnight for observation. The newspaper had gotten his permission to release the details. He blamed the taco truck just down the street for the illness. Cari frowned. Surely, others would have also gotten sick. Maybe he just ate too much or used too much salsa. Regardless of what she thought of the man, she felt bad that he was suffering. She opened her Venmo app and sent some money to the person organizing the get-well-soon basket.

Cari hadn't been able to connect with Genevieve again yesterday so they could talk about the Anerva and the two places that had recently ordered some. Cari still wasn't comfortable with the idea that a nurse or medical worker had basically poisoned people. She still couldn't see a motive for killing Jade or Eskota, unless it was jealousy because of their financial well-being.

Her list of potential suspect types had not changed from the previous afternoon and she was starting to feel like she was simply looking for something that refused to be found. *Or maybe it was never there.* She drummed her fingers on her desk. She decided to text Genevieve. Even though her friend was officially off the case, she thought she could still confer with her on it.

Have a minute to hear about Anerva?

Can't right now. Will be in touch.

Cari sighed. She thought if she could talk through some of the details with someone, she would be able to find that thread that would unravel the whole thing. She started to slip her phone back into her purse when it buzzed with an incoming text.

Did you pick out a restaurant yet? Love, Mom

Cari smacked her palm into her forehead. She had completely forgotten about dinner tomorrow night. Hopefully, since it was a Wednesday, she could find a place that wasn't already booked. She clicked on her Google app and selected the maps feature. She re-centered the map on the area halfway between her and her grandmother's and then clicked on the restaurants filter. Several places popped up and she selected one that said it served Italian cuisine. They used Open Table to do reservations, which reminded Cari that she should have just started with that app in the first place. She scrolled to Wednesday, but the only times available were after eight o'clock. She knew her parents and her grandmother would not want to eat that late. It took four or five tries, but she finally found a place that had a reservation at a reasonable time. She sent off a text to her parents and her grandmother with the time and location. She added the appointment to her phone calendar and then went back to staring at her list. She hoped Genevieve would get back with her soon.

* * * * *

Genevieve sat her phone down on her desk after reading Cari's text. She could feel Alex watching her from his desk. She bit the inside of her lip. Ending the Kastener investigation still wasn't sitting well with her. She didn't want to disobey an order, especially when it came from the chief, but she also wasn't convinced that either death was an accident. She heard Alex clear his throat and looked his way.

"Did you pull up the report on the B and E over on Carlisle?"

"Yeah, just a sec."

"What's the rising journalist worried about today?"

She signed. You couldn't hide anything from Alex. She jiggled her mouse to wake up her computer. "She's still looking into the two deaths from last week."

"Man. You weren't kidding when you said she wouldn't let something go."

"She is definitely persistent."

"You got that report up yet or what?"

"I'm getting it."

Genevieve double-clicked on the report to open it. A woman in her sixties had called to report a break-in before she and Alex had arrived that morning. The department had sent over a pair of patrolmen to take her statement and fill out a report. Genevieve scanned the document. The woman said the back door was unlocked when she got up to make her coffee. She was certain that she had locked it the night before. She claimed this had happened multiple times in the last few weeks, and she was starting to get worried about it. Genevieve started to skip to the next section when she heard someone shouting.

"This is what my tax dollars support? A week's worth of nothing more than due diligence?"

Lieutenant Grusky was already out of his office, walking quickly towards the entryway. Genevieve realized that she recognized the voice. It was Frederick Kastener. She cringed. Grusky had reached the door and pulled it open, causing Kastener's voice to echo into the squad room.

"Frederick, please. Let's discuss this in my office."

Kastener's face was red. "I never thought the day would come that the media would be more reliable than the city police. This is a disgrace."

Grusky ushered Kastener into his office as calmly as he could. Genevieve felt bad for her boss. She knew he was friends with Kastener and torn between loyalty to the job and loyalty to his friend. He gently closed the door behind them.

"Well, this is awkward," Alex commented.

Genevieve gave him the side eye. "Classy. Okay, so this B and E. It doesn't look like anything was stolen or broken. I'm getting the feeling that the responding officers don't think there was an actual crime committed here."

"How certain are we that her husband didn't leave the door unlocked?"

"The woman insists that she is always the first one up—"

Genevieve was interrupted by a door slamming into the wall. She looked over to Grusky's office and saw Kastener stomping towards the exit. Grusky ran his hand over his head as he watched his friend march angrily through the office.

"I want my daughter's phone back, since apparently no one is going to be doing anything productive anymore. You're all a disgrace. You should be ashamed of yourselves." He waved his arms around at everyone in the room as he passed them.

Genevieve caught up to him. "Mr. Kastener, I'm sorry. I can take you down to CSU to get your daughter's phone."

He whirled around and glared at her. "Oh, now you want to be helpful?!"

She winced and chewed on the inside of her lip again. "I know you're upset, sir. I'm very sorry. If you'll follow me, the elevators are over this way. We can go get your daughter's phone."

He opened his mouth to speak again, then decided against it. Genevieve led him over to the elevators and hit the down button. She felt terrible that they were abandoning this man, but didn't know what else to do. Maybe she could slip out later and call Cari.

* * * * *

Cari decided to check the news board for any additional assignments since she wasn't making any headway with the two deaths. She figured with Cardian sidelined, she might have to pick up an extra story or two this week. She knew the kick off for the annual fall festivities was coming up. The city's Committee for Culture and the Arts always organized a month-long competition for local businesses. Each participating business paid an entry fee and then would paint a ceramic duck in whatever design they chose. Community members could vote for their favorite duck through a website linked to the city's homepage. The money supported the local civic center and helped bring musicians and traveling theaters to Brenington. Cari always enjoyed seeing the brightly colored ducks around town.

The news board showed she had been assigned to call the committee chairperson back to get the details of this year's competition and festival. She also had a reminder to contact the Chamber of Commerce to get the list of restaurants participating in Restaurant Week. The city showcased many local restaurants by offering dining and drink deals the first week of October. Last year, they introduced a new feature called "sip and stroll" that invited patrons to walk up Main Street and sample appetizers and/or beverages from the participating venues. Her newest assignment was to attend the city council meeting that night and write up a summary for Friday's paper. She put a reminder in her phone. Cardian usually covered city politics, which was just fine with her. Hopefully, it would be a short meeting.

She had just saved the reminder when an incoming call came across the screen. She saw that it was Frederick Kastener and quickly answered it.

"Hello, Mr. Kastener."

"Ms. Turnlyle. As you know, the police have abandoned the investigation into my Jade's murder. I went to the station to try to

146

change their minds, but they are lazy and incompetent. I demanded they return everything that I gave them to assist their investigation and want to turn those items over to you now. Can I come by your office this afternoon?"

"That is just fine, Mr. Kastener. I'll leave a message with the receptionist that I'm expecting you to visit."

"Goodbye, then." The call ended.

Cari frowned. Kastener must have been at the police station around the time she had texted to ask Genevieve if they could talk about the case. He sounded pretty fired up. Cari wondered if he had berated everyone at the station or just the two detectives. She heard footsteps and looked up to see Ollaman headed her way.

"Good morning, sir."

"Cari, I assume you just heard from Frederick. He's pretty wound up about the police dropping his daughter's case. I promised him that we would leave no stone unturned and all that. He is a big supporter of the newspaper. I expect you understand what that means." He turned on his heel and walked away.

She sighed. Sometimes her boss was really easy to get along with and sometimes he was rather caught up in politics. She wished every story mattered as much as the next, regardless of how much one supported the newspaper or not. She did have some updates to share with Kastener, but wasn't sure if she would just be getting his hopes up for no reason if her theories didn't pan out. She hadn't read all the way through Jade's journal yet. Most of the entries were about where she wanted to travel or places she had seen while she was traveling. Cari hadn't come across a single negative word about a friend, family member, or acquaintance. She even spoke highly of the family butler, Simms. Rather than spin her wheels with the investigation, she pulled up the phone number for the committee chairperson and decided to cross some other things off of her to-do list.

* * * * *

147

Genevieve watched Kastener stomp off to his vehicle. She checked her watch and figured she could probably sneak away for five minutes to call Cari without anyone missing her. She looked over her shoulder and into the squad room. Alex was staring at his computer screen. Everyone else was either on the phone or out of the room.

"Hey, Dana, if anyone asks, I stepped outside to grab something from my car. I'll just be a few minutes."

The woman nodded and didn't look up from her sudoku magazine. Genevieve almost hadn't said anything to her, but Dana was kind of like the all-seeing mom. She was watching even when she wasn't watching. She pushed the door to the station open and slipped outside. Her car was parked in the staff lot just around the corner. Grusky had shut his office door and pulled all of his blinds closed after Kastener had finished yelling at him, so Genevieve wasn't worried about her boss spying her away from her desk. She passed by his window without glancing toward it. *"Confidence gives you credibility,"* she told herself.

She quickly unlocked the driver's door of her car and got in. Rather than cook inside her hot car, she turned it on and made sure the air conditioner was running. Cari answered immediately.

"Gen! I didn't expect you to call."

"I only have a minute or two. Kastener came by the station again today and was really mad. As you know, my lieutenant informed him of the department's decision to declare his daughter's death an accident and close the case file. He was not pleased, of course. He had given us her cell phone to look through the call log and history and so on. Obviously, he wanted it back and of course, we would have given it to him, but he got here before we could bundle everything up. We really should have been more prepared; we informed him of our decision yesterday. Anyway, it was a pretty stressful encounter. You said that you had an update on the Anerva? You called the pharmacies?"

"I did and I do. Only one of the compounding pharmacies has dispensed Anerva in the last few weeks. That's Brenington Compounding. The guy who answered the phone was really helpful. Anyway, they've had two places purchase some. One is a hospice and the other is a hospital. I have a hard time believing that someone who took an oath to do no harm would be offing people with this drug, right? What if it was someone else who had access to the medicine though?"

"Like a family member of someone on hospice?"

"Yeah, or someone who works in a non-caregiver type position at one of these places but could get access to the drugs?"

"I mean, they usually have controlled substances locked up at hospitals and there is a whole log system…ugh. I have to go. I've been gone too long. I can't meet tonight; I reserved time and space in the community garden, but can we meet for dinner tomorrow?"

"Let's do it."

Genevieve ended the call and figured Cari would text her later with dinner details. She got out of the car and locked it with the fob as she walked away. As she approached the building, she noticed that Grusky's blinds were still closed, so he probably hadn't missed her yet. Alex might have, but he knew she had taken Kastener to get the phone. He might think she just stopped to use the bathroom on the way back. She nodded in Dana's direction on her way past the front desk and quietly entered the squad room. She had barely sat down at her desk to continue going over the burglary report with Alex, when Grusky called out her name from his office.

"Viacorte. My office."

Alex gave her the side eye and put his hands up in a gesture to ask what was going on. She shook her head in bewilderment and walked over to the lieutenant's door. He opened it before she got there and waved her in.

"Have a seat. This will just take a moment."

She cautiously sat down and stared up at her boss in what she hoped looked like an innocent manner.

"I have a feeling that you aren't letting go of this Kastener case. I know you turned over the phone and whatnot, but I can see it in your eyes: you think there are unanswered questions. Officially, the department will not be paying for any time spent on a closed case. If it gets back to the chief that you're splitting your attention between your current caseload and this matter that he considers closed, there could be serious consequences for you. However, as you know, Kastener is a friend of mine and I hated having to tell him that we were quitting. I will do my best to shield you from the chief, but you will need to do your investigating on your own time. You can't be sneaking off to make phone calls in the middle of the day from your car." He looked at her pointedly.

Genevieve could feel her cheeks start to flush. "I understand sir. I have a, um, a source who is looking into certain prospective leads—"

"I don't want to hear about it. The less I know, the better. Watch yourself. Dismissed."

"Thank you, sir." She got up from the seat and walked quietly back to her desk. Alex watched her the whole way with questioning eyes.

"Well?"

"Well, what?"

"What was that all about?"

"He just wanted to know how it went with Kastener and the phone. You know. He feels bad."

Alex looked at her intently and tilted his head up and to the side. "That's it? Nothing more? He sounded pretty peeved with you when he barked your name out."

"That's it. You know how he is. He likes to speak with authority. Let's get back to this burglary report." She sat down and logged into her computer again.

* * * * *

150

Cari opened her calendar app to add her plans with Genevieve and realized that she couldn't do dinner on Wednesday evening. She was meeting her grandmother and her parents. She texted Genevieve.

I forgot about my dinner plans with my parents on Wednesday. What about coffee on Thursday morning?

Genevieve didn't respond, so Cari figured she was busy with whatever made her cut the phone call short in the first place. She added the potential coffee date to her calendar anyway and put her phone back into her purse. She fingered her locket and thought about her phone call with her grandmother on Sunday. She had said something interesting about the Bible parable, but Cari couldn't quite remember what it was. She grabbed her phone again and punched in the number.

"Cari! Your parents and I were just looking at the menu for dinner tomorrow evening. It looks lovely. I've never been there before, have you?"

"No, Grandmother, it will be new to me too, but it got good reviews, so hopefully, we will all enjoy the meal."

"We'll be together, so that will be enjoyable in and of itself."

Cari smiled. "Grandmother, when we spoke on Sunday, you said something about the parable that was covered in the sermon. I can't quite remember what it was."

"I can't even remember which parable, my dear!" She laughed.

"The parable of the talents. It was from Matthew."

"Ah, yes. Let me think back...was it the parable itself or the interpretation?"

Cari grimaced, trying to remember. "Interpretation, I think."

"Hmm, well, I might have mentioned that historically, some people viewed that parable as a call against laziness. That it was sinful to not use your gifts or work hard in life."

"That was it! Thank you, Grandmother. I have to go. I love you!"

"I love you more."

Cari set aside her notes about the fall festivities and pulled out her notebook for the investigation. She flipped through the pages, scanning her notes about both victims. Jade had put off college and any career aspirations to enjoy traveling. She had been an exemplary student in high school who was expected to excel in college, but she had taken repeated gap years in an effort to...avoid adulthood? Peter Eskota had been a rising star in the financial world. His business was doing extremely well, but rather than continue down the road of success, he quit and took up golf. Could someone be angry with them for not living up to their best potential? She tapped her pencil on the notebook. Was the person she was looking for some kind of religious fanatic?

Chapter 21

C ari was still theorizing about the killer being a religious fanatic when footsteps interrupted her train of thought. She looked up to see Frederick Kastener walking towards her cubicle. She quickly shut her notebook. She didn't know if sharing this information with him was the best course of action. He seemed a little impulsive and might sound the alarm when there was possibly no reason to do so.

"Hello, Mr. Kastener. Thank you for coming by my office."

"I brought Jade's phone. How is it going with her journal? Did you find anything helpful?"

Cari stood up and rolled an extra chair over to her desk from a cluster against the wall. The newsroom was fairly vacant as most people were still at lunch. Cari hoped her own growling stomach wouldn't be loud enough for Kastener to hear.

"Why don't you have a seat? I have read through Jade's journal and while it was interesting to read about her many adventures, it did not have any clues as to what might have happened last week. She never mentions anyone being unkind or angry with her. Everything is very lighthearted and, well, jovial."

Kastener took a seat and his shoulders drooped upon hearing Cari's words. "So, the police are right? It was just an accident? Just another horrible way that the universe is trying to beat me down?"

Cari cringed. "Well, I don't know that I'm ready to say it's an accident exactly."

"You have evidence? Did you share it with the police? Are they reopening the investigation?"

"Mr. Kastener, I can't say really one way or the other. I have a few theories and ideas, but I need to look into them more to see if they're relevant or plausible."

"Well, let me hear them. I can tell you if they are plausible."

She tried to smile but was pretty sure it came off as more of a grimace. "Sir, Mr. Kastener, I mean, I really think it's better if you let me work on this and get it a little cleaner before—"

"Oh, for Pete's sake! Do you have anything or not?" He clenched his fist. Cari glanced around wishing the newsroom wasn't as deserted after all. Her stomach gurgled loudly and she saw his eyes flick towards it and away quickly.

"I have some theories that I'm trying to tease out. I need to talk them over with a couple of people who are more knowledgeable than me. I promise you, if something pans out, I will call you first."

"After the police, of course, even if they are useless and lazy." He paused. "Have you eaten lunch yet today? Might I treat you to my favorite café in town?"

Cari hesitated. She didn't want him grilling her about leads and evidence for another hour. She was about to answer when another voice beat her to it.

"Ms. Turnlyle would be honored to join you for lunch, Frederick."

"Ollie!" Kastener exclaimed, shaking her boss' hand. "I didn't even hear you walk up. Would you like to join us too?"

Ollaman's face reddened slightly upon hearing the nickname. "Thank you for the offer, but I just finished lunch. I'll have to take a rain check." He nodded and walked to his own office.

"Shall we, my dear?" Kastener asked.

Cari exhaled and nodded. She quickly locked her computer; Lionel might be in the hospital, but that didn't mean she should develop sloppy habits. She picked up her messenger bag and slipped her purse and notebook inside.

"Lead the way, Mr. Kastener. I'll be right behind you."

* * * * *

Genevieve read Cari's text and sighed as she put her phone back into her pocket. She wished she knew which hospice and hospital had purchased Anerva from the compounding pharmacy. She might be able to get a list of employees from them and use it to cross-reference with the people working at the dentist's office. Maybe someone worked two jobs and that was the overlap between the two victims. Alex's voice snapped her back to attention.

"Hello, earth to Genevieve. Are you still with us?"

"Who is us? You got a mouse in your pocket?"

"No, I keep it on my desk."

Genevieve's eyes flared until she realized that he meant his computer mouse. "Always with the dad jokes."

He smirked. "As I was saying, this burglary that was reported—did the woman claim that anything had been stolen?"

Genevieve looked at her computer screen and scrolled down to the correct section. "No, she said that she hadn't come across anything that was missing."

"It seems like at the very worst, it's breaking and entering."

"Isn't that what you called it from the get-go?"

"Yes, but I just wanted to make sure you were keeping up. You seem distracted today. Is everything okay?"

No, everything is not okay. I'm working a case behind the chief's back and I don't even know if it's worth the time! She thought. "I'm fine. I'm just a little rattled by Kastener and how upset he was. I feel bad for the guy. First his wife, now his daughter?"

Alex nodded. "Yeah, grieving families are hard to take sometimes."

"I feel like we let him down."

"We did our best, G. We can't produce clues from thin air. Accidents happen. He will learn to accept it."

"What if we're wrong, though? What if we just didn't ask the right questions?"

"The chief said to close it, G. You have to walk away. Leave it be."

She nodded. Apparently, she was lying to her partner now too. Perfect.

* * * * *

Kastener dropped Cari off in front of the newspaper office after lunch. She was relieved he hadn't tried to pry more information from her during the meal. They had gone to The Yellow Duckling for lunch, a local café that had been in Brenington for over one hundred years. Kastener knew the owner and manager, so they were seated at a special table. Cari wondered if the restaurant's name had some sort of influence over the ducks that were used in the fall festival. She realized she didn't know much of the city's history even though she had been living in it for two years already.

She got back to her desk and made a quick note to see if there was any connection between The Yellow Duckling and the ceramic ducks. She would look into it more later. Before getting back to her theory about Jade's killer, she checked her work email. There was one quick update on Cardian: he would most likely be discharged tomorrow. They weren't able to determine the cause of his sudden illness, but he was regaining strength and would probably be back at work by Monday.

She decided to call Bob and bounce her theory off of him before pursuing it any further. The call rang once and went straight to his voicemail. While listening to his recording, she debated about leaving him a message.

"Bob, it's Cari. Just wanted to talk through a theory with you. Thanks."

She couldn't think of a succinct way to quickly put her theory in a voicemail, so she hit the message icon and sent him a text instead. It took her a few iterations before she was satisfied with it to hit send.

Do you think that the killer could be targeting people for being lazy? Like with the parable from church this week? Almost like a religious fanatic?

She figured he must be in the middle of something, so she didn't wait for him to respond. She knew he would get back to her when he could. She went back to her historical query about Brenington while she waited to hear from Bob. Rather than using a Google search, she went to the restaurant's website first. Most places had an About Us section that talked about the restaurant and when it opened.

* * * * *

Genevieve sat down on her sofa and twisted off the cap of the beer she had grabbed from her refrigerator after getting home. The afternoon had drug on and she had struggled to stay focused. It almost felt like she was leading a double life. She sat the beer bottle on the coffee table and opened her laptop. While she waited for it to boot up, she texted Cari to ask for the names of the two places that had ordered Anerva.

Which hospital and hospice got the Anerva?

Mercy Hospital and Home Hospice. At council meeting. Can't chat.

Genevieve frowned. She didn't think Cari usually covered city politics and wondered why she would go to the council meeting. She shook it from her mind and went back to her laptop. She knew it was unlikely that either place had a list of their employees on their website, but figured it couldn't hurt to check. She figured it was more likely that the hospice would than the hospital, so she started there first.

Home Hospice had a rather out of date website. Genevieve tried the site map to look for an employee list, but couldn't find one. It did have an employee login screen, but that was useless to her. She was not skilled enough with computers to even consider hacking into their system. Plus, it was illegal and she was already lying to enough people right now. Just as she suspected, the hospital didn't list its employees on its website either. She drummed her fingers on the table. Eyeing her phone, she remembered she still had Chris' cell number from the CSU in her contacts. He had given it to her earlier this year when they were working a different case. He seemed pretty proficient with computers. Maybe he could point her in the right direction. She picked up her phone and scrolled to his name in the contact list. He answered on the second ring.

"Detective Viacorte?"

She was relieved that he had saved her in his contacts too. Otherwise, he probably wouldn't have answered. "Hi Chris. Yes, it's Genevieve. Um, I'm calling about a computer issue—"

"You should call the IT department."

"Oh no, it's not with my computer. Um, it's um, well, it's about using a computer to search, um..."

"Yes?"

She gave up being vague and cut to the chase. "I'm trying to find a list of employees at two different facilities in the area, but of course, neither place lists them on their website. Any advice?"

"Is this for a case? I'm actually not at work."

She cringed. "It is...not for a case exactly. It's something I'm looking into for someone else."

When he didn't respond, she tried a different approach. "I have a list of people that I want to cross-reference with the employee lists from these two places."

"Do you have a warrant?"

She groaned. "No. I'm exploring a theory."

"Well, if you know the name you're looking for, you could try LinkedIn and see if they list either place on their profile."

"I don't have a specific name yet."

He sighed. "Okay. What are the two places? If either place has a board of directors, we might be able to find a list through some back routes."

"Like hacking?"

He didn't respond.

"I don't want you to get in trouble by helping me, Chris."

"You called me, remember? I didn't have to answer."

She sighed. "Mercy Hospital and Home Hospice. Both in Brenington."

She heard him typing and wondered if he had been sitting at a computer before she called. She felt guilty about interrupting his evening, not to mention possibly asking him to break the law. After a few minutes, the keyboard clicking abruptly stopped and Chris spoke.

"Where should I send them? Your work email or…?"

"You found it? Okay, great, um, no, not my work email. Let me give you my personal email."

She recited her email for him.

"Great. Just sent it over. Let me know when you get it."

"Already got it. Thank you, Chris. I really appreciate it."

"Glad I could help. Have a good one." The call ended.

She opened the two lists and then found the one she had saved on her phone from the dentist's office. The dentist office didn't have many employees, but the hospital and hospice both had a lot. Genevieve knew there was probably an easier way to compare the lists using a spreadsheet search function, but she had no idea how to do that. Manually searching was her only option. She remembered that Isabelle had seemed a little off to her when they met her at Dr. Santer's office, so she looked for her name first. The hospital had a nurse named Isabel and a custodian named Isabela, but no Isabelle. The number of employees at the hospice was smaller than at the hospital, but no one was named Isabelle in any spelling. She sighed. This was going to take a while. Rather than get distracted by incoming spam calls or texts, she clicked her phone over to silent. She scribbled the names from the dentist's office onto a piece of scratch paper and set the phone aside. She

159

checked Isabelle off the list and went to the next name.

* * * * *

Cari knew she should probably get her bedroom back to looking like someone wasn't squatting in the apartment, but she couldn't get her new theory out of her mind. She barely stayed focused enough to write a coherent summary of the city council meeting. She submitted the summary to her editor and pulled her notebook back out of her messenger bag. Genevieve had texted earlier about the Anerva connection. It was already well past nine o'clock; Genevieve always struck Cari as someone who went to bed early. Still, it seemed like she had been working on the case. Maybe she was still awake. She tried her phone, but it rang a few times and went to her voicemail. She decided to call Bob instead.

"Hey, Cari. You're staying up later than usual tonight. What's up?"

"I had an idea about a motive for the murders."

"You're calling them murders now."

"What? Yes. Listen. I was thinking about the sermon and Bible passage on Sunday—"

"Oh! I got the information about how to sign up for a volunteer shift at the shelter. We have to complete a background check first and—"

"Bob!"

"What?"

"I'm trying to talk about my theory, not volunteering."

"Sorry."

"Anyway, as I was saying, the parable of the talents. Grandmother told me that some people used to interpret that parable in kind of a judgmental way. They believed that if you weren't using your gifts or talents to your greatest potential, then you were guilty of sinning."

"Like slothfulness?"

"Maybe, sort of? What if the killer thinks this way? What if he is a religious fanatic?"

"You think it's a he?"

"I don't know. Aren't most killers men?"

"Yeah, I suppose so."

"What do you think? What if the killer he—or she—is angry that people have skirted their duty to use their gift?"

"You think someone would kill for that?"

"I know, it's a bit out there, but it fits. Jade didn't go to college and was just having fun and traveling. Eskota quit his successful career to be a leisurely golfer."

"Don't people do that all the time? Take a gap year? Retire early?"

"I'm sure they do, but maybe the killer hasn't met them yet."

"I don't know, Cari. It feels like a stretch. How do you find this person? Search church directories?"

She laughed. "That feels like an insurmountable task, but I'll put it on the list of options. Honestly, though, I don't know how to find the person. I need to keep thinking about that part."

"Well, good luck. Did you want me to forward you the information about the shelter?"

Cari cringed. She had already implied to her grandmother she was going to sign up, but she still didn't think she had time. "Uh, sure. Send it over."

"Great! I'll check my calendar and see which Saturday would work best for me. Saturdays are okay for you, right?"

She could hear the eagerness in his voice and didn't want to disappoint him. "Yeah, Saturdays are usually pretty free."

"Great. Well, I guess I'll talk to you later." He ended the call.

Cari sighed. She wasn't ready to give up on her theory yet, even if Bob wasn't sold on it.

Chapter 22

G enevieve yawned at her desk. She had gone through the lists of names twice, trying to find one that was common. She still couldn't believe neither list overlapped with the employees from the dentist's office. Out of the corner of her eye, she noticed Alex watching her. She turned her head and glared at him.

"What?"

"You seem especially tired this morning."

"I stayed up too late last night."

"Did you binge-watch another show?"

"No," she said almost too quickly. That would have been a great cover story. *Too late now!*

"Well, the woman from yesterday phoned again. She wasn't able to find anything out of place or missing. She is still worried about the door being unlocked."

"Do they not have an alarm system?"

"She said that her husband thinks it's a frivolous expense, but she thinks he is wrong."

Genevieve stopped herself from glancing at her pocket when she heard it buzz with an incoming text. "I can't remember. Did the responding officers check the lock for evidence of tampering?"

"You must be really tired. The officers reported that they couldn't say conclusively one way or the other. The house is old, so the door and the lock are probably old too."

Genevieve rubbed her eyes. Her pocket buzzed again.

"You gonna check that or what?" Alex asked.

She frowned. She had been hoping that he couldn't hear it.

"In all seriousness, is everything okay? I've never seen you like this before. You're distracted, constantly getting text messages. Are you sure you don't need to take a few days or something?"

"I'm fine. I appreciate your concern. I just need some more coffee and I'll be fine."

"I thought you were fine."

"You're still not funny."

Genevieve left him smirking and walked to the break room with her coffee mug. She rolled her head around and tried to wake herself up some more. Once she was out of sight, she pulled her phone out of her pocket and checked her messages. She felt bad about missing Cari's call the night before. She hadn't taken her phone off silent until after it switched to do-not-disturb mode for the evening. By then, it had been too late to return her friend's call. The incoming text had been from Cari.

Did you find anything about Mercy Hospital or Home Hospice last night? No worries about missing my call. I know you go to bed early.

Genevieve glanced around the breakroom before responding.

Nothing useful.

She wanted to say more but didn't want Alex to wonder why it took her five minutes to pour one cup of coffee. She slid her phone back into her pocket and went back to the squad room. Alex was watching for her to return.

"Why don't we swing by the woman's house and see if we can figure out anything new or at least let her know she is safe?"

"Okay, but I'm driving."

"I was going to suggest it. You never know when we might need to parallel park and since the department still hasn't updated our cruisers, you're the best person for the job."

"As long as you know who the better driver is," she said to him as she grabbed the keys and headed towards the door.

"That is *not* what I said at all."

"That's what I heard, so that's what I'm saying."

* * * * *

Ollaman had emailed Cari that morning to say that her summary was suitable for the newspaper. She got the feeling he wasn't going to be switching her over to city politics any time soon. She also had an email from the newspaper that Cardian was still on track to get discharged at some point today. She wondered if she were a nicer person if she would have called to check on her co-worker. Her nose crinkled on reflex to that thought.

Genevieve had texted Cari earlier that morning, apologizing for missing her call. Cari read Genevieve's response and wondered what her friend had been looking at in regard to the hospital and hospice. She opened a browser window and typed the hospital's name into the search window. She clicked through their webpage, uncertain of what she was looking for. She didn't want to echo Genevieve's efforts, but she decided to call over and ask about the Anerva. It seemed like they would have to report it if any had been stolen or gone missing. She started to call the 1-800 number and then hung up the receiver. She would probably have more luck if she called the hospital pharmacy first. The call rang twice and was answered by a recorded message which gave her options on how to proceed. She picked option two: speak to a pharmacist. The recorded voice told her that they thought her call was important and it would be answered in the order in which it was received. She cradled the receiver between her ear and her shoulder to free up her right hand. While she was waiting, she looked up the website for the hospice. It had a few photos and testimonials of families who had used their services. She jotted their phone number down just as someone picked up from the hospital pharmacy.

"Mercy Hospital Pharmacy. This is Tara, how can I help you today?"

"Hi, Tara, this is Cari Turnlyle with the Brenington Beagle. I had a question today about a medication I'm researching."

"Okay, what's the med?"

"It's called Anerva. It's my understanding that hospitals get this medication from compounding pharmacies," She paused, gathering her thoughts.

"That's correct."

"Okay, great. If some of it were to go missing, what procedure would your facility follow?"

"Is there something that I should know about? Should I confer with legal first?"

"Oh no, ma'am. This is purely hypothetical."

"Okay, well, first we would try to figure out how much was missing and for how long. If we couldn't track it down through the log system within a reasonable amount of time, then we would be required to report it as missing or stolen."

"And has this ever happened at your facility?"

"Not that I am aware of. We typically use whatever we order rather quickly. It's not often that we have any in storage."

"Do you have any in storage right now?"

"Let me check our records…let's see. We most recently ordered some two weeks ago and we have used all of it already. Obviously, I can't tell you any more details than that."

"I understand. Thank you for your time." She replaced the receiver and drew a line in her notebook through the hospital's name. It seemed unlikely that they were the source. She quickly punched in the number for the hospice and waited for someone to answer.

"Good morning. Home Hospice. This is Jaime speaking. How can I help you today?"

"Hi, Jaime. This is Cari Turnlyle with the Brenington Beagle. I'm researching a medication called Anerva. I understand our facility occasionally orders this from a local compounding pharmacy?"

"Anerva, you said?"

"Yes, Anerva."

"Let me just pull up our records. Yes, we use the medication. What would you like to know about it?"

"If some of it were to go missing, what steps would your facility follow?"

"Missing? Like someone stole some? All of our meds are locked up and only our trained staff members have the combination to access them. There's a very specific procedure involved when it comes to dispensing medications."

"Are you saying that you have never had a discrepancy in your log books or anything of that nature?"

"I have been working here for twenty-three years and have never heard about that happening."

"Okay, but surely you have a procedure if it were to happen."

"Yes. The person who noticed the discrepancy would report it to our chief of staff. If the amount could not be recovered, then we would report the loss to the medical board. An investigation would ensue."

"Thank you. You answered all of my questions. I appreciate your time." The line clicked dead before Cari took the receiver away from her ear. It seemed like Jaime was a little too anxious to end the conversation. Cari wondered if there had been a discrepancy recently that had been brushed under the rug. She decided to keep Home Hospice on the list of possibilities for now. She wrote possible discrepancy next to Home Hospice in her notebook and then drummed her pencil in place. She knew that they wouldn't release a list of clients they had served as that would violate their HIPAA policy. Cari sensed someone watching her and looked up from her notes to see Ollaman headed her way.

"Cari! Thanks again for covering that council meeting last night. Lionel should be back next week from what I can gather. Hey, how was lunch yesterday? How are things going with the Kastener story?"

Cari noticed that when Ollaman was pleased with her, he called her by her first name. "Thank you, sir. Lunch was nice; he took me to a local café called The Yellow Duckling—"

"That's one of his favorites since he was a child. The owners are long-time friends of the Kasteners."

"It was great food. I actually looked up some of the history of the restaurant after I got back yesterday. I had always assumed that the fall festivities used a duck for the chamber competition because that was the mascot of the first high school here. In actuality, the family that founded The Yellow Duckling is responsible for it. They started the competition back in the 1950s to try and rejuvenate tourism in Brenington after the depression and the war."

"That's right. The high school already had the mascot, so that influenced it too, but the Allertons really paved the way."

Cari nodded. "Everything I read said that Brenington wouldn't have survived without the Allertons and the Kasteners."

"I don't want to be one of those micromanaging-pain-in-the-ass type bosses, but how are things moving with your investigation into Jade's death?" Ollaman ran his fingers through his thinning hair as he spoke, then shoved both hands into his pockets as though he couldn't get comfortable.

"It's a little tricky still. I might have stirred up a reasonable lead, but it could also be nothing."

Ollaman seemed to take the hint that she wasn't ready to reveal her hand, yet. He nodded his head slowly as though agreeing with himself before speaking. "Great. Keep at it. Let me know if you need anything."

Cari watched him walk back to his office, resisting the urge to roll her eyes at her boss' quirks. He definitely went through the gamut of emotions on a daily basis. She never knew if he was going to be angry, upset, excited, or something entirely different. She looked at her notebook and tried to remember her train of thought before Ollaman stopped by her desk. If the hospice place had a portion of their Anerva go missing, had it been a hospice worker that took it, or a family member of one of their clients? She wondered if Anerva had any addictive properties. It seemed like a muscle relaxant might fall in that category. She texted Bob.

Could someone get addicted to Anerva? At a lower dose?

She didn't expect him to respond right away, but thought that Jaime from Home Health might be covering for someone with a previous addiction. Then again, would someone with a history of drug addiction be allowed to access other addictive medications? Cari wasn't sure. She hoped Bob would know. She certainly didn't think Jaime would tell her.

* * * * *

Genevieve had lost out to Alex and was stuck writing their report about the burglary. When they arrived at the home, the husband met them in the driveway. He had apparently been watching from the front door, waiting for them to pull up to the house. She stifled a grin as she remembered the conversation.

"Are you still laughing at that old man?" Alex asked.

"You're going to defend him?"

"I mean, his wife sounds a little neurotic, if you ask me."

"She's neurotic because she checks to see if their house is locked?"

"I'm just sayin'."

"You're *just sayin'* a lot of things. He is obviously sneaking out of the house after she falls asleep to go see someone else. If it were just a friend or something innocent, he would just tell her where he was going. He's either cheating or living a double life or both."

"Oh, agreed, but who am I to judge? What are you going to write in the report?"

"I'll just say that the spouse admitted to leaving the door unlocked and that no burglary occurred."

"What do you think he told his wife?"

"He's clearly not a rookie when it comes to lying. I'm sure he'll say that he forgot to take the garbage out and inadvertently left the door unlocked."

"That's good. Did you sneak out a lot as a kid? It seems like you've got the reasoning already worked out."

Genevieve narrowed her eyes at him. "Don't push your luck, or you'll get to write the report."

"I still have seniority over you, G. This report is definitely all yours." He smirked at her. "Think of it as another learning experience."

She glared at him as she sat down at her desk. Her mind was still somewhat distracted by the other case. She knew Chris had gone out on a limb for her in digging up those employee lists and hoped whatever he had done to find them wouldn't get either of them in trouble. She absentmindedly pulled up the form for the report and started filling in her information. Genevieve still thought it was reasonable that the killer worked two jobs. Her eyes widened as she realized she was at least subconsciously thinking that the two people had been killed. She blinked and tried to focus on the report again. She didn't realize that Alex was watching her with mild amusement.

Before entering any more information into the report, she pulled out her cell phone and made a note about doing another search for job overlap between Kastener and Eskota's activities. She didn't know much about either victim's weekly habits. It might be a challenge to piece together which places either one had visited that had led them into the killer's path. As she slipped her phone back into her pocket, Alex's amusement faded into concern. If Genevieve had looked up, she would have seen her partner observing her and questioning her new habits.

* * * * *

Cari had just returned from eating lunch in the break room when her phone buzzed with an incoming call. She saw that it was Bob calling and answered immediately.

"Bob! Hey! I have another Anerva question for you. Thanks for calling me."

"Hi, Cari. What's your question?"

"After speaking with people at both the hospital and the hospice place, I got the impression the woman at the hospice place was hiding something. Anyway, it felt like she was covering for someone and it made me wonder if Anerva was addictive."

"Off the top of my head, I can't say one way or the other, but because it affects the nervous system, I'd say the odds are in favor of it being addictive. What does Anerva being addictive tell you in regards to the case, though?"

"I'm not sure, actually. Her behavior just really struck me as though she were trying to keep someone else out of trouble."

"Okay and what does that tell you?"

Cari was mentally running through a multitude of possibilities and discarding them. "What if one of the people on their staff has a history of drug abuse?"

"Okay. Are you saying you think the killer is a drug addict now?"

"No. I think possibly the staff member, maybe a nurse or someone like that has a history of drug abuse and maybe there is some sort of zero tolerance policy for them."

"Oh, I see where you're going. You think if one of the nurses had some Anerva or other controlled substance go missing on their watch they could lose their job if they also had a history of drug abuse in their file."

"Yes! So, it wouldn't get reported properly and no one would be the wiser."

"I suppose that is possible. It's a lot of maybes, though. Also, the person that stole the Anerva from the nurse or whomever, are they knowledgeable enough to use it?"

"Who's to say they aren't?"

"I think you're getting somewhere, but it's still a lot of conjecturing."

"I agree, but I'm not out of ideas yet. Thanks for your help, Bob."

"You're welcome, Cari. I've gotta run. I know you'll probably ignore this, but please be careful."

"Of course. I'm just making phone calls. How can I get hurt? Thanks again." She ended the call.

Cari wanted to bounce her ideas off of Genevieve but wondered if she was causing her friend issues by texting her during the work day. Surely, if she were being a nuisance, Gen would tell her. She thumbed off a text.

Have a new theory about Anerva and Home Hospice. I'll explain in the morning. Call if you can.

She drummed her fingers on the desk, hoping Genevieve could take a break and chat for a minute. Her phone stayed silent. Cari thought back over her theory. If the killer was a family member of a hospice patient, there was a chance that their family member had died recently. She decided to pull up the recent obituaries and see if any of the names looked familiar.

Chapter 23

G enevieve clicked the save button on the form and sent it to the squad room printer. She pushed back from the desk to grab it. She and Alex had to sign it before it could be submitted to the lieutenant for approval. This could be done electronically, but Alex preferred paper copies. She squeezed a staple into the report and slid it in front of Alex on his desk.

"Finished already? Let's see if you made any mistakes." He teased.

While she waited for him to read through it, she opened a database program on her computer. She wanted to search for reports of lost or stolen Anerva in their area. She set the parameters to include anything for the last six weeks and within forty miles of Brenington. She tried to will the little spinning circle to work faster. It wouldn't take long for Alex to read through the short report. She was tapping her heel on the floor rapidly, anticipating the results window. She heard Alex flipping all the pages back to the front and was about to give up when the screen flashed. Your query returned zero (0) results. She frowned.

"Lose at solitaire again?" Alex's voice startled her.

"No..I was looking up an address for later." She lied and closed the database.

"Couldn't find it?"

She blinked at him, initially forgetting what she had said. "No, it's just further away than I expected. Everything okay with the report?"

"Looks good to me. Do we have to e-sign it or whatever?"

"Yes, Grandpa, we have to use the computer thingies to do a

digital signature."

"You're not funny."

"I just emailed it to you. Do you need me to walk you through the steps again, or can you handle it on your own this time?"

"I can do it. I'm not a dinosaur. I don't see why we can't just sign this printed one though."

"Because then, someone would have to take a few more minutes and scan the report so the department has a digital copy that can be referenced in case something comes up again."

He rolled his eyes. "Whatever."

"Did you eat lunch yet?"

"Yeah, I grabbed a taco from the stand while you were finishing the report."

"I haven't had mine, so I'm going to go eat now. I have my cell if something gets called in before I get back."

"Roger that."

Genevieve grabbed her lunch from the break room and walked quickly out to the parking lot. She could eat her sandwich while she made a few inquiries and possibly check in with Cari. She had waited to take her lunch break until a little after one o'clock in hopes that she would catch people at their desks and not on their own lunch breaks. She was still surprised that the database didn't have any reports of missing or stolen Anerva. She had been certain that one of the two facilities was going to pop up on the list. She had the address for the office of Home Hospice. It was only a few minutes from the station. She decided to drive over and speak with them in person. She turned on her vehicle and put it in gear while fastening her seatbelt. She was halfway finished with her sandwich when she pulled up to their office.

The hospice was located in what looked to be a former single-family home that had been converted into an office space. "Home Hospice" was etched on the door along with their hours of operation. Genevieve pulled open the door and saw a woman with light brown curly hair seated behind a desk. She looked to be in

Leslie A. Piggott

her late forties and had bright red reading glasses on a chain around her neck.

"Welcome to Home Hospice. I'm Jaime. How may I help you today?"

"Hi, Jaime. I'm Detective Viacorte. I'm trying to determine if a certain medication has gone missing from any of our area hospitals, pharmacies, or hospices."

"What's the medication?"

"It's called Anerva. That's A-N-E—"

"I know how to spell it. Let me look it up." She typed on the keyboard. "No reports of any missing Anerva."

"What time frame did you search? Can you search for the last two months?"

She typed some more. "Nothing. It's all accounted for."

"What would happen if some had gone missing? How often do you do an inventory check?"

"We check it every week. We use several controlled substances with our patients experiencing end of life care. If we had repeated unaccounted for loss of these meds, we could lose our hospice license."

"I understand. Here's my card. If you notice any discrepancies, please give me a call."

The woman took the card and smiled weakly at Genevieve. "Thank you, Detective. I will certainly let you know."

Genevieve returned the smile and left the office. Something about the woman's responses seemed off to her. She was friendly but in a forced way. For some reason, the woman never used her reading glasses when conducting the two searches on her computer. Maybe they were just part of her outfit, but it seemed suspicious. Without a warrant, Genevieve couldn't access their records and see if she was telling the truth. She got back in her car and took a bite of her sandwich before buckling herself in. She had been gone from the station for about twenty minutes and needed to get back before Alex got too curious.

174

* * * * *

Cari checked her watch. She decided to give Bea a call and see if there was anything she should know before eating dinner with their parents that evening. Occasionally, there were sensitive topics or family members that got one or both of her parents all riled up. She wanted to avoid that if at all possible.

"Hey, Cari. I heard you're having dinner with our parents and Grandmother tonight."

"Hey, Bea. I am. How are you doing today?"

"Same as usual. It's hot, so the kids are eating some popcorn and watching a movie from the couch. Robby and I are taking them to the beach this weekend. At least we can cool off somewhat in the ocean."

"That sounds fun. Which beach?"

"Panama City Beach. It's a couple of hours from here. We rented an Airbnb for the weekend."

"Nice. Well, anything I should know before I meet them for dinner?"

"Let's see. Daddy's pretty fired up about something at church. I can't remember what it was. Maybe a committee thing. They are also both concerned that you're still single, so be ready for a lot of questions about that."

"Oh good. Guess I can't do much about that on the fly."

"You could lie and say that you're dating Bob. I'm sure he'd pose as your boyfriend for you."

"Bea! I would not ask Bob to do that. How shallow do you think I am? Don't answer that."

Her sister laughed. "Well, it sounds like the movie is ending, so I've gotta go. I'm sure there are a thousand popcorn kernels lurking in my sofa cushions now. Love you, Cari."

"Love you too, Bea. Hug those kiddos for me." She ended the call.

Cari had about thirty minutes before she needed to leave for dinner. She had spent a little time that afternoon getting her article together for the feature about the fall festivities. The chairperson had been really helpful in providing her with a spreadsheet of all the businesses and their contact info as well as an outline of the scheduled events. Her computer dinged with a new email, so she clicked over to see what it was.

Bob had forwarded her the information about signing up to volunteer with the shelter and soup kitchen. She drummed her fingers on her desk nervously. Maybe volunteering wouldn't be that bad. It sounded like they only had to do it once a month and it would probably only be an hour or two each time. She clicked on the register to volunteer button. A new tab opened with an electronic form for her to fill out. It asked for her name, address, birthdate, and social security number. She hesitated. Was the website secure or was she about to have her identity stolen? Next to the little box was a green checkmark. She hovered the mouse over it and read the bubble that popped up.

All of your information is secure and will be encrypted.

She frowned, but decided that if Bob was okay with it, then she was too. She continued filling out the form. Near the bottom of the page, it said background checks usually take a few days to return. Once you were approved, they would email you with a confirmation form that gave available times for volunteering. She lightly flicked her fingertips on the keys. *Now or never, Cari.* She clicked submit and slowly let her breath out. She hadn't realized she had been holding it. Hopefully, Bob would be able to go with her. She didn't think she was up for going by herself.

* * * * *

Genevieve pulled her leftovers out of the fridge when she got home from the station. She washed a tomato she had harvested from her garden the evening before and sliced it to put on her salad.

She wanted to look up some background information on the receptionist from Home Hospice. Jaime hadn't answered Genevieve's question about what happens if they have a discrepancy in their records for controlled substances. It made her wonder if Jaime was trying to protect someone or possibly protecting herself. She set her plate down on the coffee table next to her laptop and logged in.

She had saved the employee lists from Chris into a folder on her desktop. She double-clicked on the one for Home Hospice and scrolled through the names to find Jaime. Jaime Shunnister. Genevieve minimized the list and opened up the National Crime Information Center (NCIC) database. She didn't want to stay in the database too long because the department was charged for using it. She typed Jaime Shunnister into the name section and added New York for the state. She clicked back over to the employee list to get her address in case the search pulled up more than one person. Her search came up with one result. Shunnister was a person of contact for another person in the database: Matthew Lupsen. She clicked on Lupsen's name to pull up his record. Scanning the record, she read that Shunnister was Lupsen's mother. He had been arrested for drug possession six years ago when he was eighteen. She clicked back over to the employee list again. Shunnister was only nineteen when Lupsen was born. Genevieve scrolled up on the list. *Bingo!* Lupsen was also on staff with Home Hospice. He was a nurse.

She drummed her fingers on the table. Lupsen didn't have any other charges on his record besides the one drug possession. It looked like he had successfully pled the charges down to a misdemeanor even though he easily could have been charged with a felony. It must have scared him straight as he was now a nurse. She double-checked the employee list and saw that he was even a board-certified-registered nurse. He had gotten the four-year degree. Genevieve guessed that his mom had pulled some strings to get him that job. She pulled out her notebook and scribbled his name into it. Maybe he was the connection they were looking for. She picked her dinner up and had just taken a bite when her cell phone buzzed with an incoming call. She didn't recognize the number but decided to answer it anyway.

"Detective Viacorte speaking."

"Is this the woman who came to the hospice today?"

"Yes, I can barely hear you. Who is this?"

"I work at the hospice. I heard you asking about the Anerva."

"Okay, I'm sorry, what did you say your name is?"

"We did have some Anerva go missing, but they altered the records to hide it."

"Who did?"

"I can't say, but the person who did it is a really nice person, but they have a history, you could say."

"Like a record?"

"I'm not totally sure, but they checked out a vial of Anerva and their report from the patient only listed them using a portion of it. However, the vial was basically empty when they checked it back in. Rather than report it and possibly get this person in trouble, someone changed the report to read like they had used more than they really had."

"How do you know this? Did you watch them do it?"

"I file the reports at the end of the day. Another person enters them into the system. When I heard you asking about it today, I double-checked the file. It had changed."

"Can you give me your name? I'd like to speak with you in person if possible—"

The call ended.

* * * * *

Cari pulled into the restaurant's parking lot with ninety seconds to spare. Knowing her grandmother and her parents, they already had a table and had been waiting for her for at least five minutes. She locked her car and hurried into the restaurant. Looking past the hostess, she spotted her mom waving from a booth to the right. She smiled and indicated to the hostess she was meeting an already seated party.

"Cari!" Her mom exclaimed, jumping up from the table. "It's so good to see you. How are you? How was the drive? Did you run into a lot of traffic?"

"Good grief, Patricia. Let her get a seat before you bowl her over with questions. Hi, sweet pea. How's my girl?"

Her grandmother sat silently in the booth with an amused look on her face. This happened every time they got together. She blew Cari a kiss from the corner of the booth. "Hello, my dear. Great to see you. This restaurant is lovely. How did you find it?"

"Google," Cari shrugged. "Thank you. It's great to see all of you too. I'm doing well. The drive was easy, almost no traffic. Did you already order drinks?"

"We only barely sat down. Here comes the waitress now."

Cari ordered a water, but her mom and grandmother got a cocktail to go along with their waters. Her dad always drank unsweetened iced tea. It really bothered people where they lived in the south, which pleased him all the more. They caught up over appetizers, her mother sharing photos from their various stops along the east coast.

"Your grandmother was telling us you're going to start volunteering at a soup kitchen or something?" Her dad asked.

Cari bit her lip before responding. "Yes, actually I filled out the registration form and background check right before I left to come here."

"Oh, that's wonderful, my dear. When will you start?"

"They said that once I cleared the background check, they would send a schedule with their openings for volunteers. It could take up to a week or so, I think."

"And you're going to be volunteering with Bob?" Her mother asked.

Cari tried to fight off a blush and hoped that she had succeeded. "Yes, he got the information from the church and helped make the initial contact for us to sign up."

"I'm glad you won't be going alone. You never know how unstable some of those homeless people can be."

"Darren! That's rude and inappropriate." Her grandmother chastised him.

"But not untrue."

Cari cleared her throat and decided to try changing the subject. The waitress had just returned with their entrees, so the conversation had paused anyway. Her cousins were usually a safe topic. "Grandmother, I haven't asked you about Zachary and Aaron in a while. How are they doing?"

"Well, let's see. Zachary is getting his doctorate in neurology or some such complicated topic. I don't understand half of what he tells me. He's still over on the west coast, um, Portland. Aaron is gradually making his way through college. His mother thinks he's getting pretty serious about his girlfriend. They got to meet her last time they visited. He's been working two jobs this summer to try to save extra money for school. This will be his fifth year of college. I think if he takes a full class load both semesters, he can graduate in May."

"Did he sign up for a full load?"

"I'm not sure. His mother didn't share that with me and he seems to be always working. I don't hear from him a lot."

"Two jobs? What kind of jobs?"

"I think he checks in patients at a dental office from eight until four, Monday through Thursday. Then on the weekends, he works with a DJ at a club nearby his school."

"And they'll just let him quit next week when classes start?"

"I'm not sure, Darren. Like I said, I don't get to talk to him very often."

Cari frowned as she thought about her cousin working two jobs. Of course! The killer could work two different places. That was why she couldn't find any overlap between the victims. The killer must have more than one job.

"Earth to Cari…is everything okay, dear?" Her grandmother asked.

"What? Oh. Sorry! I was just thinking about something you said. It makes more sense…never mind."

"Did you hear your grandmother say that Aaron is getting engaged soon?" Cari's mother asked.

Cari struggled with her emotions again and somehow avoided rolling her eyes. "That's very exciting. Is this the young woman he has been dating since high school? What was her name…Liza?"

"Good memory, my dear. Liza Penfer. She is in art school right now."

"That sounds fun. Well, I hate to eat and run, but I have an early morning coffee date tomorrow—"

"With Bob?" Her mother interrupted.

"Uh, no, with Genevieve. You remember her from high school, right?"

"Oh yes, Genevieve. Is she married?"

"No. She's a detective, remember? She helped with that story earlier this year?"

"Oh right. Well, tell her we said hi. We'll be checking in at the hotel around four on Friday. What time will you get off work?"

"Probably around six. I'll call you if it's earlier."

"Should we make a dinner reservation? I really liked that place you took us last time. What was it called?"

"Not the bar again, Patricia."

"It's a pub, *Darren*. They have good margaritas."

"We don't need a reservation at O'Zook's." Cari told them. "I really have to go. I love you. Thank you for dinner."

"I love you more, sweet Cari." Her grandmother called out after her.

* * * * *

181

Cari called Bob as she walked out to her car. She couldn't wait to tell him about the two jobs. It helped explain so much. He answered on the first ring.

"Cari? I thought you were eating dinner with your family tonight?"

"I was. I just finished. Listen, Bob. My grandmother was telling me about my cousin Aaron who works *two jobs* to help pay for college."

"Okay, sounds like a hard worker. That's great."

"Bob! Two jobs! *TWO JOBS!*"

"Oh! You mean about the case. Of course, we could have missed an overlap because the unsub works in two places."

"Exactly. Wait just a sec. The call is going to switch over to my car's Bluetooth. Okay, there it is. Maybe we could use their cell phone history to track their locations for their last twenty-four hours and see what places they went. Then we can get a list of all the people that work at those places and—"

"Woah, Cari. If this was still an active investigation, we *might* be able to do all of that, but it's not. There's no way anyone is going to approve the cost or the time for someone at the department to do all of that."

"And you can't just access it?" She asked slowly.

"Every time I access a database, I have to log it in my timesheet according to which case I was working. I wouldn't be able to put it with this case because the case is closed."

Cari groaned. "Ugh. Could Genevieve get it reopened if I found new evidence?"

"Maybe? It's pretty rare that they reopen cases. They wouldn't do it for circumstantial evidence."

She sighed. "Okay. I get it. I feel like I'm really close to finding something big on this one, Bob."

"I know your heart is really in it, Cari. Hey, not to change the subject, but did you see my email about the shelter?"

Her heart lurched a little towards her stomach, which seemed to be rolling a bit too. "I did. I filled out the form already. Did you fill it out too?"

"Oh great! Yes, I submitted mine this morning. The woman from the church said the background checks go a lot quicker than they say on the form. We could hear back as early as tomorrow!" He said eagerly.

"Oh wow! I wouldn't be able to volunteer until next weekend since my parents will be in town."

"That's fine. Like I said, I'm sure they are flexible when it comes to volunteers. Maybe we could try next Saturday; it's the first one in September."

"Is it already so close to September? Wow."

"Yeah, this Monday is the first of the month."

"Okay, well, I'll keep you posted about the background check or whatever."

"Me too. Have a good night, Cari. Drive safe on your way home."

"I will. Thanks." She ended the call. She hoped Genevieve had some good news to share with her tomorrow.

Chapter 24

Cari had placed her order through the Starbucks app before she got in the shower the next morning. She knew Genevieve would get there a few minutes early and already be sitting down when Cari arrived. As she entered the parking lot, she spied her friend's Expedition parked near the front door. Cari took the spot next to her.

Sure enough, Genevieve was already sipping her coffee at a table to the far left of the door. Her back was to the wall as usual. Cari knew she liked to be able to see the entrance from wherever she sat. She grabbed the bag and cup with Cari written on them from the mobile orders counter and joined her friend at the table.

"Good morning, Cari. How are your parents and your grandma?"

"They're doing well. My mom said to tell you hi. She asked if you were married."

"What?"

"She asks if everyone is married."

"Oh, okay." She swallowed. "I know you wanted to tell me more about the Anerva, but I've found something interesting on my own too."

"Awesome. I had an idea last night that maybe the killer has two—"

"Jobs." Genevieve finished for her. "I had that idea too. I searched the employee records—"

"How did you get those?"

"I have a friend who...never mind the details. Anyway, I have the records for both the places you told me about that had ordered

Anerva recently. I also have the employee list from the dentist's office, which is one of the only places Jade Kastener went the morning she died."

"Okay, and?"

"No matches. There is no employee overlap."

Cari's shoulders slumped. "I thought you said you found something interesting?"

"I did. Let me get there. I thought there might be a chance that one of the two places had reported a loss or stolen quantity of Anerva. I looked for reports of that in a forty-mile radius from Brenington and there were none."

"I had that idea too! I called both places to ask and they both told me they did not have any history or record of medication being stolen or lost. The woman from Home Hospice kind of rubbed me the wrong way, though. I think she was lying."

"Yes! I actually went there in person on my lunch break yesterday. You're talking about Jaime, right?"

"Yes, that's the woman who answered the phone."

"Okay, I felt like she wasn't being completely honest or forthcoming about their records. She was possibly already on alert after getting your call. Anyway, I ran her through the NCIC—"

"The what?"

"It's a database with criminal records. I ran her name through it and she doesn't have a record, but her *son* does, and it's for drug possession. Anyway, long story short, her son works for the hospice too—as a nurse."

"Okay, but you said that no one works at the dental office too, so where does this get us?"

"There's more. After I made this discovery, someone from the hospice called me. They told me that a report had been doctored and they had lost some Anerva. They refused to give me their name, but I'm guessing it was the son that lost it. He'd probably lose his job if they had to report him being the party responsible for a missing med."

"Okay, so maybe he was the hospice nurse and was using Anerva with a patient and someone took some—"

"What?"

"Shh…that voice. Do you—"

"Don't turn your head. Keep talking to me as if you don't hear them."

"I know that voice. I heard it at the spa and I heard it on the phone with the receptionist at the dentist's office. That's the person. She works at both places! You can arrest her." Cari whispered to Genevieve.

"I can't just arrest her. For what? Working two jobs? Lots of people work two jobs. We need some real evidence that ties her to both of the victims and that she has a motive. Just because you think it's the same voice doesn't mean it is. We have to verify it with recognition software or an employee list. Then we could maybe get a search warrant and see if she is in possession of the Anerva."

"But you must know her name. You interviewed people at the office, right? She must have been the hygienist who worked on Jade that morning. You have the employee list from the dentist, right?'

"Yes, but—"

"We can get her last name and then search the archives for someone who died recently. I bet that was the trigger. See, I have this theory…"

Cari explained to Genevieve about the parable and how it might relate to the case. She could tell Genevieve was listening while also keeping a close eye on the woman ordering coffee. At some point, her friend relaxed noticeably.

"Did she leave?"

"She's gone."

"Did she see us?"

"She never looked this way. She didn't see us."

"Phew. Okay, so we need some evidence. Oh my goodness.

Cardian!"

"What did that creep do now?"

"Well, he's been in the hospital for starters."

"The hospital?"

"Yeah, we thought he had food poisoning. You know what? It's trash day. I have to go. Sorry! I'll be in touch." She jumped up from the table and rushed out the door leaving her friend wondering what trash day, food poisoning, and a creepy senior reporter had in common.

* * * * *

Opening the door, the helper scanned the counter for signs of the barista, but instead saw a different familiar face.

"Hello, Marian. I didn't realize you worked here," the helper said to the woman behind the counter.

The woman frowned at first but smiled when she recognized the helper. "Oh, hey. It's been a while—high school graduation was what, eight years ago?"

The helper nodded, waiting for the woman to respond to her statement.

"Uhh, right. Well, I got pretty frustrated with the costs of medical school and all the politics of finding an internship and residency. I decided to step away and reconsider my options."

The helper nodded again. "I understand. I guess I'll order a tall, drip coffee today. Black." They pulled exact change from a small wallet and slid it onto the counter.

Marian filled the paper cup and slid a sleeve onto it. She placed the lid on carefully and stuck the little plastic green tab into it. "Here you go. Good to see you. Oh, by the way, I heard about your dad passing away. I'm really sorry. I know he was a big part of your life."

The helper struggled not to frown at the barista. What did she know about the old man? "Thank you."

The helper took the coffee and left. The barista had graduated in the top five of their class, just one spot ahead of them. She was no longer living to her fullest potential. How many patients had she abandoned by leaving the medical field? Marian was now at the top of the list.

* * * * *

Cari raced over to the newspaper office and quickly parked her car in the garage. She took the stairs to their floor rather than waiting for the elevator. She needed to see if the envelope was still on Cardian's desk. If it wasn't, then she needed to rescue it from the dumpster out back before the trash truck came through. It was still early in the morning, so the odds were in her favor for now. She hurried over to his desk and frantically looked around. A notebook was open right in front of his chair with the words spa employee written on it in sharpie. She wondered if he had visited the spa too. She couldn't imagine him getting a massage. She looked under the desk for his wastebasket. It was empty. Someone must have discarded the packaging for him and the custodial staff emptied the garbage at the end of the day. She looked down at her clothes. They were about to get ruined.

This was her first time dumpster diving and she was glad to see the newspaper used clear bags for its garbage. She could see the blank newsprint pages inside some of the bags as well as the Styrofoam cups that had the newspaper's logo on them. It would be easier to spot the manila envelope through the bag. She had grabbed a pair of latex gloves from the first aid kit in the break room before running back down the stairs and into the alley. Unfortunately, the garbage bin was really full, but at least she still had a chance at finding the packaging. If it had any residue on it from the coupon Cardian received, Bob could test it and connect it to the killer. *Here goes nothing.*

She was glad the dumpster was open; otherwise, she wouldn't

have been able to climb into it to pull out the bags. It seemed like the dumpster was shared by the newspaper office as well as whatever business was on the first floor. Their garbage was in black bags, so Cari pulled all of those first and tossed them aside. She could throw them back in later. Her hair was getting in her eyes, so she grabbed the elastic that she always had on her wrist and wrestled it into a bun of some sort on the back of her head. She was already sweating and it had only been a few minutes.

She started grabbing the clear bags and tossing them over her head, out of the dumpster. She didn't want to tear any of them open and get any messier than she had to for now. She had just tossed the tenth bag over her head when she heard someone laughing. She climbed on top of a box in the dumpster and peeked out. Ollaman was standing beside the dumpster and laughing.

"Cari Turnlyle, what in tarnation are you doing?"

"Sir, I'm looking for an envelope that was discarded earlier this week—"

"I got a call from security saying that there was a vagrant nosing through our dumpster and who do I find out here but my newest reporter?"

"Yes, sir, I know this looks odd."

"It looks disgusting. Is that a banana peel on your shoulder?"

Cari looked at her right shoulder and shuddered. Sure enough, she had a discarded banana peel on her shirt. She brushed it off with her gloved hand.

"I need to find an envelope in here. I think it will bring the whole Kastener case to light or at least get us closer to the finish line."

"Okay, as long as you don't need my help." He turned to walk away and then stopped short. "Um, don't come back inside the office like that. Go home and shower first…but call me. Tell me if you found whatever you're digging for."

"Okay. Thank you, sir."

She went back to grabbing bags and tossing them over her

head. Thankfully, there were only three left from the newspaper office. She tossed them over and then stood on a box to gain some leverage out of the dumpster. Cari peered over the edge of the dumpster to the ground below. It hadn't seemed so tall when she first approached it. She wondered if she could extricate herself gracefully. She looked down at her shirt, already ruined by stains from not-quite-closed garbage bags. Sighing, she hoisted herself up to the edge of the dumpster and half-slid, half-fell back to the ground. A rough spot on the metal container had left a scratch on her arm that looked like it might bleed. She looked down at herself to assess any other damage.

"I am so disgusting right now."

"You can say that again."

Cari whirled around to see who was speaking to her. An older woman stood a few feet away near the exit of the alley. She had a small shopping cart stuffed with blankets and bags. Her greying hair was tussled and her skin was weathered by the sun.

"I'm sorry?" Cari asked her.

"You said that you were disgusting. I'm agreeing with you. What are you up to? Did you lose a winning lottery ticket?"

Cari gave her a confused look. "No, I'm looking for some packaging that was mistakenly thrown out earlier this week. Do I know you?"

"My name is Dorothy. I'd shake your hand, but like you said, 'disgusting'."

Cari laughed. "I'm Cari. I hope I'm not bothering you. I'm kind of in a hurry though, so I can't chat."

"I understand." The woman turned her cart around. "If you find anything valuable, let me know. You can find me a block over on Philip St."

"Will do."

Cari looked at the pile of bags and counted thirteen in total. Thankfully, it wasn't windy, so she wasn't going to be chasing loose garbage around the rest of the day. She opened the first bag, gently emptied it onto the dirt, and started poking through its contents. It had a lot of shredded newsprint paper, but no manila envelopes. She scooped it back into the bag as best she could. Five of the bags looked to have only shredded newsprint. She pushed those aside and started with the first one that had an assortment of colored paper, envelopes, and discarded coffee cups. One of the envelopes had an address that was still legible. She noticed that it came from the floor above hers and decided to move on from that bag as well. She stretched the plastic of the next bag so that she could read the address on the closest envelope. Bingo! This bag came from her floor. She poured it out onto the dirt and saw the envelope immediately. She could still read Cardian's name on the outside of it.

Cari picked up the envelope and put it inside the plastic bag she'd grabbed from the wastebasket under her own desk. Then she carefully put the rest of the garbage back into the bag and tied it back up. She pulled off one of her latex gloves and fished her phone from her pocket. Luckily, it hadn't been damaged when she crashed out of the dumpster. The cut on her arm was starting to sting as her sweat dripped into it. She ignored it and called Bob.

"Hey, Cari! Did you—"

"Bob! I need you to come over to my office right now. I found the envelope that Cardian got on Monday. I think he was drugged. I think the killer sent it to him. You need to come get it and test it for DMSO and Anerva or maybe digoxin. Anything."

"Slow down. What?"

"Genevieve and I went to coffee this morning and the killer was there. I just know it."

"I'm still confused. Can you start at the beginning?"

Cari took a breath and explained what had happened at Starbucks and how it connected back to Cardian and the two deaths.

"Okay, you think the killer drugged Cardian to get him sidelined enough to stop snooping into the Eskota death. Let me check with my boss. Like I said before, there isn't an open case, so I don't have anything to charge the work to right now."

"Okay. I need to throw all these garbage bags back into the dumpster. I'll wait for you in the alley."

"The dumpster? I don't want to know. I'll call if something changes."

Cari ended the call and immediately dialed Genevieve. The call went to her voicemail. Cari groaned. She knew there was something about chain of custody when it came to evidence and she didn't want to mess that up. Before throwing the garbage bags back into the dumpster, she used her phone to photograph the area as well as the envelope that she'd pulled from one of the bags. It only took her a few minutes to get the bags back into the dumpster. She grabbed the smaller bag she'd set aside with the envelope and headed back to the parking garage to get out of the sun. Bob would have to park there anyway, so she would see him coming.

* * * * *

Genevieve heard her cell phone buzzing with an incoming call but chose to ignore it. After Cari had rushed out of Starbucks that morning, she had gone straight to the station to look a few things up on her own. Alex wouldn't arrive for another thirty minutes or so. She knew the dental hygienist's name was Isabelle. While Cari had recognized the voice, Genevieve had met the woman and knew her from their interview at the dental office. She went to the spa's website and clicked around to see if she could find the names of their masseuses. Unfortunately, they didn't list them anywhere that she could access. Frustrated, she pulled out her phone to call Chris. Maybe he could help her find an employee list again.

"Detective Viacorte, I presume."

"Chris. I need your help. Can you get me an employee list from Relax and Relief Massage? It's in Brenington too."

"Just a moment. I'll send it to your inbox. Should I use the same one as before?"

"Sure. Thanks, Chris! I owe you one."

She drummed her fingers on her desk waiting for the email to show up. Cari hadn't left a voicemail, so whatever she had called about must not be an emergency. She would call again if she needed something. Genevieve repeatedly refreshed her browser screen, willing the email from Chris to appear. Her phone buzzed with an incoming text.

Check your inbox

She hit refresh again and there it was: an email from Chris. She opened the attachment and scanned the list of names. Gotcha! Isabelle Plackard. This would at least make her a person of interest. She looked over at her boss' office and saw he was in already. Rather than call, she decided to speak to him privately. Technically, she wasn't supposed to be working this case, so she didn't want anyone to overhear her part of the conversation.

She was just about to knock on the door when she saw his face. His eyes were wide and he was waving her away from the door. She saw that his desk phone was up to his ear and wondered who he was talking to. She turned to go back to her desk and almost bumped into Alex. He flicked his head at her, indicating she should follow him. His long stride left her scrambling to keep up. When they reached the parking lot, he whipped around to face her.

"What's going on, G?"

"What do you mean?"

"I know someone in the chief's office. They keep me apprised of anything I might need to know. Is there something you'd like to tell me?"

She bit the inside of her lip, unsure what to say. "Maybe you could point me in the right direction."

"The chief is all sorts of angry because people have been using departmental access to various databases but not coding their time. It's costing the department money."

She looked off to the side, trying to think of what to say. "How many people?"

"That I don't know. What I do know is that *your name* is on the list. Why would your name be on the list, Detective?" He spat out the last word.

"Grusky's got me working on something."

"If Grusky authorized it, then it should have a code that it's logged under."

"Damnit, Alex. I don't know what to tell you."

"You better hope that Grusky covers for you. My contact says that the chief was talking about culling some names from the staff list."

"Firing people? Can he just do that?"

"If someone can't justify what they were using the databases for, he can kick them to the curb, no problem."

She tucked a stray lock of hair behind her ear. The lieutenant had her back, but this could go badly for Chris; she needed to warn him. "I need to call someone, Alex. Thanks for the heads up."

"That's it? We're partners, Gen. What are you hiding?"

"I wish I could tell you, Alex. I just...I need to work some things out first."

"Is this still the Kastener-Eskota thing? You're working on it on the side?"

"Not right now, Alex. I've got to go."

She walked around him to her car and got in it. Before calling Chris, she locked the doors so Alex couldn't try to get in. She hit send on his number and drummed her fingers on the dash while she waited for it to connect.

"Hey, I only have a second. They just called an unexpected meeting for all of CSU. What's up?"

"I heard from a friend that the chief is mad about people using their departmental access to the databases without filing it under a specific code. My source said that he wants to fire people if they can't justify their use."

"This happens every now and then. Don't worry about it."

"I hope I haven't gotten you into trouble."

"Nah. I'll be fine."

Her phone beeped with another incoming call. She pulled it down to see who it was. LT flashed on the screen. "Sorry, Chris. Gotta take this." She switched calls.

"LT?"

"Where are you, Viacorte?"

"In the parking lot. Do you need me?"

"I just got a tongue-lashing from the chief. He keeps a tight hold on expenditures, especially any overhead. When he ran for Chief of Police, he promised not to show favoritism to the wealthy or well-connected in the community...that every case was just as important as the next. Fiscal responsibility and all that. The guy before him really ran through the budget every year and the city had to skimp on some things to cover our paychecks year after year. The city council outed him to the local news and it was a big outrage. Anyway, I think I smoothed it over with him for now, but you can't access any of the databases for the Kastener case anymore."

"LT, I think we have a suspect."

"What? Already?"

Genevieve explained about seeing the woman at Starbucks, but left Cari's name out of it. She didn't know how he would feel about her working with someone from the media. She explained that the woman worked at both the dentist's office and the spa that Eskota had frequented.

"I don't know. That's pretty thin. A lot of people work two jobs; it's not a crime."

"I had the same thought, but this whole time, we hadn't been able to find a location that overlapped between our two victims. What if it wasn't a place, but a person?"

"I understand what you're saying, but I don't think it's enough to reopen the case."

"Which means we don't have a code, so I can't spend time

writing up an arrest warrant." She sighed.

She heard him suck air in between his teeth. "I would really like to just throw caution to the wind and have you go pick her up, but it's just too thin right now. Come back in and tell me what else you know."

"I'll be right there."

She ended the call and almost dropped her phone when she looked out her window. Alex was bent over, staring into her window. She resisted opening the door into his face for scaring her. Instead, she glared at him and slowly opened the door.

"What are you doing?" He glared at her.

"Lay off right now, Alex." She pushed past him and walked quickly back inside to see Grusky.

He was watching for her when she entered the squad room and waved her into his office. She followed him inside and closed the door behind her.

"Okay, I don't have a lot, yet, but I have made some progress." She walked him through the idea of the killer using DMSO as an agent to drug the two victims. She summarized what Cari had told her about Anerva and the compounding pharmacy that had dispensed it in the area.

"I had an anonymous caller phone me last night to say that the hospice did lose or misplace some Anerva recently, but they altered their records so that they didn't have to report it."

"Okay, are you thinking the hospice worker took it or someone took it from the hospice worker?"

"I think it was taken from the hospice nurse. My next step was going to be looking through recent obituaries to see if any names correspond with the employee records."

"Okay, but you can't use the department's access to look up those records."

"Not a problem. I already have them."

"Great. Keep me posted. And, uh, send Runimoss in here. I know he's probably curious, but I don't want to put any more people on this because of the chief's outburst today."

She nodded and left the office.

"Runimoss! LT needs to see you."

He looked at her in a questioning manner. She shrugged and went straight to her desk. She pulled up a browser window and searched for obituaries in the area. It would have been faster to use the database to find who had died recently, but that was off limits. Hopefully, she wouldn't get in trouble for doing the search during her regular hours. She pushed the thought aside and started scrolling through the list. She barely noticed Alex stomp out of the room toward records.

Chapter 25

*C*ari looked at her watch for at least the thirteenth time. She still hadn't heard from Bob, nor had Genevieve called her back. Thankfully, her arm had only bled a little where she had cut it. She probably still needed to get a tetanus shot to be on the safe side.

The day was growing warm quickly, but she really didn't want to get into her car without some sort of barrier between her clothing and the seat. She sighed and continued tapping her foot on the concrete with impatience. She was holding onto the plastic bag with the discarded envelope with her left hand and her cell phone with her right hand. She hadn't realized she could feel more disgusting, but sweating in her business clothes after digging through a dumpster took it to a new level. Smiling suddenly, she tucked her phone back into her pocket and popped the trunk of her car. Next to her yoga mat, her gym bag greeted her. She carefully set the evidence next to the yoga mat and pulled out her gym bag. She could use the lobby bathroom to change out of her clothes and into her yoga outfit. She kept the bag in the car in case she ever decided to attend an evening class instead of her regular morning one.

It took her just a few minutes to peel the funky clothes off. She didn't want to smell up the bathroom, so she pulled the whole bag from the garbage can and stuffed her clothes into it too. The custodial staff kept extra bags at the bottom of the can, so Cari pulled one loose and fixed it into place before replacing the lid. Regardless of how skilled the dry cleaners were, these clothes were never going to be wearable again. She slung the bag over her shoulder and walked back to the dumpster. Just as she was tossing it in, she felt her phone vibrate with an incoming text.

Can't run any tests right now. Big uproar at the station today.

Cari balled her hand into a fist. How were they going to stop this woman if they couldn't gather evidence against her? She started to call Bob, but decided he probably couldn't talk about the problem at that moment. She scrolled to Genevieve's name again. It rang four times before she answered.

"Cari, sorry. I meant to call you back, but I got sidetracked. What's up?"

"You said that you needed evidence to arrest that woman. Well, I found some. Earlier this week, Cardian got a coupon in the mail for a taco. I noticed him wipe his hand on his pants after touching the coupon, but didn't think much about it. Taco trucks are greasy places, right?"

"Right..." Genevieve wasn't following.

"Okay, stick with me. After he went to get the taco, he got really sick. We all thought it was food poisoning, but it occurred to me this morning that she could have drugged him too. He took the call about Eskota's death and then he kind of downplayed it as a non-newsworthy story. I suspected he might be looking into it without saying anything because he didn't post the report on our news board right away. But knowing what I know now—"

"You think he was drugged by the same woman! I bet she used digitalis this time. At certain doses it can cause vomiting and other digestive problems." Genevieve exclaimed. "How do we prove it though? I'm sure it's out of his system by now."

"I found the envelope that it came in! It was in a dumpster...long story. Anyway, I thought maybe the lab guys could test it..."

"That could be an issue. Our chief is all nutso today about non-coded charges."

"What do we do then? This could be what we need!"

"We also don't have any evidence that she sent it to Cardian.

It's all circumstantial. Let me make a phone call and I'll get back to you. Where are you right now?"

"I'm in the parking garage at my office."

"I'll call you back." The call ended.

* * * * *

Genevieve grabbed her office phone and punched in the lieutenant's extension.

"Find something?"

"Sort of. I just learned of some potential evidence linking this woman to the deaths."

"What kind of evidence? Where?"

"It's kind of a long story, but it sounds like she may have tried to drug Lionel Cardian to get him out of her way."

"Ugh, I hate that guy. Okay, let me think. Wait—how does the newspaper know that this Plackard woman sent the package to Cardian?"

"They don't, sir. They are just conjecturing at this point."

"Hmm, well, that changes things a bit. Let me look up this person's address and find the mail drop nearest her. Maybe we can catch her on a security camera at the post office or the street outside. I'll call down to CSU and have them send someone over to—where is the evidence again?"

"In the parking garage at the Brenington Beagle, sir."

"To the parking garage to collect the evidence."

"Thank you, sir. Are we reopening the cases then?"

"Oh, shoot." He cursed under his breath. "You're right. We can't get CSU involved yet. Find that name, Viacorte."

"Okay, I'm still looking through the obituaries. I'll keep you posted."

Genevieve started to scroll through the list again when she thought of something else. She called Cari back.

"Genevieve! Are you on your way? It's getting pretty warm

out here and I'm pretty ripe—"

"Cari—look at the envelope that you found. Can you see the markings on it from the post office?"

She could hear Cari rattling around on the other end of the line. "Let's see. I took a photo of it. It looks like it was post-marked on Saturday. There are some numbers. I'll text it to you."

"Perfect. Thanks, Cari." She ended the call.

She saved the photo to her phone and then emailed it to the lieutenant. She switched back over to the obituary results and jumped when she heard something slam onto the desk next to her. She looked up and saw an angry, red-faced Alex scowling at her.

"I've been assigned a cold case. What the hell?"

"I don't know. Things are, um, weird today." She turned back to the computer screen.

"Whatever." He opened the binder and started flipping through it angrily.

* * * * *

Cari wished she had some more water. She had already drained the one in her car she typically brought into work. Ollaman had come outside earlier to look for her again. She should have asked him to grab her a cup of water, but hadn't realized it would take so long for Genevieve to call her back. She used the back of her hand to wipe more sweat from her forehead. She had been outside for about an hour since changing her clothes and her patience was wearing thin. She pulled her phone out to check it again for a possible missed text or call. Nothing. She was about to call Genevieve again when she heard a car approaching. Her eyes lit up when she saw who it was. She shoved her phone back into her pocket and ran over to the driver's door.

"Bob! I didn't know you were coming. You said—"

"Hey, Cari. I'm on my lunch break. I'll gather the evidence. The buzz around the lab is that Viacorte is working this case off the record but is close to finding something."

"What does that mean?"

"It means that I'm collecting this evidence during *my* time and if we get cleared to run it, then we'll have it."

"Okay, well, here it is."

She led him over to her trunk and popped it open again.

"I put the envelope in a plastic bag. I never touched it with my bare hands either. Cardian did of course, but he didn't know it was evidence."

"I understand. You did a good job, Cari." He pulled the bag from the car and closed the trunk for her. "I'll drive this over to the lab and if we can, we'll get it tested."

"And you'll let me know what you find?"

He bit his lip. "I'm not sure I can do that, Cari. You'll have to get with the detectives on that."

Her shoulders slumped a bit, but she knew he was right. She didn't want to jeopardize his job. "I understand. I'll wait for her to call. In the meantime, I'm going to run home and shower. I feel disgusting."

"I wasn't going to say anything, but…"

"Bob!"

"Just being honest."

"How long do you think it will take?"

"We have an assay that we can run to test for the presence of DMSO. As for digitalis, it will take a chemical analysis with a mass spectrometer. The same is probably true for Anerva."

"English, Bob."

"The assay, I mean the test for DMSO is pretty fast, but we don't have a mass spec. We'll have to send that out to the state lab."

"How long will that take?"

"It depends on their backlog. It sometimes takes a week."

"A week?!"

"Let's just take it one step at a time, okay, Cari?"

He grabbed the plastic bag with gloved hands and slid the envelope from her bag into an official evidence bag. Then he put a strip of red tape across the opening and wrote his name over it.

"I'll get this over to the lab and secure it for the time being."

"I'm going to go take a shower and come back to start writing some of my notes up. I'll talk to you later."

She waved goodbye and got into her car. She still felt like a layer of refuse was clinging to her skin and hair. Getting into the shower was going to feel so good.

Chapter 26

C ari heard her phone buzzing when she turned off the bathroom fan after her shower. She had run the water as hot as she could for as long as it lasted. She wasn't sure if she'd gotten all of the grime from the dumpster off, but she at least felt clean again. She saw on the screen that Ollaman was calling.

"Ms. Turnlyle, I see you are no longer standing guard of our dumpster. Did you get your evidence taken care of?"

"I did, sir. I was planning to call you as soon as I got cleaned up. I was pretty disgusting."

"I won't argue with you. Now, was Lionel drugged or what?"

Cari explained that the case was kind of in limbo because the police had filed the deaths as accidental. She was hopeful they would get it reopened and could process the envelope.

"Is it time sensitive? If they aren't on this tomorrow, we're going to write up a story about negligence and wasting taxpayer dollars!"

Cari cringed. She didn't want her friends to get attacked that way, but was frustrated that she didn't have an alternative to having the envelope tested.

"I'm going to call over there and talk to that idiot in charge of the department. He thinks he's being all fiscally responsible, but he's risking lives here! Lionel could have died!"

He hung up. Cari sighed. She hoped she wasn't making things harder for Genevieve or Bob. She quickly got dressed for the fourth time that day and gathered her belongings to go back to the newsroom. The cut on her arm looked better after she'd washed it in the shower, which was good because she didn't own any bandages anyway. Hopefully, Ollaman would be in a better mood when she arrived.

She pulled into the same spot from earlier in the day and slung her bag over her shoulder. She had a lot of notes that she needed to organize before she could start putting her story together. She felt certain Isabelle Plackard was the killer, but couldn't write about it until the police confirmed it with the evidence. She flipped through her notebook and opened a new document on her computer to put together an outline.

Cari wanted to start with the idea that things were not always what they seem. Two deaths that seemed wholly accidental at the time had been revealed to be the work of a crazed fanatic. It was another case of someone playing the role of judge, jury, and executioner.

* * * * *

Genevieve looked at the clock. It was almost five in the afternoon and she still had several names of obituaries to comb through. Alex had ignored her the rest of the day, which was better than him glaring at her. She wished she could get his help but didn't want to put his career with the force at risk. She had reached the letter 'P' in the alphabet and was scanning the names in the family lists when a familiar one jumped out at her. *Isabelle Plackard. I should have just started with your name.*

She grabbed her phone and called Grusky again. He didn't answer, but opened the door to his office and waved her over.

"I found a name."

"Same woman?"

"Same woman. I didn't make it to the end of the list. Should I make sure?"

"How many more names could there be? Finish sorting through them. I should have this reopened by the time your shift starts tomorrow."

"Can I talk to Alex about this yet?"

"Tomorrow." He opened the door and she showed herself out.

Alex glanced up when she returned to her desk. She started putting her stuff in her messenger bag and shut her computer down. She could finish the search at home. She jumped when she heard Alex slam his binder closed. She hoped once the cases were reopened, he would forgive her.

When Genevieve got to her vehicle, she pulled her phone out of her pocket. She wanted to give Cari a call and see if they could collaborate a bit on the case. Maybe it would help her to hit the ground running tomorrow. She started her car and then hit send on Cari's number.

"Genevieve! Tell me that you've reopened the investigation."

"We're really close, Cari. My boss is working on the paperwork right now. It should be a go tomorrow."

"I hope that whatever is in that envelope is stable until tomorrow. I have no idea if any of it is time sensitive. If she used Anerva on Cardian, then it's gone for sure. If she used something else, it could still be there."

"Cari, are you free tonight? I thought maybe we could compare notes and see where we stand on all of this. I can get a pizza delivered. I've got beer in my fridge."

"Right now? Send me directions and I'll be on my way."

"I'm over on Washington Avenue in the Ridgeway Apartment Building."

"Why don't you let me order the pizza and you focus on driving?"

"It's a deal. I'll see you in a bit. Oh, and I eat anything but fish or fruit on my pizza."

"Oh, of course. Text me your address and I'll make it happen."

* * * * *

Isabelle Plackard pulled the front door closed behind her. It had been a long day at the dental office. Thankfully, tomorrow was Friday and they were only open until noon. She didn't want to rush her experience with Marian at the Starbucks, but she also didn't know the woman's hours. She could stop by and pretend to just want a cool place to read a book if Marian wasn't behind the counter.

She went to her room and opened the small refrigerator where she kept the Anerva she had swiped from the hospice nurse. She had fasted for three days after swiping the medicine, drinking only a small amount of water each morning to avoid dehydration. She needed the medication for her work and when the opportunity arose to take it, she couldn't pass it up.

Isabelle pulled four one-dollar bills from her wallet. She pulled a small piece of tape from her dispenser and folded it over the edge of the first bill, then repeated it for the other three. Then she put on a new pair of latex gloves. She picked up a small brush and squeezed some of the DMSO onto it. After brushing the ointment onto each bill, she used a syringe to draw up the Anerva from the vial. She carefully dripped it onto each of the bills and waited a minute for it to be absorbed by the DMSO. She delicately lifted each bill by the corner where the tape was and placed it into a small Ziploc bag. After removing her gloves, she placed the sealed bag in the refrigerator. She would put them in her purse with a small ice pack to keep it chilled tomorrow. Putting it in her lunch bag seemed like too big of a risk.

* * * * *

Cari finished placing the pizza order and then changed into more comfortable clothing. She had pulled up Genevieve's address from her text messages before placing the order. She grabbed her messenger bag and slipped her phone and keys into it before leaving her apartment.

Genevieve's building had a parking garage next to it with

designated visitor spots. Cari picked the one nearest the elevator. The building used an intercom system for guests of the residents. Cari pressed the button next to two-oh-four and waited for her friend to respond.

"Two-oh-four?" Genevieve asked.

"It's Cari."

"See you in a moment."

The door buzzed and clicked. Cari pulled it open and hit the up button for the elevator. The entryway was small and probably only had room for a handful of people. The building had two elevators and of course a set of stairs on the opposite side. On the second floor, a small placard indicated that apartments two oh-one through two-oh-six were to the left and the larger numbers were to the right. The hallway reminded her a bit of a hotel. She knocked on two-oh-four and Genevieve let her in.

"Fancy building," Cari remarked.

Genevieve shrugged. "I picked this place because it has a community garden on the roof. The security features are nice, but they seem a little over the top sometimes."

"Right, I always forget that you're into gardening. The pizza should be here in the next fifteen minutes. Do you want to wait for it or dig into our notes right away?"

"Let's get started. That way, when the pizza is late, we won't feel like we've wasted any time. You can use the outlet on that wall to plug in your laptop."

Cari followed her over to her kitchen table and got everything she needed out. "What's your WiFi password here?"

"The network is ViaGen325 and the password is Sunshine123. Let me tell you what I've discovered today while you finish setting up. I verified that Plackard works at the spa through employment records. The rest of the day, I have been weeding through obituaries in the area from the last six weeks to look for any names on any of the employment lists that I have."

"Don't you have a database that you could access that lists the

208

deaths?"

"We do, but I couldn't access it because of this issue with our chief."

"Oh right. I heard a bit about that. You probably would still need to read obits to find the family member's names."

"Exactly. I made a list of all the names and put them into a spreadsheet first. I've been filling it in as I read each obituary as to whether any names of interest pop up. I made it to letter P before leaving the station today."

"Did you find her; did you find Isabelle in there?"

Genevieve nodded and smiled. "I did. I just wanted to clear the other names so that we're sure."

"Makes sense. Should I start at Z and work up while you keep going down from P?"

"Works for me. Let me share the spreadsheet with you. It's a Google sheet. One of the tabs in the sheet has the names of people who have died and the other has the names of the employees at the spa, the dental office, and the hospice. It's probably overkill to look at all of them, but luckily the three employee lists are pretty short, so you can get through the names pretty quickly."

Cari opened up her Google drive and accessed the spreadsheet Genevieve shared. She typed the last name on the list into a search window and found the obituary. She scanned the list of family members and then referred back to the employee list. None matched, so she repeated the process with the next name up on the list. She had moved through four letters of the alphabet when the pizza guy buzzed the intercom.

"Two-oh-four?" Genevieve asked again.

"Pizza delivery."

"Come on up." She hit a button to release the door.

"That's a clever way of answering your intercom."

Genevieve smiled. "I figured that they already know they pushed two-oh-four. If they can't tell me why they are here, then I don't let them in. I made it through the letter S, where are you?"

"I just finished with W, but X, Y, and Z had almost no names, of course."

"Do you care if we work and eat?"

"Not at all."

Cari grabbed the pizza from the delivery guy while Genevieve pulled out some plates and napkins.

"That smells amazing. Do you drink beer? I have a local IPA or I have water as the other option."

"I'll try your IPA; why not?"

They each got a couple of slices and then went back to sifting through the list of names. It was a bit tedious, especially when only one name was on more than one employee list. Cari moved through the letters V and U quickly.

"I'm into the letter T now. Looks like we've only got four more names to cross off."

"Make that three," Genevieve responded.

It had taken them almost ninety minutes to plow through the last ten letters of the alphabet. Cari rolled her head around to release the tension in her neck.

"Okay, I didn't find any names that matched the employee lists, so where does that leave us?"

"The one name we were looking for—Isabelle Plackard—showed up in the obituary of a Mr. Ronald Plackard. Let me pull it up so you can see it too."

Cari leaned over to look at the laptop screen. "The obit mentions Home Hospice of Brenington! That connects her to the drug."

"Exactly. I know the name of the woman whose son was most likely the hospice nurse for Mr. Plackard. Assuming my lieutenant has this case reopened in the morning, we can get a warrant for the medical records to confirm the daughter's connection to the hospice."

"It would be great if you could actually find the Anerva in her home."

"You're not wrong there. Here's what I have, feel free to stop me and fill in any blanks. Plackard's father died two and a half weeks ago. This triggered something in the woman that led her to poison or drug the two victims."

"The obituary mentioned a church where the family has been long time members. Wait, did it say anything about the man's wife?"

Genevieve scrolled back up and skimmed the obituary again. "It says he was married back in the late nineties, but then it doesn't list his wife as a survivor or as someone that preceded him in death. I guess she left them? Odd."

"Okay, continue with your summary."

"We know that Plackard was Kastener's hygienist on Monday. We believe that she drugged her by rubbing the Anerva-laced DMSO onto her cheek at some point. Then on Thursday, Eskota got a massage from Plackard at the spa where she also allegedly drugged him."

"Then Cardian stuck his nose into things, which concerned her. I think she put something on that taco coupon. I wonder if anyone at the taco truck got sick from touching it when he claimed his free taco."

"It's definitely possible. It seems like she is choosing her victims based somewhat on chance."

"What do you mean? I don't think it's random."

"Not random. I mean that she isn't looking through social media posts and trying to find people that fit a certain criterion or something like that. She is allowing her chance encounter with them to influence her selection. She has probably been cleaning Jade's teeth for a few years."

"Oh, I see. I found out from Eskota's friend that he's been getting massages for a few weeks too. I know you don't do a lot of chatting at either place, but you do get to know the person somewhat in both situations."

"I think Eskota was selected not only because he quit his job, but also because he quit supporting charities."

"I bet you're right. He was no longer doing good in the community."

Genevieve nodded. "I think that's about all I can do tonight. I would start filling out an arrest warrant application, but I don't want the time stamp to get me into trouble later. I'll hold off until tomorrow."

"Keep me posted?"

"Of course. My lieutenant is close to this case, which goes completely against the way the chief wants to work cases, but that's a different story. What I'm trying to say is that I'm pretty sure he'll let me share information with you for a story before we put out a press release."

Cari smiled. "Thanks, Gen. Thanks for hosting. I'm going to head home and get some of this typed up in anticipation of good news from you tomorrow. Where should I put my plate?"

"I'll take care of it. Thanks for coming over."

Cari packed up her messenger bag and slung it over her shoulder. "Talk to you tomorrow."

Chapter 27

*G*enevieve got to the station early again on Friday. She was anxious to hear if Grusky had gotten permission to reopen the investigation. His office door was closed when she walked in, but she could see him sitting at his desk. She knocked on the door.

"Viacorte. Good news and bad news."

"What's the bad news?"

"The chief is pretty displeased that we continued to work these cases after the deaths were declared accidental. He was pushing for a suspension, but clearer heads prevailed. He said he was going to put a note of insubordination in both of our files as well as a few other people who also couldn't justify their use of departmental resources."

Genevieve grimaced. She knew that probably meant Chris and hoped that it wouldn't hinder his career in any way. She wondered briefly if it would keep her from getting promoted in the future, but she was more interested in the case at hand.

"Insubordination? Can I appeal it? Should I appeal it? This case should never have been closed."

"He hasn't done it yet. It could be an empty threat."

"Okay, well, the dust will settle. What about the case?"

"I talked him into it. Tell me where we stand."

Genevieve pulled out her notebook and walked him through what she knew of Isabelle Plackard, her relationships with the victims, and the theory about what drove her to do it. She told him about the hospice nurse and the access to the drug.

"You did all of this yourself?"

"I mean, some of it was with Runimoss initially. I had a little outside help too."

Grusky tilted his head. "Outside help? Never mind, as long as everything is clean and we can use it in court, I don't care."

"I'd like to fill out an app for an arrest warrant and a search warrant."

"One step ahead of you, Viacorte." He looked through the office blinds before continuing. "Call Runimoss in here."

She stuck her head out the door. "Alex!"

Her partner looked her way. She could see that he was curious but also still angry about her actions the last two days. He set his bag down and walked over to the office door.

"What's up?"

"Have a seat, Runimoss." He paused while Alex pulled a chair around and sat in it. "I see you're a bit peeved with Viacorte, but give us a chance to explain. She was only following my instructions." They brought Alex up to speed on the investigation.

"First, I want you two to look through video footage of the street near this Plackard woman's home. There's a mail drop there and from what we can tell, it was postmarked last Saturday. Start on Friday evening and see if you can find her putting that envelope in the mail drop. CSU is going to test it for prints and DMSO and whatever else they can do. If we can get her on using the drug on Cardian, it will save us some time searching her house for evidence. After you finish with the videos, I want you to figure out where the Plackard woman is working today and pick her up. I'll get these applications submitted and keep you posted."

They left his office and settled in at their desks. Alex grabbed their empty coffee cups and looked Genevieve in the eye.

"Yes, please. I went straight to his office this morning and haven't had a drop yet."

While she waited for him to return, she pulled up Isabelle Plackard's DMV photo to help remind them of her face. Isabelle Plackard stared back at them on the computer screen. Her

214

expression was blank just as it had been at the dental office. The pale, grey eyes seemed to be looking right through them. Next, she opened the database with the footage from all the street cameras. She found the correct camera and scrolled back through the files to the previous Friday.

"Can I see the photo of the envelope? Did she print her own mailing label and just drop it off or did she wait in line?"

Genevieve pulled up the photo and showed it to Alex. He enlarged it and looked at the label.

"I think it's a label that was printed at home, which means she didn't stand in line. She probably wore gloves the whole time."

"You never know. They're dusting it for prints anyway."

She sat down at her desk while Alex leaned over her shoulder to watch the footage. It started at nine in the evening. She sped it up to five times the regular speed and the images flashed across the computer. She watched for the manila envelope as it would be easier to spot because of its brighter color.

"There. Take it back a bit." Alex pointed at the screen.

She moved it back a minute and slowed it down. A few seconds later, a thin woman in a hoodie with a manila envelope passed by the camera. She froze the image and zoomed in on the face.

"We got her. That has to be her with the package."

"We can't see his name on the label, so it's possible she just mailed something else in the same kind of envelope, Alex."

He groaned. "Let it roll forward a little bit further. Maybe we can see some of the label at some point."

Genevieve put it at quarter speed and hit play again. The woman seemed to know there was a camera nearby and never looked up again. Just as she opened the mail chute to drop the package in, a light flashed across, possibly from a vehicle's headlights. Genevieve hit pause and enlarged the image.

"Perfect! That definitely says Lionel on it. Let's go pick her up."

"Okay, but we still do not have confirmation that she drugged him. Let's see if Grusky has that warrant for us, yet."

Before they could knock on his door, he banged out of it with his thumbs up. "We got approval on the arrest warrant. I'm still waiting for the search warrant."

"Anything from CSU yet?"

He shook his head. "Go pick her up, wherever she is."

Genevieve grabbed the keys to the departmental cruiser and rushed out of the station with Alex. She hoped the woman was still at work. It had taken some time to review the footage. Alex called the dentist's office first since they were more familiar with the staff there.

"Hi, Sonia. This is Detective Runimoss. We spoke last week in regard to Jade Kastener. We have a few more questions for Ms. Plackard." He paused. "She is working today? You close at noon. We are almost there. Please don't alert her before we arrive. No, you are not in danger." He ended the call. Genevieve started driving towards the dental office once it was clear that Plackard was working there today.

She stopped in front of the dentist's office and put her vehicle in park. Alex was already out of the car and walking up to the front doors. He pulled the door open and stood to the side to let her enter first. She nodded at him on her way past. Sonia was seated at the receptionist's desk and looked at Genevieve with wide eyes as she approached.

"Your partner said that you need to speak with Isabelle again?"

"Yes, ma'am. If you could page her now, we would appreciate it."

They waited while Sonia spoke into a microphone attached to her earpiece. She requested that Isabelle come to the receptionist's desk as soon as possible. Genevieve could see Dr. Santer's door from the desk and saw it fly open. The dentist walked quickly over to Sonia's desk, then halted when she saw the two detectives staring at her. She opened the door from the waiting room to the offices and exam rooms and let them in.

"Why do you need to speak with Isabelle again?"

"I'm sorry, ma'am, uh, doctor, but we can't discuss an active investigation," Alex told her.

Before Dr. Santer could respond, Isabelle stepped into the hallway from one of the exam rooms. Genevieve noticed a flash of panic cross her face before her normal expressionless façade returned. She saw the muscle in Alex's forearm twitch and knew he had seen her face too.

"Ms. Plackard, we request that you accompany us down to the station to talk about Ms. Kastener again."

"Am I under arrest?"

"We'd like to do this as easily as possible, ma'am, and cause you the least amount of embarrassment. If you could just step outside with us."

"And if I refuse?"

"We're going to have to put you in handcuffs here, in front of your co-workers."

The woman's shoulders slumped. "Very well then."

"We need to check you for weapons, please."

"Weapons?!" Dr. Santer exclaimed.

"This will just take a moment. If everyone could remain calm," Genevieve said.

"Please remove your lab coat first, Isabelle."

They waited while the woman shrugged off the lab coat and handed it to her boss. Then Alex stood next to Isabelle while Genevieve gently patted her down. She was more concerned that she might have a syringe than a gun or knife.

"Can I bring my purse? It has my phone and wallet in it." She asked.

"I can grab that for her," Dr. Santer offered. She walked quickly down the hallway and soon returned with a black purse. Isabelle reached out to grab it, but Alex stopped her.

"We'll hold onto that for you, ma'am."

They escorted her back to the cruiser while Sonia and Dr.

Santer stared after them in shock. Genevieve opened the back door and made eye contact with Alex. He pulled a little card from his wallet and recited the Miranda warning to Isabelle. Then, he walked around to the opposite side and sat next to the woman in the backseat. Genevieve opened the trunk and placed the purse inside. They didn't know what was in it, but didn't want to risk her gaining access to something potentially deadly.

* * * * *

Cari tried to busy herself by typing up her story while she waited to hear from Genevieve. She would rather get confirmation about their theory before she had the story written. Plus, she was worried that if they left the Plackard woman free for too long, she would find a new victim and attack again. She looked up when she heard Ollaman's office door close. He was walking her way. She minimized her document before he reached her desk.

"Any news from the police?"

"Not yet, sir. Were you able to speak with anyone?"

"They refused to put me through to the chief of police yesterday. Told me that I could wait on a press release if they had one to release."

"That's frustrating."

He sighed. "Okay, well, keep me posted. Did you finish that bit on the fall thing already? And the Restaurant Week announcement?"

"They should be in your inbox."

"I'll go look. I've been spinning my wheels all morning wanting to know if the police are ever going to do their jobs!" He stomped off.

Cari started to open up her document again when she heard her phone vibrate in her purse. She waited for Ollaman to get settled in his office before pulling it out and reading the message. It was from Bob.

Case reopened. Testing envelope now.
Great news. Thanks.

She decided to hold off on telling Ollaman for now. He was so riled up he'd probably issue his own press release and spoil the whole thing.

* * * * *

Alex was getting Ms. Plackard settled in the interview room while Genevieve stopped by Grusky's office to update him. The woman had remained silent for the entire car ride back to the station. Genevieve saw her glaring at her from the review mirror whenever she glanced at it. She hoped that the woman's level of agitation would get her talking sooner rather than later.

"Hey, LT. We picked up Ms. Plackard. Alex is escorting her to the interview room now."

"Sounds good. I just heard from CSU that they have started testing the envelope."

"Keep us posted on their results, if you can. It might help us get her to talk. She seems pretty angry right now."

"I'll let you know as soon as I hear something. Are you going in right away?"

Before she could answer, Alex knocked on the door with one knuckle before stepping into the office. He nodded at Genevieve and closed the door behind him.

"How is Ms. Plackard?"

"I told her that we would be back shortly. She hasn't said anything, yet. She didn't even ask for a lawyer."

"Have you gotten the search warrant?"

"I'm still waiting. Let me give my friend over at the courthouse a call and see what they say."

Genevieve took that as a signal to exit. Alex held the door for her and they walked over to their desks. She had goosebumps just anticipating the interview.

"Before we go in there, are we cool? I know you were pretty angry with me yesterday."

"We're cool, G. I get it. I don't like that it had to go down that way, but I get it." He put his fist out for a bump. She tapped her knuckles into it.

"What do you think, Alex? Do we ask about Eskota first? Do we start it as a conversation about her jobs? Do we ask her about working with DMSO?"

Alex raised his eyebrows. "Can you feel the rage boiling within her?"

"I can. I think with the right words, we can get her to talk. What do you think about our theory for her motive?"

"It was a little out there. How did you come up with it?"

"Well, um, Cari did, actually. She heard this sermon at her church the other day and it was on this Bible story with a master and three servants—" She flipped through her notes.

"The reporter woman goes to church? Never would have guessed it. That sounds like a—"

"It's a parable. The parable of the talents."

"I'm familiar with it. The reporter woman thinks this Plackard person is offing people because they didn't live up to their potential, because they squandered their God-given talents?"

"That's her theory."

"Pretty far-fetched."

"I agree, but I don't have anything better. If the DMSO pans out, the LT can probably get us a warrant to search her home. Maybe it will have something that indicates that she is a religious fanatic of some sort."

Alex nodded. "Should we just keep making her wait until they get the result from that?"

"I think if we start talking about the two victims, we'll get her fired up enough to speak."

"After you," Alex said as they both got up from their desks.

Genevieve tapped on the door lightly before entering the

interview room. She signaled to the uniformed officer that he could go. Alex remained standing while Genevieve sat in a chair across from the woman. Her mouth was pinched into a frown, but her eyes stared blankly ahead.

"Hello again, Ms. Plackard. You remember Detective Runimoss, and I'm Detective Viacorte. We just have a few questions for you today. Can we get you anything? Water? Soda?"

The woman gave a faint shake of her head and blinked once. Genevieve plowed on.

"I just want to remind you that you don't have to speak to us. That is your right. You can ask for a lawyer at any time."

The woman glared at Genevieve, but didn't ask for a lawyer. "It has come to our attention that you saw Jade Kastener and Peter Eskota just hours before they died. Were you aware of this?"

The pale, grey eyes flashed briefly, but the woman did not speak. She continued staring straight ahead, almost as though she didn't see Genevieve at all. Genevieve could feel Alex growing frustrated and hoped he wouldn't jump in yet. She drummed her fingers on the table.

"Did you notice anything strange about their mannerisms that day? Did anything seem off?"

At this, the woman's frown deepened and Genevieve could tell she was considering responding, as though this was a harmless question. "They were both the same as they have always been."

"Is it customary for you to use DMSO with your massage clients? Do other masseuses do that as well?"

"Relax and Relief has a policy of only using it after massage alone has not relieved the pain that the client is experiencing."

"How frequently would you say DMSO is required? One in five, ten? Less?"

"I could not tell you the prevalence."

A faint knock on the door interrupted Genevieve's thoughts. Alex cracked the door slightly and listened to someone speaking. He locked eyes with Genevieve, then stepped towards the woman.

"Ms. Plackard, I just spoke with my associate from the crime lab. You see, we came across this envelope earlier today that was sent to a Mr. Lionel Cardian at the local paper. Do you know Mr. Cardian?"

The eyes narrowed briefly, but no words were spoken.

"I'll take that as a yes. If we're being honest—ouch!" Genevieve kicked Alex in the shin before he could say something derogatory about Cardian in front of the woman.

"As I was saying, someone sent him a little package earlier this week with a coupon for a taco. Mr. Cardian got very sick after getting his taco. He thought it was a bad case of food poisoning, but wouldn't you know it, our lab buddy found DMSO in that envelope. He is having it tested for some other compounds too."

"Maybe you're wondering why we are going off on a tangent about some old guy's mail and tacos, but it turns out that we have evidence of you mailing that package. That combined with your interactions with the two victims from last week, doesn't look very good for you."

Geneveive noticed the woman was digging her fingernails into her palm. She wondered if it was to keep herself from speaking or possibly as some sort of punishment. She decided to share Cari's theory now.

"Ms. Plackard, correct me if I'm wrong, but I'd like to tell you a story of what I think happened. Now, remember, if you want a lawyer, just say the word. You don't have to talk to us, okay?"

A blink.

"I have a hunch that these two seemingly unrelated people, that is, Ms. Kastener and Mr. Eskota actually have quite a lot in common in your mind. Both of them are financially well-off, but I don't think you are jealous of that. Lots of people have money, right? Let's see, both of these people were also very intelligent, gifted, some might call it. Now, Mr. Eskota, he started out a little differently in life than Ms. Kastener. He went to college and got a degree, then became a very successful day trader. He was making money hand over fist, but then one day, he just walked away and quit. He started golfing and living a leisurely life.

"Ms. Kastener, on the other hand, after graduating at the top of her class, decided to take what some people call a gap year. She was getting ready to start her third gap year, however. From the sounds of it, she didn't seem to want to go to college even though that would be all it took to take over her father's business and lead a successful life.

"I think that bothered you, Ms. Plackard. I think you felt like they were *sinning* by not using these gifts, these *talents* of theirs. Is that right, Ms. Plackard?"

The woman's eyes had narrowed to mere slits. Genevieve could feel her hatred of the two people coming off of her in waves. She sat still and waited for the woman to speak. She knew that she wouldn't stay silent this time.

"This was *my calling*! You sit there and judge me for what I've done, but I have done what is right, what is *best!* I gave up everything to care for that old man and they had every opportunity in life. They were willing to throw it all away, so I took it from them. They didn't deserve it. To those who use well what they are given, more will be given in abundance. But the one who does not have, all will be taken from them."

Genevieve flinched when spittle flew in her direction from the woman's mouth. Alex's eyes were wide with surprise. He yanked his handcuffs from his back pocket as he stepped back from the table. Then he pulled the woman to her feet and placed the cuffs on her wrists. Genevieve stood and opened the door for them to exit.

Chapter 28

*C*ari heard her phone buzzing when she turned off the bathroom fan after her shower. She had given up at the office and went to a midday yoga class instead. None of the people from her regular class were there, including the instructor. She felt a little guilty about avoiding the other class, but still didn't have answers for them. She saw on the screen that Genevieve was calling.

"Cari! I'm glad I caught you. You are not going to believe this, well, actually, you might."

"What? Did you get her?"

"Here's the condensed version: we picked up the woman that you identified at Starbucks after we scanned video footage of the postage drop near her home. She sent that package to Cardian; we could see his name on the envelope in the video."

"Did they test it? I told Bob, um, the CSU guy—"

"Let me finish. It tested positive for DMSO, which was enough for a warrant to search her home. She recently inherited her family's home after her father passed away from a chronic illness. We think it was some kind of cancer, but we're still going through everything. He was apparently big into religion, and just like you thought, that parable was like his creed. He drummed it into all of his children and this woman held it as the gospel truth. Bad choice of words, sorry. Anyway, she had to quit college during her first year to take care of her dad and seeing these people just give away their opportunity at life was too much. She was convinced it was her calling in life to render justice to those who were '*sinning*' by not living up to their fullest potential. *And*, get this, she had cash in her purse, separate from her wallet, coated in DMSO and positioned next to an ice pack. We sent a sample off to the state lab. I'm certain it will have Anerva on it. I don't know who she was planning to give it to or how she was going to keep from touching it, but that really sealed the deal. Well, that and the vial of Anerva we found in her refrigerator. It had a homemade label on it, like she had taken it from another vial and put it in her own. God knows where she got her own vials or her own syringes. She must have taken some of the medication from the hospice nurse when her father was dying."

"What did she drug Cardian with?"

"They sent that off to the state lab too. It will be a few days before we hear anything. My lieutenant is calling Kastener now to let him know. He's probably going to get in touch with you after that. If you have a minute to come by the station, I can give you our official statement before we put it out to all the news outlets."

"I'll be right over. Thanks for thinking of me, Gen."

"If it weren't for you, we never would have caught her. The department had given up on it days ago. I'll see you soon."

Cari quickly toweled off and threw on some clothes. She was about to run out the door when she remembered that her parents were going to be visiting that weekend. She hastily put her towel up on the rack and tossed her clothing into her hamper. Then, she grabbed her phone, purse, and keys and raced out the door. Her phone started ringing right as she was starting her car.

"Mr. Kastener?"

"Hello, my dear. I just spoke with Lieutenant Grusky. Have you heard? They found the person responsible for my Jade's death. A woman! Pretty rare from what I've read. I know you were the one that made this happen. You went the extra mile on this. I can't thank you enough. It won't bring my little girl back, but at least people will know that she wasn't careless. She had her whole life ahead of her…" He choked on the last few words.

"Mr. Kastener, I, um, I'm so very sorry for your loss. I'm going to rewrite my article about her death. It will be in this weekend's paper. I'm sorry for any pain I caused you with my first one. Thank you for giving me a second chance."

"I know you will do her memory justice." He ended the call.

Cari was almost to the station when her phone rang again. The Bluetooth told her that it was Bob calling. She pushed the button to answer it.

"Cari! Do you have a minute?"

"I actually just pulled up to the station. I'm meeting Genevieve."

"Oh, well, did you get the email from the church? I got an email from the lady in charge of the volunteers for the shelter. She sent over the schedule. I saw your email on the list, so I guess we both cleared the background check. Do you still want to try it out next weekend?"

"Um, sure. Text me with the times. Can we ride there together?"

"Of course. I know you're a little hesitant about doing this, Cari, but it will be great."

"Ok, I'm just glad I'm not going alone."

Epilogue

*B*ob parked his car in the spaces designated for volunteers. Cari drummed her fingers on her knees with nervous energy. She had never been to a shelter or soup kitchen before and didn't know what to expect. Bob seemed completely calm as usual.

"Ready to go inside?" He asked.

She nodded.

"I know you're a little nervous, Cari. The lady from the church told me that all of the coordinators here are really nice and easy to work with."

Cari smiled and tried to sound enthusiastic. "Let's go see what tasks they have for us today."

They walked up to the building and entered through the door labeled volunteers. Two people were filling out information on clipboards while a dozen or so other adults were sitting in chairs and chatting. A woman waved Bob and Cari over to the table.

"I just need you to enter your name and the organization you're associated with. Then, you can grab a nametag and we'll get started in just a few moments."

They did as she instructed and then sat down with the others. Cari stifled a yawn. She wondered what they would be assigned to do. She knew that they served three meals a day here, but they also had places for people to sleep at night too. She looked up to see the woman who gave them instructions approaching the front of the room.

"Good morning, everyone! It's great to have you here this morning. I know it's early and I really appreciate you donating your time today. We have a lot on the docket today. For my first-timers, if you have any questions, look for someone with a lanyard and nametag like the one I'm wearing. We have three supervisors here today and we'll be rotating through the building this morning. Let me give you your assignments and then, I'll take any questions you might have."

She flipped through the pages on her clipboard and started reading names off her lists. They needed people for gardening work, kitchen work, and general cleaning. It sounded like some of the volunteers had been coming for a while and had familiar assignments. The woman started with the cleaning crew. She gave them instructions and sent them off.

"For our community garden, we're building a couple of raised beds today as well as pulling some weeds from the already established beds. Let's see…Bobby Hursley?"

Bob raised his hand. Cari looked at him in bewilderment. *Bobby?*

"My mom named me Bobby Gene, but no one knows that. I go by Bob, and everyone assumes it's short for Robert." He whispered.

Cari smiled and tried to catch the other names the woman had said while Bob was explaining about his name. Three other men had raised their hands and were standing up. Cari started to stand along with Bob when the woman began to speak again.

"I have two pancake flippers today. Cari Turnlyle?"

Cari felt her cheeks flush and she turned to look at the woman. Surely, this was a mistake. She and Bob had signed up together. Wouldn't they get to work together? She looked around and another woman had also stood up from her seat. She smiled at Cari and started walking to the front of the room. Cari flinched when she felt Bob grab her hand.

"It will be okay. I have my phone if you need anything. You can flip pancakes, right? I'll just be right outside." He said to her quietly and gave her hand a squeeze before releasing it.

She didn't want to cause a scene or look like a baby, so she just nodded and followed the other woman up to the front. This was not starting out well, but she had watched her grandmother make pancakes hundreds of times. She could do this. The other woman seemed to know where she was going, so Cari followed her out of the volunteer room and down a hallway.

"The kitchen is just at the end of this hall. They serve breakfast for about two hours on Saturdays. The kitchen has been certified by the health inspector, which means that someone else mixes up the batter. We're in charge of getting the batter onto the griddle and flipping the pancakes. The guests will come through the line and we give them each two pancakes."

They reached the kitchen and Cari could smell the pancake batter. Her new friend turned to her to hand her an apron.

"I almost forgot. My name is Regina. I've been volunteering here for about three years. I don't come every weekend, but I try to be here as often as I can. I'm a fourth grade teacher at Burke Elementary during the school year, but in the summers, I spend a lot of time here. It's a great facility."

"I'm Cari. This is my first time. I work for the Beagle." She shook Regina's hand and then put on the apron. It looked like there were two griddles for making pancakes. Regina showed her where the utensils were and how to adjust the heat on the griddle.

"They should be coming inside any minute now, so we'd better get started."

The two women each grabbed a bowl of pancake batter and walked over to the griddles. Cari watched as Regina coated her griddle with some butter before ladling out the batter, so she did the same. She had just laid out six circles of batter when she heard people entering the eating area on the opposite of the counter. Cari tried to remember what her grandmother had shown her when she made pancakes. She felt foolish for not knowing how long to leave it on the griddle before flipping it. She could see that the line of people stretched outside and felt like she was holding things up.

She decided to just flip the cakes and see what happened.

"You're doing that wrong." A vaguely familiar voice said to her.

Startled, she looked up and saw the woman from the alley frowning at her. "Dorothy?"

This triggered a smile. "Have you never flipped pancakes before, woman?"

"Um, it's been a while, I guess."

"As in never, I'd guess," she said pointedly.

"You need to wait until all those little bubbles form on top. When they start to pop, that's when you flip it. Otherwise, it's going to be paler than..." She winked.

Cari reddened and looked at the five remaining pancakes that she hadn't flipped yet. They all had bubbles, so she started to slide her spatula under one.

"No! Not yet."

Cari jumped. She looked at the circle of batter again. None of the bubbles were popping yet. She stole a glance over at Regina's griddle and saw that she was starting to flip her pancakes. She pushed the spatula back under the pancake.

"There, that's right. Gently flip it over." Dorothy told her.

Cari watched as the other pancakes' bubbles were bursting and carefully flipped them over too. She wondered how to know when they were finished on the other side. Maybe she could just peek under the first one.

"Don't do it! I see you wanting to peek at that first pancake. It's probably *almost* ready. You need to give it almost two minutes on each side. I can't believe you've never made your own pancakes before. You got a maid at your house or what?"

Cari blushed again. "No, I just, well, I don't usually eat pancakes except with my grandmother."

"And then *she* makes them, is that right?"

Cari smiled. "Yes, she always pampers me when I visit."

"Okay, well don't burn 'em now. Flip them over and put them

on the plate. We're getting hungry over here."

Cari stuck the spatula under the first two pancakes and slid them onto Dorothy's plate. The woman smiled at her. Cari saw that she was missing a molar on her upper right side.

"Thank you kindly, Ms. Cari. Will I be seeing you at the dumpster this week?"

Cari's eyes widened, but the woman just laughed and walked away. She flipped the four remaining pancakes onto the next two people's plates and started cooking some more. Before she knew it, the line had vanished and she was out of batter. Regina was carrying her empty bowl over to the dishwashers, so Cari grabbed the bowl and spatula and joined her.

"How did it go?" Regina asked.

Cari wondered if she had overheard any of the interaction with Dorothy. "It went pretty well. I didn't realize that two hours could go by so quickly."

Regina smiled warmly. "I'm so glad that you had a good experience. Dorothy wasn't too hard on you, was she?"

Cari smiled. "She was very helpful. I needed a few tips."

"Oh! It looks like your boyfriend is back from the garden area."

"My boyfriend? Oh, you mean Bob? We're not, um, we're just friends."

Regina tilted her head and almost frowned. "My mistake. Do you think you'll be coming back to volunteer?"

"Definitely. I was a little nervous about coming, but it was really fun."

"Hey, Cari, are you ready to sign out?"

"I think so. Are we all set here, Regina?"

"We are. Part of the certification for the kitchen requires that licensed people operate the dishwashers, so we just leave the items over here and someone else will run it through."

"Sounds good. Thanks for guiding me through the process. I'll see you next time."

Cari walked with Bob back out to his car. He had some dirt

smeared across his forehead and his arms had a couple of scratches on them too. He was holding work gloves in his left hand.

"You're kind of a mess, Bob-*by*."

"Hey! No one's supposed to know about my name. It's just my legal name."

"Okay, okay. I won't tell your secret. What did you do this morning?" She asked as they got into the car.

"We worked hard, but it was fun. I'm glad I had my work gloves in my trunk or my hands would be covered in blisters right now. We built two above ground beds and cleared the weeds and dead plants from several of the others. What about you? Did you have fun?"

"I did. Regina was really nice and everyone was friendly that came through the line. Did you get to work with any of the guests, or just the volunteers?"

"Just volunteers for me. Do you want to come back? I can email the lady from the church and let her know."

"I'd love to come back. Thanks for encouraging me to do this, Bob."

"I knew you would enjoy it if you gave it a chance. Hey, do you have plans for the rest of today?"

"No, not really. Why?"

"I, um, well," he cleared his throat and started again. "I have tickets to see "Chicago" at the local theater and thought you might want to join me. And, uh, go to dinner first."

Cari felt her palms get a little sweaty. "Like a date?"

He exhaled and wiped his hand across his forehead, smearing the dirt some more. "Yes, I'm asking you out on a date. What do you say?"

"Are you sure? I mean, we've been friends for so long and, what if—"

"I'm sure. I've wanted to ask you out since the day I met you, but the timing never seemed right. I could wait forever for it to seem right and maybe never get there. So, what about it?"

Bob had pulled into the parking lot at her complex and was parking in a visitor space. He turned to look at her after putting the car in park. She could see the earnestness in his blue eyes.

"Okay, Bob. I would love to join you for dinner and the theater tonight. What should I wear?"

* * * * *

Thank you for reading "Forsaken Talents"! Please take a moment to leave a review.

Ready for more action from Cari and friends? Stay tuned for Book 3: Cari suspects that an arsonist is at work in Brenington, but clues and witnesses are vanishing faster than she can track them.
Coming soon! Summer 2023!

Visit https://leslieapiggott.com for more information and to join my newsletter list.

Acknowledgments

Thank you to my amazing editor, Jennie Rosenblum! She not only finds those typos that I miss, she helps me tell these stories in a much-improved way. Thank you, Jennie!

To my friend Desiree: you listen to my story ideas, read through my rough draft and find typos, and then STILL buy my book once it's published.

To my mama, Suzanne, who realized that I had initially named my pharmaceutical "weapon" after a real medication before I published the book. Close call!

To Harold Sheely: Congrats on winning the contest and getting a character named after you! Hope you enjoyed the experience.

To all of the authors and crew with Indies United Publishing House, you are fantastic! Thank you for your support and encouragement. Best of luck with all of your future books.

And finally, to my beautiful family: Brad, Abby, and Simon. You make my world go 'round. I love you so much.

About the Author

Leslie A. Piggott lives in the Austin, Texas area with her husband and their two children. She is a scientist-turned-mom who received her doctorate in Biomedical Sciences from the University of Texas Health Science Center at Houston. In addition to writing, she also enjoys running marathons, quilting, knitting, singing in the church choir, and watercolor painting. She has previously published two watercolor and poetry books, both in 2021: *Poems in the Pandemic*, and *Art in Words*. Her first novel, *Rising Pressure* was published in January of 2022. She began publishing her first mystery series with *Chasing the Edge, book 1 of the Cari Turnlyle Series* in July of 2022. To sign up for her newsletter, you can visit her website at https://leslieapiggott.com.

www.ingramcontent.com/pod-product-compliance
Lightning Source LLC
Chambersburg PA
CBHW010737130726
47899CB00015B/3358